PLENTY OF GUILT

BY

SUZANNE FLOYD

COPYRIGHT

Cover by Bella Media Management

I dedicate this book to my husband Paul and our daughters, Camala and Shannon, and all my family. Thanks for all your support and encouragement.

CHAPTER ONE

"I'm Detective Dan Tobin. May I help you?" The man was over six feet tall with dark blonde hair and Paul Newman blue eyes. No one would call him Hollywood handsome, but his rugged features were striking all the same.

"Yes, I'm Jillian Connors."

His jaw dropped open, before he regained control, and snapped it closed. For a minute, he didn't say anything, but surprise lifted his eyebrows. In his late twenties or early thirties, he seemed too young to be a detective. "What are you doing here?" He finally found his voice, staring at me like he was seeing an apparition.

"When I talked to you yesterday, I told you I would be here sometime today or tomorrow." I didn't know why he was surprised. Something wasn't right causing my stomach to twist.

His sandy-colored brows came together in a frown. "Could I see some identification?" It was my turn to frown at him, but I pulled my driver's license out of my purse. What did he expect that to prove? He took his time examining it, looking at my picture then at me like he was comparing the two. I must have passed muster because he finally handed it back to me as he took a big gulp of air.

"Um, we seem to have a small problem here. Let's go into my office." He turned away without waiting to make sure I would follow him. His tight fitting jeans hugged his backside and long legs. In other circumstances, I might appreciate the view, but today my mind barely registered that fact.

He waited in the doorway of the office he'd come out of just moments before. Whatever was going on, I wasn't going to find out by standing in the hallway.

Seated behind his desk, he continued to stall for several seconds before starting again. "We have a little problem."

"So you said. Just tell me what the problem is so I can see my sister's...body." I stumbled over the last word. I still hadn't come to grips with the fact that she was really dead.

"Um, well, you see, that's the problem. Her body is no

longer here."

"What?!" I stood up so fast the chair tipped over with a resounding crash. "How do you lose a body?"

"W…we didn't lose it, exactly," he stammered. His face paled beneath his dark tan.

"Where exactly is Claire's body, if it isn't here?" I stared down at him with my hands braced on my hips. My green eyes had to be shooting daggers at him by now. Ever since I received the call telling me that Claire was dead, I went from grief to anger to guilt and back again. Anger was winning right now.

"We received a fax sometime during the night instructing the morgue to release her body for shipment back to South Carolina. The mortuary picked her body up about an hour ago."

"Who sent the fax?'

"Presumably you did."

"You're wrong there. I didn't send any fax. My instructions were *not* to release her body until I got here. You knew I was coming."

"Your fax said you had changed your mind." He stood up so I wasn't looking down at him, and giving him the advantage of height.

"It wasn't *my* fax. I didn't arrive in Tucson until close to midnight. I spent the night there until I could drive here this morning. Where did it originate from?"

"Well, we assumed it came from you since it had your signature."

"Assuming is always a good idea, isn't it?" I asked with sarcastic sweetness. "I'd like to see that fax." I held out my hand, tapping foot to tell him he'd better hurry up.

He opened a folder on his desk, looking at the top sheet of paper. "Ah, I can see the signature on this doesn't match the signature on your driver's license."

"Right, so it would be a wise move on your part to get on the telephone, and call the mortuary. They are *not* to embalm her body. Do I make myself clear this time?"

"You can't ship a body across the country unless it has been embalmed," he pointed out.

"Claire will be buried here next to her late husband, but first there will be an autopsy performed." He started to object, and I held up my hand to stop him. "You don't have to worry about your budget. I'll pay for it."

"What do you hope to prove? Your sister has been under a doctor's care for the past three or four months. He signed the death certificate."

"I intend to prove she didn't kill herself. If that fool of a doctor thinks he's going to get away with putting that on any legal form, he has another think coming." Remembering my last conversation with Claire, guilt ate at me. *Would she still be alive if I had dropped everything as she wanted, and come here?* It was something I would never know.

"You can't be certain of that," he argued, breaking in on my thoughts. "How long has it been since you saw your sister?"

"Her name was Claire, Claire Wilkins, and I didn't have to see her to know she would never kill herself. That isn't something she would do."

"I'm sure she didn't mean to do it, Miss Connors. The doctor said she was in a lot of pain. Many people take an accidental overdose in an effort to stop the pain." He bristled at my attitude while my hands curled into fists at his condescending tone. We were at an impasse.

"I know she had been sick. I also know she would never take something that would make her even sicker." She had told me a lot of other things that I wasn't ready to reveal to this man. He wouldn't believe me anyway. "That phony fax suggests, to me at least, that someone wanted to stop an autopsy from being performed. Who else knew I was having that done?"

"No one, we don't make a habit of releasing that kind of information to the general public." He acted like I had insulted him, his blue eyes turning icy cold now.

"Are you going to investigate where it came from, or do I

have to do that as well?" I didn't give him a chance to answer. "Are you going to investigate her death as something other than an accidental overdose now?" We were glaring across his desk at each other. He was convinced Claire had taken the overdose herself, while I was just as convinced she would never do something like that. She wasn't stupid. She wouldn't take enough pills to kill her.

"Is there a problem, Detective?" I turned to see a burly man in his fifties standing in the doorway, his hands braced on his broad hips, his belly hung over his belt nearly hiding the buckle.

"Who are you?" I didn't give Detective Tobin the chance to comment. I didn't care if I was being rude. Something was going on here, and I intended to get to the bottom of it.

"I'm Jeffery Daniels, Chief of Police here in Bisbee." He puffed out his chest in an effort to show his importance. "What is the problem here?" he asked again, looking at Detective Tobin.

"Um, this is Jillian Connors, Claire Wilkins' sister. She came to claim her sister's body, but..." His voice trailed off.

"But your department released her body to a mortuary without my permission," I picked up his sentence where he left off. I didn't want him making excuses for what had happened.

The chief grasped my hand with both of his, a look of sadness on his face. "Claire was a dear friend of mine, of everyone in town. I'm very sorry for your loss." I knew that for the lie it was. Someone had killed her; that didn't seem very friendly to me.

I pulled my hand out of his. "If that's true, why aren't you looking for the person who killed her?"

He took a step back, shock registering on his face. "No one killed her, Miss Connors. She took an overdose of pain pills."

"She would never do that!" I snapped, stomping my foot in frustration. I wished people would stop saying that, and listen to me for a change. "It would be a good idea if someone got on the phone and had her body brought back here. ASAP,"

The last came out as an order. Both men scrambled for the phone, but Detective Tobin won.

It took another hour before I was assured that Claire's body had been returned to the morgue. I would finally be able to see her.

When the morgue attendant removed the sheet covering Claire's face, I gasped, swaying slightly. I had told myself I was prepared to see her like this, but I was wrong. The detective took my arm to keep me from falling over, leading me to a chair. It took several minutes to get myself under control enough that I could walk over to the cold metal table where she laid. "Oh, Claire, I'm so sorry I didn't believe you," I whispered. "Someone is going to pay for this." Her cheeks were sunken, and there were dark smudges under her eyes. She was so thin her cheek bones stood out, and her skin was pale and wax-like. Tears ran down my face now as grief replaced my anger, but not my guilt. I should have paid more attention to her.

"Miss Connors, no one did anything to her." I'd forgotten I wasn't alone, and the detective's voice startled me. I jerked around to stare at him. "She took an entire bottle of pain pills," he said quietly. "The empty bottle was on her nightstand beside her bed."

My anger came roaring back. At only five foot five I had to tip my head back to look him in the eye. I glared up at him. "I don't care where the pill bottle was, Claire would never do something like that. The fact that someone knew I was having an autopsy performed and tried to stop it, should tell you that something is wrong with this assumption of yours. Did you even bother to check for fingerprints on that bottle?"

He sighed. "There was no need. She lived alone, and she didn't have a caregiver taking care of her."

"That means you aren't even going to check this out."

"Her doctor said…"

"I don't care what her doctor said," I cut him off before he could finish his sentence. I felt like shaking him in an effort to get him to listen to me. "I'll be speaking to him later.

Something was making her very sick, but he wasn't interested enough to find out what. She told me she was going to see a specialist in Tucson next week. Whoever did this, didn't want that to happen anymore than they wanted an autopsy done."

This piece of news appeared to surprise him, and he was silent for a long moment. "If she was sicker than you thought, you can't say for sure what she would have done." I shook my head. He would never convince me that she had taken those pills of her own freewill.

"Why don't we wait for the results of the autopsy to make the final determination on how and why she died?" The mocking tone in my voice caused his spine to stiffen. The glare he shot in my direction was the only indication that his temper was reaching the boiling point. He did a better job of keeping his temper in check than I did.

"I'll speak to the chief." His tone was stilted and cold.

"You do that. Until then, I'd like the keys to her house." I held out my hand like he had them in his pocket.

He looked unsure whether he should give them to me. "Since you don't think a crime has been committed, why would you object to me going into her house? It isn't a crime scene," I said, mocking him. "I'll be staying there until this has been resolved." Reluctantly, he took me back to his office, handing over the keys.

~~~

"How did she get here so fast?" he muttered. "I just got rid of her nosy sister yesterday." He stared out the window of the small café as the woman walked across the street to her car. She looked enough like her sister to cause his heart to skip a beat. If she had arrived a day later, there wouldn't have been anything to autopsy. He shrugged. There was nothing he could do about it now. If she started causing trouble, he'd have to take care of her like he had her sister.

He didn't know how much that bitch had known, or if she had even realized what she saw. By that time she was in pretty bad shape from whatever was wrong with her. He hadn't been willing to take the chance that she'd guessed what they were doing though. He'd had to take her out.

How much had she told her sister? He shrugged his shoulders. It didn't matter. He wasn't taking chances with this one either. She would also have to be disposed of when the time came. He had to figure out if she'd told anyone else what she knew. That thought caused his hands to shake so bad hot coffee sloshed over the rim of the cup. Things were coming undone. He only needed a little longer, and he could get out. No one would ever be able to connect him to any of it.

~~~

A shiver moved down my spine, and I looked around for the cause. It was the first of June; the sun was shining without a cloud in the sky. The temperature was edging its way into the nineties. There was no reason for the chill.

I dismissed the feeling with a shrug, and got into the rental car. I had more important matters to handle. Somehow I was going to have to return this car to the airport in Tucson. After that I could use Claire's car that was in the garage until I got this sorted out. For now I needed to go to Claire's house, the place she died, where she was killed. I choked back a sob. There would be plenty of time for tears once her killer was behind bars, I told myself.

Pulling into the steep gravel driveway leading to Claire's house, I stayed in the car with the engine running for several minutes letting the air conditioning blow on my face. The cool air felt good. Arizona was much warmer than I was used to. My shoulder length brown hair was plastered to my neck, and I wished I had put it in a ponytail before leaving Tucson this morning. A trickle of sweat made its way between my breasts.

Drawing a deep breath for courage, I turned the car off, and stepped out. The huge old house Claire had lived in since marrying Thomas Wilkins six years ago sat atop one of the many small hills that made up the town of Bisbee, Arizona. The neighboring houses were either further down the hill or up another one.

I rang the doorbell instead of unlocking the door and going in. I could hear the musical chimes through the heavy door.

Did I really expect someone to answer? Claire had lived here alone since Tom passed away two years ago.

Jake, Tom's son from his first marriage, had been visiting her recently. She never said if he was staying in the house with her, or at a hotel. They hadn't parted on good terms when Tom disowned Jake. Of course, he'd blamed Claire, calling her a gold digger, only after his father's money. Since she was thirty-five years younger than Tom, many people agreed with Jake's assessment.

Why had he come back now? Was he the one who had been trying to kill her? Until I could find out what was making her so sick, it was a guessing game. I had been worried about him being here, but she had been convinced he no longer hated her.

For a long while after Tom's death, Claire had been desolate, unsure what she was going to do with the rest of her life. In the last year, she had decided to turn the big house into a bed and breakfast, and had been working towards that end. She'd even had a small area just down the hill paved for a parking lot for her prospective guests. Had Jake come here now to stop her from doing that? Was that why someone had given her those pills?

My breath suddenly caught in my throat, and I stepped back several paces when something or someone moved behind the heavy beveled glass window in the door. When the door remained solidly closed, I cautiously reached out and twisted the knob. Of course, it was locked. I'm not sure what else I expected. The police wouldn't leave the house open for anyone to walk in.

Turning my head slightly, it looked like something moved inside again. "It's just an illusion through the wavy glass." I spoke out loud to bolster my courage, hoping I was right. Looking around, I tried to determine if anyone was watching me. I drew another deep breath, and inserted the key in the lock.

I had barely closed the door when there was a soft knock. Pretending no one was home wasn't an option. Whoever was there must have been watching for me to arrive.

With a weary sigh, I pulled the heavy door open again. "Yes? May I help you?"

"Oh, you must be Jillian. I am so sorry for your loss." The small woman barely reached my shoulder. She wrapped me in a hug before I could stop her. Standing stiffly in her embrace, I wasn't sure what I was supposed to do. Finally the bird-like woman released me, stepping back to stare up at me. Tears glistened in her faded eyes.

"Forgive me. You must think I've lost my mind. I live next door." She pointed down the hill to a house where only the top floor could be seen. There didn't seem to be a flat piece of land in this part of town. "I'm Irma Grover. Maybe Claire mentioned me?

I nodded my head. "Yes, Claire spoke of you. You were a good friend to her." I vaguely remembered seeing the small woman at Claire's wedding and Tom's funeral.

"She was such a sweet girl. We did so enjoy our tea parties," Mrs. Grover went on. "She spoke of you so often, and she was always showing me your picture. I feel like I know you already."

Her assertion surprised me. Claire and I were polar opposites and until recent years hadn't been that close. I should have listened to her, I told myself again. Guilt ate at me as tears blurred my eyes.

"Oh, you poor dear," Mrs. Grover took my hand, leading me into the living room. Sitting down beside me on the plush couch, she patted my hand. Her kindness was going to do me in. I needed to stay angry if I was going to get to the bottom of what happened to Claire.

I wiped my face, and blew my nose before turning back to the small woman. "What can you tell me about what happened? The doctor didn't know what was causing her so much pain. I know she had an appointment with a specialist."

"I wanted her to go to one sooner, but she wanted to wait." She sniffed back her own tears. "That stupid doctor ran all kinds of tests, but when they didn't find anything wrong with her, he just threw a bunch of pills at her. If it was up to me, you'd sue the pants off the man."

"Once I find out what was making her so sick, I just might do that." That wasn't high on my to-do list, but I didn't think any doctor worth his salt would let his patient suffer without finding out what was wrong. I wondered if Claire had told Mrs. Grover, or the doctor, that she thought someone was trying to kill her.

Turning my mind back to the small woman, I considered my next question. "Claire said Jake was in town. Do you know if he's still here or where he's staying?" I didn't know how much she knew about the situation between Jake and his father, but I was hoping she would supply the answers to my unasked questions.

"Yes, he's still in town, at least part of the time. I assume he has a job somewhere." She shook her head. "When he showed up on her doorstep, I was worried about what he was going to do. He had been very vocal about his dislike for Claire when she married his father. As you know, he didn't attend the wedding or his own father's funeral." She tsked at that.

"Now he wants to make up for the way he acted back then." She shook her gray head. "He claims he's changed. Claire was smart enough not to invite him to stay here with her."

"Did Claire believe him? Do you?" She seemed pretty sharp even though she was well up in years.

She lifted her shoulders in a shrug. "I'm not sure if it's true or not. But Claire believed every word out of his mouth. She was too trusting for her own good." I nodded my head. That sounded very much like my sister. She was more trusting than I was, taking people at their word until proven otherwise. Maybe that had been her undoing.

"I was told a friend found her. Was that you?"

Her eyes teared up again as her head bobbed up and down. "We made a habit of checking on each other every day. When she got sick, I came over every morning to make sure she was all right. When she didn't answer my knock, I used the key she had given me. She was in her bed. She looked like she was sleeping, but when I touched her I knew." She sniffed sadly.

Tears rolled down my face again. I vowed to get to the bottom of this, even if it meant moving to Bisbee, and hounding the police until they did something.

Several minutes later, Mrs. Grover stood up. "I'll leave you alone now, dearie. I wanted you to know how sorry I am about Claire. If you need anything, all you have to do is call me. I'm right next door." She chuckled softly at that. "Of course in Bisbee that means a lot of stairs to climb, and I don't do that very fast any more. Call me anyway if you need something. My number is beside the phone in the kitchen." She opened the door to leave, but turned back to me. "Claire went to church with me every Sunday. Would you like to join me this week?"

"I'd like that very much, Mrs. Grover, thank you."

"Oh, dearie, please call me Irma. I'll see you soon." She hobbled down the driveway to the steps leading to her house.

The one thing Claire and I had in common was a strong faith in God. He had sustained us after our father died when we were little, and again when our mother died of cancer while I was in college. He would see me through this as well.

CHAPTER TWO

The house had been in Tom's family for several generations. Consequentially, he had kept it in the divorce from his first wife. I knew very little about Tom's former wife. If Claire knew what caused the divorce, she kept it to herself. I only knew that it had been messy.

When Tom passed away, Myriam had tried again to get the house. Fortunately, Tom had a trust preventing her from kicking Claire out of her home. What would happen now that both Tom and Claire were gone was anyone's guess. I didn't know enough about estate planning to predict what will happen.

What had Jake thought of Claire's plan to turn his family home into a bed and breakfast? Had he done something to her to prevent that from happening? Would he try to claim the house as his own now?

Moving through the different rooms, I could see where Claire had begun making preparations to open her bed and breakfast. Bathrooms had been added to the extra bedrooms upstairs, and she had moved her room to the third floor. This was still so surreal to me. I kept expecting her to walk down the stairs at any minute.

Once again I couldn't stop the tears from streaming down my face. Her plans for the house had been good for her. It gave her something positive to think about instead of dwelling on the past. I wish I had seen that before it was too late. "Oh, Claire," I whispered. "I am so sorry I didn't listen to you. Who would do this to you? Who sent that fax hoping to stop me from having an autopsy done?"

Someone was worried about what an autopsy would prove. Why couldn't the police see that? How many people knew I was going to have it done? Detective Tobin said no one in the police department would have said anything, yet someone knew about it. Would they even investigate to find out who sent the fax? Was I the only one who could see this was proof that she hadn't taken those pills on her own? I was more determined than ever to prove that someone else had done this to her.

Regaining control of my emotions, I continued my tour of the big house. Claire's room was just as it had always been while we were growing up, disorganized to the casual observer, yet she knew right where to find anything she was looking for. Her Bible was on the night stand beside her bed where she always kept it.

Our parents had given each of us one when we were little. Mine was as rumpled and well-read as the one here. She never went to sleep without reading it first. It was the one thing that never changed with either of us. I picked up the small book, holding it to my chest, tears burning behind my eyes. It would join the one on my night stand.

Standing in the center of the large room, I turned in a circle. In this organized chaos, where would she keep her important papers, such as a will or a living trust? I needed to find something that would answer even my most basic questions. Going through the drawers of the dresser was a waste of time. They contained nothing but clothes.

When the chimes on the front door sounded on the ground floor, I stood up with a heavy sigh. Why couldn't people leave me alone? Answering the door meant I had to go down two long flights of stairs. Would the person even be there by the time I made it down? I was debating whether to ignore the chimes when they sounded again. Whoever was at the door knew I was here. The car in the drive was a dead giveaway.

Not used to the mile high altitude of Bisbee, I was out of breath by the time I made it to the door. The room had been warm, and sweat was beaded on my upper lip. I took a second to mop my face.

Through the beveled glass on the door, I could make out the figure of a tall man. Butterflies attacked my stomach. Maybe this was Jake. What was he going to do? Had he really changed, or was he planning to claim the house for himself and his mother?

13

I opened the door, staring up at the tall man. At six feet three or four, he was almost a foot taller than me. "Y…yes?" I stammered. His intense stare was unnerving as his dark eyes bore into mine. If the detective's rugged features placed him out of the running for Hollywood handsome, this man was leading man gorgeous. His hair was as black as night, and one lock fell onto his forehead in a calculatedly casual way, giving him a boyish look.

He was dressed casually in jeans and a long sleeved shirt with the cuffs rolled up to reveal tan, well-muscled arms. I imagined there was a set of six-pack abs hidden under that shirt.

For several long seconds, neither of us spoke. I'd never met Jake the few times I visited Claire, and could only guess that's who this stranger was.

"You're Jillian, right?" He finally broke the silence. His voice was well-modulated and cultured.

"Yes, may I help you?"

He flashed a dazzling smile, and I took a step back. This was a man accustomed to getting what he wanted on his good looks and charm alone. I wasn't going to fall into that trap.

"I'm sorry. Claire spoke of you so often, and she had so many pictures of you, that I feel like I know you already." He voiced the same sentiment Irma had just a short time ago. "I'm Jake, Tom's son." He offered his hand for me to shake.

I hesitated for a split second before placing my hand in his much larger one. He held my hand longer than necessary, causing jitters to dance in my stomach. What was he going to do?

"Um, come in." I stepped back allowing him to enter, pulling my hand away in the process. I turned away, leading him into the living room.

My eyes were red and puffy, and my face was splotchy from my recent crying jag. I had pulled my shoulder-length hair into a ponytail while I looked through Claire's things. Tendrils were beginning to escape the band holding it up, curling on my neck and around my face. I wished now that I had used a comb instead of simply finger-combing it into the band. I gave myself a mental head slap. What did it matter what I looked like? I wasn't here for a beauty contest.

"I'm so sorry about Claire," his voice broke in on my thoughts. "I was just getting to know her when she became ill. She was a nice lady."

"Yes, she was." People kept telling me that, yet someone had hated her enough to kill her. After the way he had treated her when she married his father, it was difficult being civil to him. I didn't know if this was all for show or what he was up to.

Sitting down in the recliner, I watched as he wandered around the room. The large portrait of Tom still hung above the fireplace. He stopped, looking up at his father's face.

As the silence began to draw out, I fidgeted in the chair. Was he ever going to say something? Maybe he didn't know what to say any more than I did.

Finally sitting down on the couch, he smiled sadly. "This room was always so stuffy and formal. My mother wasn't into comfort, just fancy. I like what Claire did with it. She managed to turn this old house into a welcoming home."

"You didn't always feel that way."

He chuckled softly. "You don't pull any punches, do you?"

"Sorry, I shouldn't have said that." I wasn't really sorry though.

"Maybe not, but it's the truth. I'm sorry for the way I treated her when she married my dad, and I told her that. I was wrong. I wish my father had lived long enough to see that I had changed." He looked up at the portrait again. "I hope he would be pleasantly surprised by the transformation. Maybe even a little proud." Sadness placed a heavy hand on his shoulders. *Was this all for show?* I wondered again.

"My dad was ten years older than my mother, and I don't think either of them planned on having children. Neither of them knew quite what to do with me." He gave his dark head a shake. "I grew up listening to them argue about their different opinions on how to raise me." For a minute he was lost in the past before picking up his narrative again.

"My folks divorced during my junior year of high school. It wasn't a fun time for any of us. They pitted me one against the other, both of them trying to buy my affection and hurt the other one. Like any kid, I took advantage of that situation." He continued to look up like he was talking to the man in the portrait. I didn't know why he was giving me this history lesson, but I let him ramble. Maybe he would say something that would help me figure out why Claire had been killed.

He turned back to me, those dark eyes boring into mine once again. "After Claire came into our lives, there was another war between my parents. My mother had received a sizable settlement in the divorce, but the thought of another woman living in the house she considered hers made her furious.

"I'm not proud of the fact that I had flunked out of most of my classes the first two years of college. Claire pointed out that by paying for the education I was wasting; Dad was enabling my playboy lifestyle. That's when Dad cut me off. He told me I had wasted my inheritance. I wouldn't be getting any more. Of course, this added to my mom's anger." He shook his head again. "Anyway, suddenly I had to toe the line, and support myself. I don't think any twenty-one-year old would take kindly to that sort of thing."

"So you still say what happened was Claire's fault," I snapped. "She wasn't a gold digger! She loved your father." He was the one thing besides her faith that she was devoted to.

"No, that's not what I'm saying. I don't blame her. I'm very grateful for all she did for him. I wish they could have had many more years together. I know she really did love him."

He sounded sincere, but could I believe him? There were too many question marks in what happened to her. It would be interesting to know if his mother still held a grudge against Claire. Until I had some answers, I wasn't going to trust him or anyone else in this town. I didn't know how long it would take for the results of the autopsy and toxicology report to come back, but I needed to be cautious.

He stood up again. "I didn't come here to cause trouble, for Claire or for you. I came here to make amends. I'll be in town for a while. I have a few questions of my own I'd like answered. If there is anything I can do for you, give me a call." He handed me a business card. "My numbers are there. I'm sorry about Claire."

What had he meant? Did he want to know what had been making her sick? Had Claire told him she suspected someone was trying to kill her? I had no idea where he worked or lived. It would also be nice to know where his mother lived. If she still held a grudge against Claire, would she go so far as to try to kill her? Is that what he wanted to find out?

I stayed in the recliner as he walked out. When I heard the door close behind him, I went to the window overlooking the long driveway. He was getting into a black Land Rover parked behind my rental car. Either he had money of his own, or he was putting on a good show.

What had brought him to Bisbee at this particular time? Was it just a coincidence that Claire became ill right after he arrived, or did he have something to do with it? Would he try to claim everything Claire had as his rightful inheritance? I needed to find legal papers or an attorney who could give me some answers.

If Jake had done something to Claire to make her sick, I didn't want him to benefit from it. Hopefully, the autopsy would give me some of the answers I needed.

I was halfway up the stairs, when the chimes on the front door rang again. Releasing a heavy sigh, I turned back around. If nothing else, I was going to get plenty of exercise this way.

The chief was at the door this time, looking all official. "Good afternoon, Miss Connors. Mind if I come in?" He didn't give me the chance to answer as he stepped inside, forcing me to step back or get run over. "You made some very serious statements this morning. I was hoping you could explain."

"Which statements are you talking about?" I remained in the entry instead of inviting him into the living room.

"You're accusing someone in my town of being a murderer."

"The fact that someone sent a fax to release her body, when I had clearly said not too, should indicate that someone in your town didn't want to have an autopsy performed. Someone knew I was having that done. Are you even going to investigate to find out who sent it?"

He lifted his heavy shoulders. "That's on the county morgue. The people in my department know better than to release confidential information to the public."

"So the answer is no, you aren't going to investigate."

He shrugged again, like it didn't matter one way or the other to him. Instead, he went back to his original questions. "I'd like to know exactly where you get the crazy notion that someone killed her. Claire died of a self-inflicted overdose."

I bristled at his pompous attitude, but clamped down on my temper. "I got that crazy notion as you call it from Claire. She told me someone was trying to kill her." Unfortunately, I hadn't believed her until it was too late, I reminded myself. That was on me.

He staggered back several steps as though he had been punched in the gut. Gathering himself, he glared at me. "Why did she think someone was trying to kill her?"

I shook my head. "I don't know why she thought that." *That was part of the reason I hadn't believed her,* I thought guiltily.

He gave a derisive snort, but pushed on with his questions. "And just when did she tell you all this?"

"Three days before she died."

"And you were so concerned that you waited until you were notified of her death to come rushing out here." His sarcastic tone was pushing my temper to the boiling point.

"I'm a teacher. I had three days left before the end of the school year. I had already made my airline reservations when I got the call that..." My voice trailed off. It was still hard to accept the reality of her death.

He gave a disbelieving sniff at my statement, but didn't argue the point. "Did she tell you who was trying to kill her or why?"

"She didn't know the answer to either of those questions."

"Why did she tell you instead of coming to the police? There was nothing you could do for her in South Carolina."

"Maybe because she didn't trust the police," I suggested, arching an eyebrow at him.

"She had no reason not to trust the police," he stated indignantly. "It seems a little like the ramblings of a very sick woman to me." My fingers curled into fists at his thoughtless comment. "Can you even give me a motive for someone to kill her?" He seemed unaware or unconcerned of the effect his words had on me.

"Isn't it your job to find the answers to these questions?" His pudgy face got red at that, but I didn't give him the opportunity to say anything. "I came here to prove that she didn't take those pills herself, and that someone had been trying to kill her for the past several months. It would be nice if you did your job and found her killer."

"I spoke with her doctor an hour ago. He assured me that no one was trying to kill her. All the tests he ran came back negative. He couldn't find anything wrong with her."

"I'll deal with the doctor in due time," I snapped. "What could she gain by faking her illness?" The question was for me as much as it was for the chief. She had a knack for being overly dramatic. I had thought it might be more of the same now, and I hadn't listened when I should have. Obviously I was wrong, so was he. I had to put the guilt aside for now until I could find her killer.

He lifted his broad shoulders in a careless shrug. "Sometimes single women get lonely, and they do silly things to get attention."

"Just moments ago you thought her idea that someone was trying to kill her was nothing more than the ramblings of a very sick woman. Now you say she faked being sick to get attention. You can't have it both ways, Chief. I think it's time for you to leave." My voice was low and menacing. "Get out."

"Calm down, Miss Connors. You're putting words into my mouth."

"I doubt that. I'd like you to leave. Now!" When he still didn't move, my temper boiled over, and I gave him a shove.

"Careful there, Miss Connors, or I'll have to arrest you for assault." I hadn't even been able to move his hefty frame, and he was going to accuse me of assault?

"Then leave, or I'll file a complaint against you for trespassing." I opened the door, sweeping my arm to show him the way out. His rump was barely out the door when I slammed it closed.

He turned, glaring at me through the glass.

I watched until his car was out of sight. I wanted to make sure he was really gone. I hadn't gone far from the door when the chimes rang again. Now I was really mad. I yanked the door open again. "What part of leave…" I stumbled to a halt. It wasn't the chief standing there. "Oh, Detective Tobin, you just missed the chief. I'm sure if you hurry, you can catch up with him."

"I'm not looking for the chief. I'd really like to talk to you."

I released a heavy sigh, stepping back to let him in. All I wanted at the moment was to be left alone. It didn't look like that was going to happen any time soon.

Leading him into the living room, I sat down in the recliner, pulling my feet under me. "What can I do for you, detective?" Even my voice sounded weary. Although it was only two in the afternoon in Arizona, it was five at home. I hadn't slept much in the last twenty-four hours, and my energy was beginning to wane.

He sat down on the couch close to my chair, leaning forward so that his elbow was almost resting on the arm of the recliner. "Please, call me Dan," he smiled at me. Once again jitters danced in my stomach. He waited for me to nod consent. "First, I came to apologize for my attitude this morning. After receiving that fax, I wasn't expecting you to show up. I am sorry for your loss."

He drew a deep breath. "I would also like to know why you're so certain Claire was murdered. You seem convinced she wouldn't take those pills on her own. I think there's more that you aren't telling."

"I just went over this with the chief. Maybe you should talk to him," I sigh.

"Humor me, please Miss Connors."

"Jillian," I interrupted. If I was going to call him Dan, he might as well call me Jillian.

His smile was devastating, sending my pulse into overdrive. "If you don't mind repeating what you told the chief, I'd like to hear it for myself."

For the next several minutes, I went over my conversation with the chief. "He didn't believe a word I said," I finished. "That's precisely why I want the autopsy done. Someone killed her, and no one is doing a thing about it." A single tear traced its way down my face.

"You were planning on coming here even before I called with the news of her death. Why is that?"

I drew a shaky breath. "For the past year Claire has…had been trying to convince me to move out here with her. It wasn't something I wanted. I finally agreed to spend the summer with her. I already had my plane ticket when you called, but I should have come here sooner." Once again guilt gripped me.

"At the morgue you said you were sorry you hadn't believed her. What did you mean?"

I rested my head on the back of the chair, giving a tired sigh. Admitting how dismally I had failed my sister wasn't an easy thing to do. "Did you know Claire?" I asked. He shook his head, causing me to wonder again how the chief knew her.

Drawing another ragged breath, I tried to explain some of my relationship with my sister, "Claire is…was," I corrected, "six years older than me, consequently we weren't all that close growing up. It wasn't until we were adults that we became friends. Still, old habits are hard to break. With me she was the bossy big sister, always telling me what to do. She thought she knew what was best for me. When she started pushing for me to move out here, I pushed back," I reluctantly admitted. "I had agreed to spend the summer with her. When she told me someone was trying to kill her, I thought she was just trying to get me to move out here. I didn't believe her." I whispered the last, tears clogging my throat.

"But you believe her now. Why?"

"Because she's dead, isn't she? She was looking forward to me coming out for the summer. Why would she take an entire bottle of pills just before my visit when she knew it would kill her? That doesn't make sense. She wasn't just trying to get attention as the chief suggested either. She knew what was happening to her, but she didn't know why."

"You believe someone was giving her something to make her sick?"

"I don't know what else to believe," I said. There was a shrug in my voice.

His silence lasted so long, my heart began to sink. What was the point in of all this if he wouldn't believe me either? He finally nodded his head. The breath I'd been holding escaped in a rush. "You believe me?" I whispered breathlessly.

"Let me put it this way: I don't, *not* believe you. I'll do a little checking to see what I can find."

"Thank you." Tears blurred my vision as I laid my hand on his arm. The buzz of an electrical current moved through me, and I jerked back. "Sorry." I didn't know what else to say.

His crooked smile was beyond sexy, causing my heart to jerk in my chest. *What is wrong with me*, I silently asked myself. I'd never reacted this way towards any man before, especially one I had just met. A romantic entanglement was not something I needed at the moment.

His next question brought my mind back to the subject at hand. "If Claire thought someone was trying to kill her, why didn't she ever tell the police or her doctor?"

"She told her doctor, but he didn't believe her. He even

had the gall to tell the chief that he thought she was faking her illness because she was lonely. She didn't know who else she could trust." The smirk on the chief's face still made me angry, but it was very close to my initial reaction to her words. If I had just listened to her, maybe she would still be alive. Tears of anger and shame burned behind my eyes.

Detective Tobin, Dan, shook his head. "I'm sorry about that." This time he reached out, placing his hand on my arm. That same tingly shock passed between us. He didn't pull away, and neither did I. "The autopsy will tell us what was happening with her," he said quietly. "I'm glad you insisted on having it done. We will get to the bottom of this, Jillian, I promise."

"What about that fax? Someone besides your department knew I was having an autopsy done, and they wanted to stop that from happening. The chief isn't even going to look into it."

He nodded solemnly. "Maybe I can check that out as well." When he left a few minutes later, I felt like I finally had someone on my side. I hoped I wasn't placing my trust in the wrong person.

After the detective left, the chimes on the front door rarely stopped ringing as a succession of people stopped by, either to offer their condolences, or just out of curiosity. Some brought food or flowers. Only one gave me hope that he believed what really happened to Claire.

"Miss Connors, I'm Pastor Roy Bennett. Claire had attended our small church since she moved to Bisbee. I'm very sorry for your loss." He offered me his hand.

From the expression on his kind face, I was certain he had heard about the 'official' cause of death. I didn't want people to believe that about her. "What can you tell me about Claire's illness?" I hadn't contacted her doctor yet. That would come when I could present him with the truth.

He was in his early fifties, with kind blue eyes. He shook his head. "When she first became sick, she thought it was food poisoning or something like that. But it never went away. In the last week, she seemed frightened of something or someone. She wouldn't talk about it though. She had cut ties with most people except for those closest to her."

"Maybe those are the ones she should have cut off," I spoke softly. His frown drew his brows together in question.

I wasn't sure how much I should tell him. But if I couldn't trust a pastor, who could I trust? I asked myself. When I finished recounting what she had told me, shock had left his face gray. For several minutes the only sound in the room was the ticking of the big grandfather clock in the corner as he thought about what I'd said.

"Why did she believe someone was trying to kill her?"

I lifted my shoulders in a tired shrug. "I'm not sure why. She never said. I thought it was just because she was so sick. I no longer believe that to be true." Once again guilt ate at me. *I should have believed her*, I told myself for the hundredth time since this began.

"If she really believed someone was trying to kill her, why wouldn't she tell someone?" He asked the same question I had asked her.

I shrugged. "She said she didn't know who she could trust."

"She couldn't trust the police?" Pastor Roy seemed shocked by that. "Who did she think was doing this to her?"

"I wish I knew," I sighed. "I don't think she knew who was doing this or why. I'm hoping the autopsy will give me some of the answers I need."

"Why would someone want to hurt her? I don't believe she ever intentionally hurt anyone. I know she was looking forward to your visit this summer, and to opening her bed and breakfast, until she became ill."

More reasons I didn't believe she knowingly took those pills. I had no answers for him, just questions.

"I hope you'll come to church on Sunday, Miss Connors," he said as he prepared to leave.

"I'll be there," I assured him. "Irma Grover asked me to attend with her, and please call me Jillian."

He gave a sad smile, nodding his head. "Irma and Claire were very close. I know she will miss Claire, as will we all."

When the doctor in Tucson called to confirm that Claire's body had been picked up, I was hit with another disappointment. "It will be several days before we can begin the autopsy," he explained. "I already have several scheduled that need to be done first. The tox screen will be started right away. It will take several weeks to get the results back on that."

"Several weeks?" My voice squeaked. "Isn't there some way to hurry the results?" I didn't want to wait that long to find out what happened to my sister.

He gave a small chuckle. "Real life isn't like a television show, Miss Connors. These things take time. There are no short cuts in medicine or police work. From your initial phone call, I understand you suspect foul play in your sister's death. What exactly are you looking for?"

"The reason my sister died," I answered simply. "Someone killed her, and I want to know who."

"An autopsy won't show that."

I sighed in frustration. "I'm aware of that, Doctor, but I have to start somewhere. You find out what killed her, I'll figure out who did it."

For a long moment he was quiet. "A standard toxicology screen will only show the usual substances we would look for in a murder. If something more exotic was used, that will take more comprehensive testing."

"Okay, do that," I insisted.

"Those tests will take considerably longer for the results to come back."

I groaned, that meant I would have to be patient. That was one thing I was short on at the moment. Still it didn't look like I was going to get answers any time soon.

By the time the sun had sunk behind the Mule Mountains, a good portion of the population had been at the door. When my stomach rumbled, I realized I'd forgotten to eat lunch. There were few street lights on the roads winding through the mountainous town, making it difficult to see after dark. I was grateful Claire kept a well-stocked kitchen, as well as all the food people had brought throughout the day. I didn't need to worry about finding a place to eat.

Dishing up a salad, I sat down at the big butcher block table in the kitchen only to be interrupted a few minutes later by a knock on the back door. I released a frustrated sigh. "Who else is left to visit?" I asked the empty room.

"Hello?" A woman in her forties stood on the large back porch, her face draped in sadness.

"You must be Jillian, of course you are." She answered her own question. Before I could say anything, she pulled me in for a hug. "I am so sorry about Claire. She was such a special person." She continued to hold me close, pinning my arms to my sides. Everyone had a kind word to say about Claire, but one of them was lying. Someone had killed her.

For a long moment, I stood in her embrace, too stunned to move. When I pulled away from her, she was forced to drop her arms, stepping back to give me the once over. Like everyone else who stopped by, she knew who I was while I had no idea who she was.

She stepped towards me again, and it was either move back into the kitchen or risk getting caught up in her embrace again. When she shut the door behind her, a shaft of fear traveled up my spine. What she going to do? Was she the person who gave Claire the final dose of pain killers?

"Oh, I see you were getting ready to eat. I was hoping I could convince you to join me for dinner tonight." She gave a disappointed sigh. "This is the first chance I've had all day to come by. Maybe you'll let me take you out another night. You will be here for a while, right?" She finally paused to take a breath, giving me a chance to answer.

"Yes, I will." I answered only her final question. "I'm sorry, but I don't know who you are." I was too tired to care if I was being rude.

"Of course you don't. I'm sorry. I'm Dusty Reynolds. I own The Tinderbox Bed and Breakfast." She waved vaguely out the back door, to indicate where she lived. "I've been helping Claire get the house set up so she could open her own B&B." She stuck out her hand.

I placed my hand in hers. If she was helping Claire, I would do my best to be nice. Until I knew what was really going on in this town though, I would reserve judgment.

It was my guess she was at least fifteen years older than Claire. Her graying hair was cut in a short bob and her blue eyes were hidden behind heavy glasses. She was rougher around the edges than Claire. I couldn't imagine the two women being close friends.

"Claire was so excited about opening her own place until she got sick. I was helping her with different recipes to serve her guests." She gave her head a shake. "I can't believe she's really gone. Everyone in town loved her." I was getting tired of people telling me that. Not everyone had loved her. I needed to figure out who that person was.

Unaware of my thoughts, she continued. "Bisbee is an artsy-fartsy kind of town. We have everything here from Cowboy Poets to genuine artists to aging hippies. Claire had such big ideas. I know her bed and breakfast would have been a big draw." There was a hint of something besides love in her voice that I couldn't place. Was she giving me a line of bull? Her mind seemed far away for several seconds. Giving herself a shake, her smile returned. I wondered if she wasn't happy about the upcoming competition.

"What are your plans for the house now? Will you be staying in Bisbee?" Her questions surprised me.

I shrugged. "I don't have any plans beyond finding out..." I stopped myself before blurting out the truth, "why she had been so sick," I finished lamely. "If that takes a week, a month, or a year, that's how long I'll be in Bisbee." I wasn't going to tell her or anyone beyond the police and Pastor Bennett my true thoughts on the matter. I wouldn't give the killer a heads-up. Besides, I had no idea who owned the house now that both Tom and Claire were gone.

CHAPTER THREE

That night I decided to sleep in the room I'd used the previous times I'd visited Claire. But sleep didn't come easily. My mind wouldn't let go of all that was going on. Why was the chief reluctant to see what really happened to Claire? Why couldn't he see that someone had deliberately tried to stop the autopsy from being done? Was he somehow involved?

Finally falling into a restless sleep, a loud creak somewhere above me brought me wide awake. Someone was in the house with me, in Claire's bedroom on the third floor. Sitting straight up in bed, I waited for the boogeyman to come get me. For several long moments everything was silent again. I released the breath I'd been holding, forcing myself to relax. It must have been a dream, I told myself. Lying back down, I willed myself to go to sleep.

Before that could happen, another sound came, this time much closer to my room. With my heart in my throat, I crept out of bed. If someone was out in the hall expecting to catch me sleeping, they were in for a surprise of their own. I would meet them head on. Grabbing a heavy antique candlestick off the fireplace mantle, I edged my way to the door. Had it creaked when I shut it several hours ago? I couldn't remember.

Throwing caution to the wind, I jerked the door open, the candlestick held over my shoulder like a baseball bat. Whoever was out there was going to have a headache when I finished with them. The hallway was empty.

I dropped my arm, letting the heavy candlestick hang at my side. The adrenaline that had surged through my body ebbed away leaving me shaking. Another creak sounded somewhere in the house. This time I recognized it for what it was. The old house was creaking and groaning like an old man with arthritis as it settled for the night.

Feeling disappointed and foolish all at the same time, I sagged against the door frame. I had been ready to bash someone's head in all for nothing. Replacing my implement of mayhem on the mantle, I crawled back into bed. Even though I knew what was causing the sounds, I wasn't sure I'd get to sleep. Ear plugs would help drown out the house noises, but if someone really did break in, I wouldn't be able to hear them until it was too late. My dilemma kept me awake for another hour before exhaustion took over, and sleep finally claimed me.

Blurry-eyed, I stumbled down the stairs the next morning. The kitchen was equipped with several modern appliances I didn't know how to operate, including an espresso machine. It was too early in the day to try figuring out how to use any of the new appliances. Thankfully there was also a regular coffee maker on the counter. Filling the carafe with water, I went in search of ground coffee. Claire had several different flavors of regular coffee plus decaf in the butler's pantry. This morning I needed full octane.

Sipping my first cup, I rummaged through the cupboards and refrigerator for something to fix for breakfast. Most of the food brought by strangers the day before wouldn't work for breakfast. Settling on the old stand-by of bacon and eggs, I pulled out a small frying pan and set to work.

I needed to keep busy or I would go out of my mind while I waited to hear from the doctor in Tucson. What would I do if the autopsy was inconclusive? The question had been niggling at the back of my mind. I finally had to face the fact that I might never know what or who had made Claire so sick, or who had given her the pain pills. Nothing would ever convince me that she had taken those pills herself, but how could I prove it?

Nibbling on a crisp piece of bacon, I finished scrambling two eggs. These thoughts, and others, chased each other around in my brain. I had a small apartment in South Carolina, a job I loved, and many friends. How long could I survive if I had to quit my job while waiting for the police to catch Claire's killer? Leaving my apartment for an extended time would prove to be costly. Still, I didn't want to give it up if this would be solved once the autopsy and toxicology screening were done.

But they would only prove *what* had happened to Claire, not *who* did it, I reminded myself. That would take much longer. I was back to the starting point of what to do about my life in South Carolina and my job. I didn't have to decide immediately, I told myself. With school out for the summer, I had time to figure out what I was going to do.

After cleaning up my breakfast dishes, I wandered aimlessly around the house trying to think of something to do to keep myself busy. I needed to find any legal papers Claire had, but searching for them in the large house would be like looking for a needle in a hay stack. There were just too many places to hide things. Did she even have a will? It wasn't something we'd ever talked about.

The house had belonged to Tom, I reasoned. The master bedroom had been on the second floor. Was there a safe hidden somewhere in the big room? I rushed up the staircase to what had been the master suite. Looking behind all the pictures on the walls and in the closet, I came up empty. Where else would Tom hide a safe?

Duh! I gave myself a mental head slap. Tom had kept an office in the library downstairs. What better place for a safe than a home office? I traced my steps back down the long staircase.

Even before I reached the first floor, the chimes on the front door rang out. *Who now*, I wondered? There couldn't be very many people left to come around and offer their condolences.

Opening the door, Irma was standing there with a casserole in her hands and a big smile on her face. "Hello, dearie. I didn't have time to make this yesterday when I found out you had made your way to Bisbee." She held out the big dish. "It's still warm for your lunch." Without waiting for me to invite her in, she walked past me heading for the kitchen. I had little doubt she knew her way around the house.

"Mrs. Grover, Irma, that isn't necessary. I have plenty of food. People brought food over all afternoon yesterday I'll never be able to eat it all." She ignored me, placing the dish in the oven and turning the temperature to warm.

"I know, dearie. I just wanted to bring something over so you don't have to worry. People will stop by after the funeral, and you'll need the food then." She was assuming the funeral would be soon, but I had no idea when it would happen. I kept that thought to myself. A lot of people seemed to be in a rush to bury Claire. Was the entire town trying to cover up what happened to her?

Sitting down at the kitchen table, Irma didn't appear to be in a hurry to leave. She was probably lonesome, but I wanted to search the library/office for a safe. It was the most logical place to hide one.

"What are your plans for today, dearie? Do you need any help packing Claire's things? Our church has a food and clothing pantry for the poor and homeless. I'm sure they would be very grateful for anything you gave them."

"I'm not ready to clear out her things yet." My heart ached and tears burned at the back of my eyes at the thought. This was still all too new to me.

"Of course, I understand and I'm sorry. I guess old age makes me forget how upsetting death can be for the young. I often wonder why God has let me stick around this long. Maybe he has plans for me, but I know my time is short. I get impatient sometimes, wanting to hurry things along before I run out of time." She patted my hand. "You just take your time. Don't let anyone push you into something you're not ready for. Not even me." She chuckled.

Pushing herself out of the chair, she patted my shoulder. "I'll let you get on with whatever you were doing. Don't forget about the casserole." She hobbled to the front door with me following along behind like an obedient puppy dog.

Once the door was shut and locked, I headed to Tom's office. A big desk sat in front of a built-in floor-to-ceiling bookcase. The wood gleamed in the sun streaking through the windows. Casting my gaze around the room, I wondered where to begin looking for a safe.

The desk drawers held nothing of importance or any indication of where a safe might be. Next I looked through the tables sitting at each end of the leather couch and beside the big chair, hoping to find some indication of where a safe would be. Again nothing. On either side of the big windows were more built-in shelves that held books and mementos from all of Tom's travels. A big fireplace took up the last wall. A portrait of Claire hung above the mantel. Checking behind the picture, I was disappointed again.

There wouldn't be room for a safe behind the pictures hanging beside the double doors leading to the hallway, but I checked just to make sure. I wasn't surprised when there wasn't anything hidden behind any of them. There was nowhere else to search.

Sinking down in the massive leather desk chair, I leaned my head back, closing my eyes. *Where would you put your important papers, Claire?* I silently asked. A combination of little sleep and high altitude was wearing me out. The next thing I knew, the chimes on the front door rang out, bringing me out of a sound sleep.

Rubbing my eyes, confusion clouded my mind for a moment before I remembered where I was and why. When the chimes sounded again, I pushed myself out of the comfortable chair. "I'm coming, hold your horses," I muttered. I ran my fingers through my long hair, putting it in some semblance of order.

Although the tall figure was distorted in the beveled glass window, I had little doubt that it was Jake standing there. My stomach twisted. What could he want now? Was he really a good guy? Only one way to find out, I told myself as I pulled open the door.

"Hello Jillian. How are you holding up today?" He didn't give me a chance to offer any greeting before speaking. Again he was dressed casually in jeans and a long sleeved shirt. He said he hoped his father would be proud of what he'd made of himself. Exactly what was that?

I stepped aside, silently inviting him in. This had once

been his home, and could be again if Tom and Claire had left everything to him. Until I could find a will or trust, I had no idea what would happen to anything Claire had owned.

"I'm doing all right, I guess," I finally spoke once we were seated in the living room. "I'm not really sure what I should be doing right now." That much was the truth.

He gave me a sad smile of understanding. "Would you let me take you out for lunch? Or have you already eaten?"

It felt like I had just had breakfast until I looked at the grandfather clock in the corner of the room. A small gasp escaped my lips. It was already two in the afternoon. I'd slept for several hours in Tom's big chair.

"Is something wrong?" Jake's deep voice drew my attention.

"Um, no," I gave him a sheepish smile. "I didn't realize how late it had gotten." I explained about falling asleep in his father's desk chair.

"If I remember correctly, that chair was very comfortable. I used to curl up in it when I was little." A sad smile curved his full lips at the memory.

"It's still comfortable," I assured him.

"If you slept through lunch, you must be hungry now. How about going out with me?" He made it sound like he was asking me for a date.

I gave myself a mental shake. He was just being polite. Or was he trying to insinuate himself in my life to find out how much I knew, or guessed at, concerning Claire's death? Paranoia had taken over my life.

"People brought enough food yesterday to feed an army. In fact, Irma Grover brought over a casserole this morning. It's still in the oven keeping warm." I gave a small chuckle. "Unless I slept so long it's now crispy."

"Mrs. Grover used to be an excellent cook. When I was little I enjoyed sneaking over to her house to con her out of a cookie or two. I'm sure that casserole will be delicious." With that settled, we headed for the kitchen.

Fortunately, I hadn't slept so long that Irma's offering was ruined. I set the piping hot dish on the table while Jake took two plates out of the cupboard. Either Claire had kept everything in the same place it had been while he lived here, or he'd spent a lot of time here with Claire. The thought made me uneasy. Was he the one who was making her sick?

Unsure what the casserole consisted of, I took a small bite. "Oh, wow." My eyes got big. "This is good." I took another bite. "What is it?"

"It's her rendition of Mexican enchiladas."

"The Mexican food I've had is either so spicy it burns the taste buds off your tongue, or so bland it's almost tasteless."

He chuckled. "Maybe that's because you haven't had the real thing. Welcome to Arizona. We have the best Mexican food anywhere. As long as you don't go to one of those places that try to put a gourmet spin on a classic dish," he qualified.

I relaxed, trying to forget why I was in Bisbee for a few minutes and enjoy the company of a handsome man.

Finally, pushing my plate away, I leaned back in the chair. "I can't eat another bite, or I'll explode." Eyeing him across the table, I decided it was time for some serious conversation. "What brought you back to Bisbee after all this time?"

He braced his elbows on the table, propping his chin in his hands. "I've always had ties to the town. I still have a cousin living here, along with a lot of friends. I don't visit often, but I figured this was as good a time as any."

This was a revelation I hadn't known. If Tom's first wife was in Bisbee often, did she have something to do with Claire's murder? Maybe she had convinced someone in her family to do it for her. Unaware of where my thoughts had taken me, Jake continued with his reasons for being here. "As I said earlier, I come to make amends. I almost waited too long, again." He drew a steadying breath. Were the emotions I saw on his handsome features real? Would I ever be able to trust anyone in this town?

"When my father cut me off, I'll admit I was angry." He paused for a moment. "Maybe I even hated him right then. In hindsight, it was the best thing that could have happened to me.

My first two years of college had been a waste of time and money. The only thing I was interested in was partying. I had no idea what I wanted to do with my life. After Dad cut me off, I finally got my head on straight, and set out to prove to him that I wasn't worthless."

His voice took on a faraway quality, and I got the impression he was talking to his dead father instead of me. He shook his head. "I never got to tell him any of this. That's why I came back now. I wanted to tell Claire how sorry I am. I hope she believed me; that she knew I wasn't the same spoiled brat I'd been when she married my father." He drew another deep breath. "For a long time I blamed her for what my father did, but it wasn't her fault, it was mine." That was a pretty speech. I hoped it was sincere.

"What's going to happen to the house now?" I asked. The question was half test, half honest curiosity.

He lifted his broad shoulders in a shrug. "I assume that's up to you."

"What are you talking about? Why is it up to me?"

"Unless Claire left everything to someone else, you're the heir apparent."

"What about you?" My voice held surprise.

"What about me? My father disowned me a number of years ago, remember? He said I had wasted my inheritance on wild living. I wasn't getting anything else from him." He lifted his shoulders in another shrug, like it was no big deal.

Again I wondered how much of this little speech I could believe. Did he really care so little about his father's money or the house he grew up in? I needed to trust someone. Was Jake the one? An image of Detective Dan Tobin flashed through my mind, causing my heart to bump a little harder. He had no connection to this family. Was he the one I should trust?

"Don't you know how Claire structured the trust after my dad died?" Jake's words brought me back to the present.

"She never said anything to me about a trust," I admitted. "I was looking for any legal papers when I fell asleep in the chair."

"Have you looked in the safe?"

"I haven't found that either." I sighed in frustration.

He laughed. "I always thought it was an obvious place to put a safe, but it worked for Dad. If you haven't found it, I guess he put it in the right spot. Come on, I'll show you." He pushed away from the table, holding out a hand to me.

For a long moment I hesitated. I wanted to find the papers, but I wasn't sure I wanted him with me when I looked at them. If the house reverted to him, what would he do about me being here? He waited patiently for me to place my hand in his, then he pulled me out of my chair.

"Right there in plain sight," he said, sweeping his arm towards the wall of books.

"The books?" I looked at him questioningly "The safe is behind the books?"

"Well, sort of," he laughed again as he walked across the room. "More like in the books." Directly behind the desk, at eye level, his eye level, he pushed on a special book spine. Magically, two rows of what looked like books swung aside revealing a metal door with a combination lock.

My mouth dropped open in surprise. "I thought they were just books."

"That was the whole point. Look in there. That's probably where you'll find the trust papers."

"I don't have the combination. How do I get it open?"

He turned to the desk, jotting down a row of numbers with the correct number of turns before each one. "Unless Dad or Claire changed it, this is the combination. Give it a try." Bending down, he placed a kiss on my cheek. "I'll leave you to it. See you later." Before I could think of anything to say, he was gone. Was this a ploy to get me to trust him? Paranoia reared its ugly head again.

Sinking down in the big chair, I stared at the numbers. What would I find in the safe? Would it give me any answers, or just cloud the situation further? My life was on the opposite side of the country. It didn't appear like Jake was interested in the house. What would happen to it?

Folding my arms on the desk, I laid my head down. "Father God, I need some direction here. Is it safe to trust Jake? Did he have something to do with Claire's death? What about Dan Tobin? He's never far from my mind. Is he the one I should trust? Thank you for always being with me." Sitting back up, I accidentally dislodged the desk blotter, revealing the corner of a piece of paper.

Goosebumps traveled up my arms. Was this an answer from God? I pulled the paper out. My name was written in Claire's flowery handwriting.

"Dear Jilly,

"If you're reading this, someone has succeeded in killing me." I sucked in my breath, tears blurring my vision. I wiped my eyes and continued reading. *"Don't grieve for me, Jilly; I'll be with Mom and Daddy. Tom will be with me as well. I know what everyone thought; I was the trophy wife, only after Tom's money. They were wrong. We really did love each other. The age difference didn't matter to us.*

"I wish we could have had this summer together, but that wasn't meant to be. It's my time to go home to Jesus. I'm not afraid.

"I saw or heard something I shouldn't have; I just don't know what. I was too trusting, so you need to be careful where you place your trust. It's too late for me, but you need to watch your back. If you can, find out who did this, and make them pay. But please be careful. I don't want this to happen to you as well.

"I love you, and will always be with you.

"Forever,

"Claire"

For a long while I stared at the note too stunned even to cry. What could she have seen or heard that meant she needed to die? Why hadn't she gone to the police? Would Chief Daniels have believed her? Somehow I doubted that. When her doctor hadn't believed she was really sick, had she given up, or had she told the wrong person?

Reading Claire's words for a second time, my tears finally

found release. "Oh, Claire," I whispered. "Who did this to you?" I laid my head on my arms, sobs wracking my body.

When my tears ran dry, I sat up, resolve stiffening my spine. She said to find out who did this to her and make them pay. I was going to do just that, even if it meant moving to Bisbee.

CHAPTER FOUR

My first instinct was to call Dan Tobin. I reached for the phone, letting my hand rest on the receiver. Would he take the note to the chief? If he did, what would happen then? I doubted Chief Daniels would take it seriously. Jake said some of his mother's family still lived in Bisbee. What if Dan was related to her? Or the chief. I pulled my hand away from the phone like it was a snake about to bite me.

I was beginning to see conspiracies around every corner. Until I figured out all the players, I would heed Claire's warning, and be careful where I placed my trust. I needed to figure out who she had trusted, and who had betrayed her. For now, I would keep the note to myself.

Lifting the blotter, I checked to see if she had left any other secrets for me to find. Disappointed when there was nothing else there, I dropped the blotter back in place. What next? Why hadn't Claire told me about the trust, or given me the combination to the safe? Was she too sick to do anything more than leave that short note? Had someone been watching her, and that's all she could write? My head swirled with all the questions.

I had the combination to the safe, or what Jake said was the combination. If it didn't work, he could always claim that his father or Claire had changed it in the years since he left home. Still I hesitated. Other than learning who the beneficiary of her estate was, I didn't know what good it would do to find the trust papers. I doubted they had anything to do with her death. Unless someone benefiting from the trust had killed her, those papers wouldn't be any help to me.

Spinning the chair around, I looked up at the safe high above my head. What else would I find in there? Releasing a sigh, I pushed myself out of the chair. There was only one way to find out, and that was to open it.

Tom had been as tall as Jake. With the combination at eye level for them, it was too high for me to see what I was doing.

Claire had been my height. Would she have used the safe if she had to stand on a chair every time she needed to open it?

There was a small step stool in the butler's pantry off the kitchen. "Let's get this thing done," I said to the silent room. Leaving the safe's hiding spot uncovered, I headed for the kitchen. As I moved through the entry way, a shadow fell across the beveled glass window in the front door. My heart jumped, then started pounding against my ribs. Jake had left a short time ago. He wouldn't be back that fast. I'd never considered myself a coward, but right then I was feeling very cowardly.

I had no idea what Claire had seen or heard that was important enough to kill over. I could be next if the person thought she had passed that information on to me. I needed to figure out what she'd known and tell the police.

The chimes echoed through the quiet house, causing me to jump again. If they were announcing their arrival, they probably weren't here to do me harm, I reasoned with myself. Anyone with evil intent would sneak in a back door after dark instead of coming to the front door where anyone could see them.

Releasing the breath I'd been holding, I slowly walked to the door. Looking through the design in the window, I could make out a distorted image of the tall man standing there. My heart thumped a little harder, but not in fear this time.

Looking over my shoulder at the library door, I made sure it was impossible to see where the fake books had been swung aside. I turned the knob to release the lock, and opened the door. "Hello Detective Tobin, Dan," I corrected myself, smiling up at him. I swung the door open in a silent invitation for him to enter.

His crooked smile caused the butterflies in my stomach to flutter. What was it about this man that caused this reaction? "I just came by to see how you're doing today. You haven't had any problems?" He shifted from one foot to the other in a self-conscious dance.

"N...no problems," I cleared my throat before I could

make my voice work properly. "Unless you call a creaking old house trouble," I qualified, laughing at myself as I explained about the noises that had kept me awake in the night. "Can I get you something to drink? I have iced tea and lemonade."

He followed me into the kitchen where I poured two frosty glasses of lemonade. "Have you been able to trace that fax yet?" I wasn't sure if he was here on official business, or was it something personal?

He shook his head, his sun-bleached hair brushing against the collar of his shirt. He was several weeks past due for a haircut, but it looked good on him. "It was a dead end." His sigh echoed mine. "Someone in Tucson sent it from one of those copy centers that have fax machines the public can use for a fee. No one remembers who sent it."

"But doesn't that prove someone is trying to cover things up?" I pressed. I refrained from asking what the chief thought of this development.

"Yes, but I still haven't found out who said anything about an autopsy. I asked at the county morgue, but no one admitted giving out any information." For a minute he looked a little uncomfortable. "Claire's doctor did call the morgue after her body had been picked up from the house. He was told you requested an autopsy. I can't believe a respected man like the doc would send that phony fax though."

I had my doubts about the man's competence as a doctor, but I kept the thought to myself. I would hold off going to see him until I got the results of the autopsy. If he had missed something in all the tests he'd run, he might be afraid of a medical malpractice suit. In that case, he might very well have sent that fax.

"I'm not going to give up, Jillian." Dan promised, breaking in on my thoughts as he touched my hand. That familiar zing moved up my arm. "If someone in this town is guilty of murder, I want them caught." He didn't call it his town the way the chief had.

"Have you lived in Bisbee all your life?" I tried to pose the question casually, so he wouldn't know I was checking him out. I needed to know if he had any connection to Jake's family.

"No," he chuckled. "I'm originally from a town in North Dakota that's even smaller than Bisbee. We had one stop light and no police department of our own. We relied on the county sheriff for law enforcement. Right after high school, I joined the Army. I wanted to see something of the world. As it turned out, I was stationed stateside the whole time right here in Arizona as an MP. It was a good fit all the way around, so I stayed and joined the police department here. I've been in Bisbee five years now. I like the town, and the people. Most of them," he qualified. I wondered who it was he didn't like.

He stood up, "I'd better get going. Thanks for the lemonade. Remember to call me if you need anything. This town is known for its ghosts," he teased, "so if those creaking noises turn into rattling chains, I'm just a phone call away."

"I'll keep that in mind," I laughed.

I watched through the window as his car pulled out of the long drive. "Ghosts," I said. Was there anything else that could cause trouble? Did this house have a ghost lurking around? I shook my head. A ghost hadn't killed Claire. Someone very much alive had done that. Turning away from the door, I dismissed that thought, and headed for the butler's pantry and the stepstool.

With the piece of paper Jake had left in my hand, I turned the dial the appropriate number of times to the corresponding numbers. Holding my breath, I twisted the handle. It moved smoothly, and the door swung open.

The waning light coming in the big window and the desk lamp offered little help to see inside, but it was clear that the only things in there were several velvet cases holding Claire's jewelry. Hoping there was something I couldn't see, I moved them aside and I swept my hand around only to come up empty. "Now what," I asked the empty room. I didn't know where else to look.

Leaving the jewelry cases in the safe, I closed the door, and spun the dial. An attorney would have a copy of the trust;

I just had to find out who that was.

With a sigh, I flopped down in the leather chair. "I'm not a detective," I muttered. "How do I go about finding the information I need?" What was I supposed to do now?

~~~

The next few days seemed to go on forever while I waited to hear from the doctor in Tucson. He said it would take several weeks for the results of the toxicology screening to come back. It would take even longer if some exotic toxin was used to poison her. I wasn't sure what I was supposed to do while I waited.

Claire's friends continued to drop by with condolences and food. I had put most of that in the freezer for later. At this rate, I wouldn't have to buy groceries the entire time I was in Bisbee. That presupposed that the autopsy and toxicology report would point to the killer. I held out little hope of that happening. Life wasn't like a television show where the mystery got solved inside of an hour. For now my life was in limbo.

I didn't go far from the phone in case the doctor called with the results of the autopsy. I had given him my cell phone number along with the house phone, but I wasn't taking the chance of missing the call. Whatever the results, I had questions I was hoping he could answer.

Irma was over every afternoon for a 'tea party' as she called it. "I did so enjoy my time with Claire," she told me. Several times she brought over one of her sweet confections to share. If I continued to eat like that, I would need a new wardrobe before I went home.

~~~

"Watching her is like watching grass grow," he grumbled. "What does she do all day in that house by herself?" In the three days she'd been in Bisbee, she hadn't left the house for more than a few minutes at a time. What is she doing in there? How much had Claire known? How much did she tell her sister? The questions swirled in his head. "I need to get in there," he told himself, "but first she has to leave." He gave a

frustrated sigh. Panic was beginning to set in. What the hell does she hope to prove with an autopsy? Everyone knows she died from an overdose of pain meds. It won't prove who gave them to her. He chuckled at that. There was nothing that would prove she didn't take them herself. That was the beauty of this whole plan. No one knew anything about him. I'm like the invisible man which is just the way I liked it, he thought.

That nosy old biddy next door could prove to be a problem, he told himself. She watched everything that went on in the neighborhood. I might have to take her out in order to get in the house, he told himself. He watched as the old woman hobbled down the drive heading to her own house. Maybe I can arrange a little accident that proves fatal to the old bat, he thought with a chuckle.

If Claire showed her what she'd found, it would be all over. With a shake of his head, he chased the thought from his mind. If that old bat knew anything, she would have been on the phone to the police in a New York minute. Invisible or not, he was going to have to be careful. That old biddy could cause all sorts of trouble. He turned away. He'd been here too long.

~~~

If Claire had a will, I hadn't found it. Jake insisted his dad had a trust, but he didn't know where the papers would be since they weren't in the safe. The attorney who drew up the trust had passed away years ago. So where were the trust papers now? I had called the few lawyers in town without any luck. No one had any knowledge of a trust in Tom and Claire's name.

Anticipating the call from Doctor Langston in Tucson every time the phone rang was beginning to wear me out. So far I'd been disappointed each time. I'd been in Bisbee five days, and still nothing. I was beginning to go stir crazy. I'd never been good at waiting for something to happen, and this was doubly hard. After all, how long did it take to do an autopsy?

Late Friday afternoon the house phone rang. Most calls on that line had turned out to be one of Claire's friends. I'd all but given up that it would be the doctor in Tucson. "Hello?"

"Is this Miss Connors?" a deep voice asked.

"Yes, I'm Jillian Connors. May I help you?" I didn't know who would be calling for me on this line.

"My name is Zackery Edmonds. I'm the attorney for Tom and Claire Wilkins' estate." I let out a small gasp. This was the man I needed to talk to. "I've been out of town and just learned of Mrs. Wilkins' death today. I spoke with Mr. Jake Wilkins and he told me that you were in Bisbee. I would like to get together with you to discuss the terms of the trust. Would it be convenient for me to meet with you sometime tomorrow at the house?"

"Um, maybe it would be best if I came to you. Where is your office?"

"My office is in Sierra Vista." He sounded very formal.

I groaned softly. No wonder the attorneys here didn't know anything about Claire's trust. I wasn't sure how to get to Sierra Vista, but the rental car had GPS. I could find my way. If he came here, the entire town would know about the meeting before it was even over.

"There are several others involved, Miss Connors. It would be more convenient for everyone if we all met at the house."

"Others? What others? Who are you talking about?" If there were a lot of people who would benefit from Claire's death, could one of them be her killer?

"Jake Wilkins, for one. I'll explain all of that when I see you." He left his cryptic remark hanging. "What time would be convenient for me to come there?" He didn't leave me any room to argue.

I shrugged. "Any time is fine with me. I'm not going anywhere." At least not until I find Claire's killer, I added silently. Did he know about the pending autopsy? What would he think about my belief that Claire hadn't knowingly taken those pills? Had she told him that someone was trying to kill her? Was he someone else I shouldn't trust?

Agreeing that he would come to the house at one the

following day, I hung up the phone. He didn't say how many others would also be here, and I didn't ask again. I didn't know the protocol in this type of situation. Was I expected to provide refreshments, coffee, tea, cookies? This wasn't a social occasion. I decided not to worry about it.

~~~

Mr. Edmonds hadn't even arrived when Irma showed up on my doorstep. I was only mildly surprised that she was part of this dog and pony show. She was a good friend to Claire, so maybe Claire had left something to her.

Jake was the next to arrive. "Do you know why Mr. Edmonds wants me here?" He seemed puzzled by this meeting, but I didn't know if it a ruse to throw me off.

I shook my head. "He said he'd explain when he came today. I don't know who else is going to be here. Do you know if your father named other people as beneficiaries?"

He gave his dark head a shake. He was in the dark as much as I was. "Dad wasn't big on sharing information with anyone. We spoke very little after he disowned me." There was sadness in his voice, but he pushed it aside. "I guess we'll have to wait and see. This could prove to be an interesting afternoon." Interesting wasn't how I would describe it. This was more like a side show to me.

"What did he tell you when he called?" I was hoping to gain a little information before this party started.

"Only that he needed to meet with me and several others. He seemed surprised that I was in town. When he said he would be contacting you, I told him you were here."

When a fancy car pulled into the drive, I assumed the stranger inside was Mr. Edmonds. The only occupant was a man dressed in an expensive suit. As he got out of the car, I studied him through the wavy glass. He was exactly as I imagined an attorney to be; in his mid-fifties or early sixties with gray hair that he wore slightly longer than most men his age. He looked familiar, but I couldn't guess why. I quickly dismissed that thought as a trick of the old glass. In the small tourist town where everyone dressed in T-shirts and jeans or shorts, the elegantly dressed man would stand out like a sore thumb. I certainly hadn't seen anyone like that on the only day I had driven through town.

Pastor Bennett and a woman I presumed was his wife followed closely behind the fancy attorney. I held the door open for everyone. Mr. Edmonds made quick work of introducing himself, and went into the library without another word. The fact that he seemed familiar with the big house was a little disturbing to me. How many times had he been here? What would be the purpose? I turned my mind back to the others who had followed the attorney in.

Pastor Bennett came up to me, taking my hand. "How are you doing today, Miss Connors, Jillian?" I waggled my hand back and forth in a so-so gesture. "I'd like to introduce my wife, Emily," he continued. I was struck by his kindness once again. I had already trusted him with what Claire had told me. What would he think of her note? Maybe he was the one I should show it to. "Do you know why the attorney wanted us here today?" he asked softly.

I shook my head. "I have no idea what any of this is about," I admitted.

Mr. Edmonds was sitting at Tom's big desk, tapping his pen on the blotter. He was clearly in a hurry to get this over with. His fancy briefcase was open, a stack of papers in front of him. Once everyone was settled, he nodded his head in a grave manner. "I want to thank you for coming today. As I explained when I spoke to each of you earlier, this is about a bequest left to you by Claire Wilkins."

He looked down at the papers on the desk like he was reading from a script. "The deed to the church that Mrs. Wilkins attended since she moved to Bisbee is to be turned over to the church free and clear." I didn't know what kind of arrangement they had with Claire or Tom, but now wasn't the time to ask. It didn't matter anyway.

Pastor and Mrs. Bennett let out a small gasp. "That... that was very generous of her," Pastor Bennet stammered.

The lawyer turned to Irma next. "Mrs. Wilkins was very

fond of you. She wanted you to have the sterling silver tea service she always used when you came to visit her. She enjoyed your visits very much." Tears sparkled in the older woman's faded eyes. She seemed unable to speak for several minutes.

"Now to the house and the remainder of the estate held by The Wilkins Family Trust," Mr. Edmonds looked at Jake and me. "It will all remain in the name of the trust. Miss Connors can live in the house as long as she chooses. There are no stipulations for or against turning it into a bed and breakfast as Mrs. Wilkins intended. Mr. Jake Wilkins and Miss Jillian Connors are to be co-trustees. You will each receive an equal share of any monies coming in from the investments and rent on the properties held by the trust."

"No, that's not right," Jake spoke up, causing my heart to sink. His professions of not caring about his father's money were all false.

"Excuse me?" Mr. Edmonds' eyebrows shot up so high they almost disappeared into his hair line.

"Maybe you weren't aware that my father disowned me several years ago. Claire shouldn't have changed the trust." He turned to me. "Everything should go to you."

Mr. Edmonds cleared his throat loudly, drawing our attention back to him. "Mrs. Wilkins changed nothing. The trust is just as your father had it written. It was always to be divided between you and Miss Connors if both he and Mrs. Wilkins were deceased. He never had your name removed from the trust."

"Then you have to do it now," Jake interrupted. "That's the way he wanted it. This isn't right."

"I'll do no such thing," Mr. Edmonds was indignant. "Your father was aware of the fact that you were working to prove yourself to him. It's unfortunate that he passed on before you accomplished that. You will get half of the proceeds from the estate as originally stated, while Miss Connors will receive the other half. As I stated before, if either of you still want to turn the house into a bed and breakfast as

Mrs. Wilkins planned, you may do that."

Either Jake was a world-class actor, or he was being sincere. I hoped it was the latter. I didn't think he could fake the shock currently written on his face.

The proceedings concluded a few minutes later. Jake continued to argue with the lawyer, but it was no use. The legal documents couldn't be changed. "Why can't I sign my half over to Jillian?" he finally asked. "It's what should have been done in the first place."

Mr. Edmonds shook his head. "That isn't what your father, or Mrs. Wilkins, wanted. No matter what, you were still his son. Do you really want to turn your back on that? I don't think that would have made your father happy."

Jake's shoulders drooped. He'd lost the argument, and he knew it.

"Would it be all right if I left the tea service here as long as you stay in Bisbee?" Irma asked before she left. "Maybe we can have tea the way I did with Claire?" Her voice trailed up at the end in a hopeful question.

I gave the small woman a warm hug. "I would enjoy that. Come over anytime." It would be a nice way for both of us to remember Claire.

"Will you turn the house into a bed and breakfast as Claire had planned?" The others still lingering in the library turned at the question. Even Mr. Edmonds seemed interested in my answer.

I shrugged. "That's something Jake and I will have to decide." That wasn't the answer she was looking for, but it was the only one I could give her. I had no idea what Jake would want to do with the house. It would mean I had to move to Arizona. I didn't know if that was something I wanted. I had no family anywhere, but my friends were all in South Carolina. Jake never said where he lived, or what he did for a living. Did either of us want to relocate to Bisbee?

Pastor and Mrs. Bennett stopped on their way out. "It was very generous of your sister to deed the church building and property to our congregation. The building has been there for more than seventy-five years, our congregation has paid a nominal rent each year for its use."

"I hope everyone will remember this was Claire's gift to the church, not mine. But she didn't do it for her own glory or praise. If you could remind people of that, I would appreciate it." I didn't want anyone fawning over me because of her gift.

"Yes of course," Pastor Bennett agreed. "We'll see you on Sunday then. Again, we're sorry for your loss. Claire will be missed by everyone." The couple seemed in shock over the church's windfall as they left.

As he left, Mr. Edmonds handed Jake and me an envelope. "You will each receive a similar check at the end of each quarter as your share of the proceeds from the trust." He gave Jake a stern glare. "Don't even think of turning your share over to Miss Connors. It will have grave tax ramifications for both of you." With that pronouncement, he sailed out the door without a backward glance.

With the others gone, Jake turned to me, a worried frown drawing his dark brows together in twin question marks. "I hope you believe that I didn't know my father had done that. I probably wouldn't have pushed myself so hard if I'd known he was still looking out for me. Maybe he knew that, and that's why he never told me." He looked away as though looking into the past. "I wanted to prove to him, and myself, that I wasn't worthless."

"Maybe he wanted to force you to stand on your own. The fact that he didn't disown you says he knew you had grown up." I placed my hand on his arm in comfort. He looked down at me, his dark eyes intense. For a long moment, I thought he was going to kiss me.

Claire's note and her admonition not to trust anyone flashed through my mind. Getting involved with Jake, or anyone at this time, wasn't a good idea. I dropped my hand taking several steps back breaking the spell that had held us in its grip.

CHAPTER FIVE

Clearing his throat, Jake gave a weak smile. "Thank you for saying that, Jill. I hope it's true. Um, I guess we need to discuss this situation we're in." He led the way into the living room. What situation was he talking about? Maybe I had been mistaken about his intention.

"What do you want to do with the house? Claire said you're a teacher. Are you out of school for the summer?" Neither of us had bothered to look inside the envelope Mr. Edmonds had given us.

I nodded my head. Wisps of my longish hair brushed against my neck, sticking to my damp skin. "I was planning on spending the summer with Claire." I didn't tell him I wasn't going anywhere until I got the results of the autopsy and the toxicology report. I didn't know if he was aware that I had requested them. "What about you? Don't you have to go back to work? I don't even know where you live." I wanted to redirect his attention away from me.

"I still live in Tucson," he said. "After Dad cut me off, I managed to finish college with a Master's Degree in computer science. A friend and I started a computer security company about a year ago. It's small, and we work long hours to keep it growing, but I can work from anywhere. I'm just not sure I want to move back to Bisbee."

"How did you decide to get into computer security?" I asked in an effort to keep him talking about himself. The more I learned about him, the easier it would be to know if I could trust him.

"I've always been interested in all things technological," he shrugged. "It just seemed the natural progression of my interest. When one of my friends had his identity stolen by a computer hacker, I realized how much damage that can do. It took him several years to get things straightened out, and he still has trouble every now and then.

"I decided if there was anything I could do, I couldn't let

that happen to anyone else. My partner and I teach classes on computer security and how to prevent identity theft, as well as working with companies to secure their business information."

"How can you keep your business afloat if you've been here for the past two months?"

"I haven't been here the entire time," he chuckled. "When I'm here I stay with a cousin. My intention was to be here for a week, maybe two. When Claire started getting sick, I decided to come back on the weekends to check on her." He paused, looking away from me. "When she died, I was in Tucson. I keep thinking that if I had been here, she might not have taken those pills. I'm so sorry."

I wasn't sure what to say, there was plenty of guilt to go around. Either Claire hadn't told him someone was trying to kill her, or he was the killer trying to find out how much I knew. Until I knew otherwise, I would play my cards close to my vest. If he had been in Tucson when someone gave her those pills, he couldn't be the killer. Or was that simply his alibi, while a local relative with no connection to Claire managed to give her the pills? How was I ever going to prove she hadn't taken them herself? There were too many people to suspect.

He looked up at the portrait of his father again. "Memories that I always thought were bad ones have morphed into good ones. Some are rather warm and fuzzy now." He continued to look at his father's face. "I'm glad he knew I'd changed," he said softly. "It's always hurt that he thought so little of me."

He turned back to me. "Do you want to move to Bisbee, maybe even run a bed and breakfast?"

I considered the question for a moment. "That was Claire's dream," I answered the last half of his question. "I don't know that it's mine. Right now, I have all summer to decide what I'm going to do." The idea of living in this quirky town was beginning to take root in the back of my mind. I loved teaching; maybe I could get a job here if I decided to stay.

When one door closes, God opens a window. Claire's death closed that door. Had God led me here to begin the next part of my life? "If I stay here, I'll need to find a job. Or open a bed and breakfast," I added with a chuckle.

"What do you think of the idea of turning the house into a bed and breakfast?" I asked. I was still trying to figure out if he had objected to Claire's plans. I didn't know if her plans for the house had anything to do with her death. I couldn't think of any other reason someone would kill her though.

He shook his head, a stray lock of dark hair falling over his forehead. "It would be a lot of work. Right now there is no way I could help you run it. My business keeps me very busy."

"That's not what I asked. This was your home. Would it bother you to have strangers staying here on a regular basis?"

He gave a small laugh. "Unlike some people in my family, I'm not sentimental about this old place. I would rather see that happen than let it fall into disrepair like some of the old houses in town have done."

Who was he talking about? Were these family members on his father's side or his mother's side? I knew so little about Tom's family, I couldn't answer that question. Maybe one of Tom's relatives hadn't wanted the house turned into a B&B.

At the sound of merry-go-round music, Jake looked around, a puzzled frown drawing his brows together. When I pulled my cell phone from my pocket waggling it at him, he laughed, stepping away to give me some privacy.

"Miss Connors, this is Doctor Langston." The deep voice announced as soon as I said hello. When I didn't respond right away, he continued, "At the Medical Center in Tucson."

"Oh, yes, sorry. Have you finished...the autopsy?" I stammered out the word. I had almost given up on this call.

"Yes, and I'm sorry to say your assumption was correct. Her doctor didn't look very far for the cause of her illness. The initial cause of death most likely was the overdose of pills, but there is also liver and stomach damage consistent with some kind of corrosive substance. I won't know exactly what was given to her until I get the tox report back. That won't be for several more weeks, but she was definitely being given something over a period of a month or more with the intent to kill her."

I gasped, gripping the back of the chair I had just left. Jake was by my side instantly, holding me up. "You're sure? There isn't any doubt?" I asked. Although I didn't believe Claire had killed herself, having it confirmed that someone was trying to kill her, didn't give me any comfort.

"No doubts, Miss Connors. I'm sorry. I'll be sending you a copy of my report as soon as it's typed up, but I wanted to let you know what I found right away. I'll also fax a copy to the chief of police there in Bisbee along with a hard copy. She would have died within a month or less if someone had continued to give her the same substance. Her death is definitely suspicious, and should be looked at as a homicide."

The phone slipped from my fingers, and my head spun. Jake picked up the phone as he pushed me back into the chair. I could hear the doctor continue talking, but the buzzing in my ears prevented me from understanding the words.

As Jake listened, his face went gray. "Thank you for your help, doctor. As you can imagine, Miss Connors isn't feeling very well at the moment. She'll have to call you back." He didn't wait for the doctor to acknowledge his statement before hitting the end button on the phone.

Kneeling down in front of me, he gripped my hands. I felt as though I was encased in ice, his hands warm on mine. His dark eyes stared at me. "You've suspected Claire didn't kill herself all along." It wasn't a question. Tears blurred my vision. Unable to make my voice work yet, I nodded my head. "The police didn't say anything to me about doing an autopsy. Why were they keeping it under wraps?"

Anger boiled up inside me again, helping to dry my tears, and I swiped my hand across my eyes. "*I* paid to have it done. The chief didn't think it was necessary since her doctor was willing to sign the death certificate." My voice was harsh. Too agitated to sit still, I stood up, pacing across the room. "He wouldn't listen to me when I told him Claire wouldn't take those pills of her own free will."

"Was her doctor that incompetent? Didn't he even check to find out what had happened to her? I knew she had been going to the doctor, but she wasn't getting better." His dark eyes followed me as I paced across the big room.

"Who would do this? Why would someone kill her? What is going on in this town?" Jake's questions echoed the ones I'd been asking since learning of Claire's death. Unfortunately, I didn't have any answers for him.

Needing time alone to take in what the doctor had said I finally convinced him to go back to his cousin's house. Standing at the front door, he placed his hand on my cheek, bringing my face up so I was looking at him. "Don't think for a minute that I'm going to leave you alone to face this by yourself. I wasn't a very good son or stepson, but I'd like to think I've grown up some in the last few years." He placed a soft kiss on my lips.

Alone, I went back into the library, sitting down in Tom's big desk chair. I pulled Claire's note from under the blotter. Should I take it to Dan now? Would this finally convince Chief Daniels that Claire hadn't taken those pills herself? What had Claire meant that she'd seen or heard something she shouldn't have? I still had more questions than answers.

Unless Jake was lying about where he was when Claire died, he couldn't have given her the pills that killed her. But someone had been poisoning her before that. Was it simply a coincidence that he arrived days before she starting getting sick? What if one of his local relatives was working with him or for him? Claire had never hurt anyone in her life. I needed to figure out why someone wanted to kill her.

Doctor Langston said it would take another week or more to get the final lab results back. Now that murder has been confirmed, would that help speed things up? I didn't know enough to even figure out why those tests took so long.

After digesting what the doctor said, I called him back. I still had a few questions. I didn't wait for any greetings when he answered the phone. "How could someone give Claire poison without her knowing it? Wouldn't she get sick right away?"

"My educated guess is that they put it in the food she ate."

"But wouldn't she get suspicious of that person if she got sick right after she ate something they gave her?"

"Whatever they gave her was in minute amounts. It wouldn't make her sick immediately. It had to build up in her system. She wouldn't connect getting sick with any food she'd been given."

I spent the remainder of the afternoon throwing out all the food people had brought over when I first arrived. If one of them had been poisoning Claire, would they try the same thing on me? Until I knew why she died, I wouldn't know if someone might go after me next.

~~~

First thing the next morning, a distraught-looking Chief Daniels was at my door. "You were right," he began as soon as I opened the door. "The doctor in Tucson faxed me a copy of the autopsy results. I can't believe I missed the signs." He reached out to take my hand, but I moved back before he could touch me.

He followed me step for step, closing the door behind him. As the door clicked shut, my heart jumped into my throat. Was he the killer? Was he going to kill me now? He stalked across the entry to the living room, throwing himself onto the couch only to bounce back up. I followed at a safe distance. He said he was a friend of Claire's, but she had never said anything about knowing the chief of police. As it turns out, there were a lot of things she hadn't told me.

"I want you to know I am going to find out who did this and make them pay." He looked down at me. "I can't imagine why someone would do that to her. She was a kind and gentle lady, everyone loved her." He wouldn't say the word 'murder'.

"Not everyone," I contradicted. "Someone was poisoning her for several months." The doctor hadn't said poison, but it was the only term I could think to describe what had been given to her. Until I knew better, I suspected everyone, including the chief of police.

"Yes, of course. I just meant that the people who knew her thought she was a very nice lady. Did she ever give you any indication she was having trouble with someone here in town?"

"I've told you everything she said to me the last time I talked to her. She had no idea who was trying to kill her, or why." It looked like this was going to take some time. Sitting down, I drew my legs under me. Once again I debated whether to show him the note Claire left for me, and once again I decided to wait to see if he really was going to do something. Claire had no idea who was doing this to her, so the note wouldn't be much help.

Before he could ask another question, I turned his question on him. "Can you think of any reason why someone would want to kill her? You would be a better judge of the people here than I would be." I wanted to ask about Jake's relatives, but couldn't point fingers at them until I had more information.

He shook his head. "There isn't a lot of crime in Bisbee. We haven't had a murder in years."

"That isn't what I asked. I know some people were unhappy when Tom left his estate to Claire."

A dark scowl drew his bushy brows together. "You mean Myriam Wilkins. I've known her since grade school. She would never do something like this. Sure, she was upset when Tom cut his only son out of his will, but she wouldn't kill for money."

I didn't contradict him. Apparently he hadn't heard the news about the estate. I wasn't going to be the one to enlighten him. Instead I asked another question. "Have you been able to find out who sent that fax? Who gave out the information that an autopsy was going to be performed?"

He scowled at me again. "No one in my department would release information like that."

Again he chose to misinterpret my question. I didn't pursue the subject this time. Dan Tobin had already given me what little information they had. Since her doctor also knew about the autopsy, maybe he was the one who sent the fax. It was one more thing I would ask him when I confronted him with the information I now had. I wouldn't let on to the chief I knew about that. Without putting his doubts into words, I had gotten the impression that Dan didn't care much for his boss.

The chief stood up, a sad expression on his round face. "I'm sorry I didn't see what was happening to Claire. I still don't want to believe anyone I know would do something like that." With that pronouncement, he walked out, closing the door gently behind him. Was he suggesting a stranger was poisoning her? A stranger gave her those pills? I shook my head in disgust.

His promise to find the person who did this to Claire didn't hold much conviction, and I wasn't sure what to make of his visit. In a town of six thousand, he couldn't know everyone. Had he known Claire as well as he claimed? There was still a great deal I didn't know about the people in her life. I wish Claire had told me about what was happening to her before it was too late. If I had known, maybe I could have convinced her to leave Bisbee, even for a little while until she recovered.

For a long while after the chief left, I stayed in the big chair trying to sort through everything that was going on. Someone wanted Claire dead. If I could figure out why, maybe I could figure out who that person was. The chief had jumped to Myriam's defense, even though I hadn't mentioned her by name. They had grown up together. How well did he know her now? I didn't even know if she still lived in Bisbee.

The ringing of the telephone broke in on my thoughts. I decided to let the answering machine pick it up. I didn't know anyone here. If one of my friends at home was calling they would call my cell phone. I could listen to the message later.

A knock at the back door brought my jumbled thoughts to a halt. Until this moment I had forgotten about Dusty Reynolds. She had come to the back door my first night here, but I hadn't seen her since. It looked like she was paying me another visit. The shocked expression clouding her heavy features said she had already heard the news.

"I just heard what really happened to Claire," she

confirmed. "Is it true? Did someone really kill her?" She brushed past me into the kitchen. "This is terrible. I can't believe it. Who would do something like that?" Her questions came rapid-fire without giving me a chance to answer. She wrung her hands while she paced around the spacious kitchen.

Bisbee was a small town, but I was still amazed how fast the news had traveled. How long would it take before the entire town was buzzing with the news?

Dusty finally ran out of steam, throwing herself into a chair at the big table. "I can't believe someone would do this," she repeated. "Bisbee is a friendly town. This isn't like Chicago or New York where people are killed every day. That kind of thing just doesn't happen here." I didn't argue with her. The facts did that for me.

"What are you going to do?" She turned her attention back to me.

I lifted my shoulders in a shrug. "Make sure whoever did this pays for their crime." In my mind it was that simple. I couldn't do anything else.

"So you're going to stay in Bisbee? What about your job? Don't you have to go back?"

I shrugged again. "I haven't worked out all the details." I had finally gotten around to opening the envelope Mr. Edmonds gave me. The size of the check was shocking. If I received a check for the same amount four times a year, money wouldn't be a problem. Still, I would need something to occupy my time. There was always the option of opening a bed and breakfast.

"If you stay, are you still going to turn the house into a bed and breakfast like Claire planned?" she asked as though reading my mind. She looked around the kitchen as if she expected to see signs of that happening.

"The house doesn't belong to me alone," I hedged. "Jake is half owner."

"Jake?" She looked shocked by that revelation. "But I thought his father disowned him." This was one piece of news the grapevine had missed. I guess it wasn't so efficient after all.

"Apparently not," I said. If she was fishing for more information, she was doomed to disappointment. I wasn't going to give her any details.

"What is he going to do? Is he moving back here?"

"That's not up to me. You'll have to ask him."

"I just might do that. He was a spoiled, rich kid and not a very nice person most of the time. He got into all sorts of trouble. When his father married Claire, he treated her terribly. I don't know why she even let him back in her life."

"Because Claire was a very forgiving person," I stated emphatically. "She didn't hold a grudge on anyone." Maybe if she had, she would still be alive, I added silently.

CHAPTER SIX

After Dusty left, I decided I had been cooped up in the house long enough. It was time to get out and do a little exploring around town. For a little while I just wanted to be a regular tourist with no cares, no worries. I wanted to forget what had brought me to Bisbee, what had happened to my sister. I grabbed my purse and headed downtown.

The streets of Old Bisbee were as confusing as I remembered. I almost turned the wrong way on a one-way street, catching my error in time to avoid an accident. Finding a parking place, I decided walking was my best bet until I knew my way around a little better.

For the next few hours, I tried to forget about the autopsy report, and pretend I was a tourist, enjoying myself. The stores were eclectic, with everything from kitschy knick-knacks to beautiful jewelry, paintings, pottery, and so much more. There were even wine tasting rooms where I bought a bottle of wine to take with me.

When the hair on the back of my neck began to prickle, I looked around. There were people everywhere. Was someone watching me? Paying close attention to the people around me, I spotted a man I'd seen in several of the stores I visited. Was it a coincidence, or something more sinister? When he saw me looking at him, he quickly turned away. The day suddenly felt a little less fun, a little less light-hearted.

If he was really following me, I didn't want to go back to an empty house. Remaining in a crowd seemed to be a better idea. I didn't know if I should call Dan, or play it cool and see what happened. If the strange man continued to show up everywhere I went, I could always call Dan then.

Having lunch in town sounded like a good idea. Maybe the man would get tired of waiting for me, and go away. There were a number of small cafes to choose from. I settled on a cute little bistro in the heart of Old Bisbee. It didn't look like the place a man would venture into without his wife or girlfriend.

Like the rest of the town, the restaurant was crowded with tourists. I'd lost all track of time, and realized for the first time that it was Saturday. Was the town always this busy, or just on the weekend? That would be very good for any business, including a bed and breakfast. Maybe Claire had been onto something. If I was going to stay here, I'd have to think that idea through a little more thoroughly.

When a man sat down at the table across from me, I gave a surprised start. Was this some small town custom-sitting down with a stranger to make them feel welcome? But I wasn't feeling welcome, I felt threatened.

"Hello, Miss Connors. May I call you Jillian?" He smiled calmly.

"No, you may not. Who are you?" In small town America that might be considered rude, but I didn't care. I didn't know this man.

"My name is Roland Granger. I was a friend of Claire's."

"Really. She never mentioned you."

He gave me another one of his serene smiles. "No, I don't suppose she did."

"Why's that?" He was dressed casually in jeans and a T-shirt like all the other tourists in town. The hot Arizona sun had turned his face and arms a rich golden color. His reddish-blonde hair was perfectly styled without a hair out of place.

He lifted his broad shoulders. "I'm a private person. I don't like people knowing my business."

"Yet you sat down with a perfect stranger, interrupting her lunch."

"I was friends with Claire," he stated again. "I would like to be friends with you as well."

Not going to happen, I thought. I just stared at him without commenting. I let the silence stretch out until it grew uncomfortable. He finally sighed, standing up. He was very tall, probably taller than either Dan or Jake. I tilted my head back to look up at him. Like Jake, he was extremely good-looking, almost to the point of being phony.

"Maybe another time, Miss Connors." He tipped his head, walking out of the small café without another word.

That was weird. I tried to remember any time that Claire had mentioned knowing a man named Roland Granger. We talked often, but she never said anything about a man by that name. In fact, she rarely mentioned any man. Tom had been the love of her life. If she had lived, I seriously doubted she would ever have remarried.

My appetite wasn't what it had been before that little episode, but I ordered anyway. I still wasn't ready to go back to the empty house, especially if someone was following me.

I took my time over the sandwich I'd ordered. It was much later when I finally left the restaurant. I breathed a sigh of relief when the man I'd seen before was nowhere in sight. Maybe it was just my overactive imagination that had me thinking he was following me, I told myself. Roland Granger had also disappeared. Hopefully he would stay that way. Something about the man didn't ring true. I didn't believe he was Claire's friend.

I decided to drive around some before heading back to the house. If someone was following me, maybe I could lose them on the confusing streets of town. I kept a close watch on the rearview mirror to see if I could spot the same car behind me more than once.

The San Jose district of Bisbee was where all the city and county business took place, including the police department. If he thought I was going to there to lodge a complaint, it might make my possible stalker back off until I could figure out what he was up to.

It was also where the locals shopped for groceries and other items that weren't available in the small specialty shops in Old Bisbee. As I drove by the police department, Dan pushed open the door, stepping onto the sidewalk. Without conscious thought I pulled to the curb, touching the horn to get his attention.

"Well, hello there." He leaned down, looking in the passenger window. His crooked smile sent my senses reeling.

I didn't know what this man had that others didn't, but it was potent. "I was planning on stopping by to see you today. I read the autopsy report. I'm so sorry. Are you okay?"

He'd made a habit of stopping by the house every afternoon, to check up on me he said. I hoped that wasn't the only reason. I looked forward to his company.

I nodded my head as I choked back a fresh bout of tears. For a few hours this morning I had been able to push all the bad things that had happened aside. Now they came crashing down on me.

"I'm sorry," he said again. "I was just going to lunch. Would you care to join me?" He changed the subject.

I blinked away the tears, turning my mind to Dan. "Thanks, but I just finished lunch." I could feel my face heat up when I heard the regret in my voice.

"How about some iced tea then? It's a warm day."

An hour later, I pulled into the drive. The time I spent with Dan and away from the house had helped to clear my mind. I hadn't even thought to tell him about the odd feeling of being watched. *Oh well*, I gave a mental shrug. *It was probably just my imagination.* I hadn't thought to mention Roland Granger either. If the man lived in town, maybe Dan would know him. I told myself I would ask him later. Until then, I pushed all thoughts of both men out of my mind.

"Yoo-hoo," Irma waved a lace hanky at me as I stepped out of the car. She was standing at a window on the second floor of her house. She must have been watching for me to return. "Would it be all right if I came over for tea? I don't want to make a nuisance of myself." She had also been a daily visitor. If Claire had this much company, it was a wonder she ever got any work done getting ready to open her bed and breakfast.

"Of course, give me a few minutes to put some groceries away." Since I had thrown away so much of the food people brought over, I had decided to stock up while I was out. Unlocking the door, I stepped inside. With two bags full of groceries in my arms, I blindly reached out to deposit my purse on the small table in the entry. When it hit the floor, I stared at the empty space where the table had sat this morning. Now it was on the opposite side of the entry.

My stomach did flip flops, and not the good kind it did each time Dan smiled at me. Had the ghost he teased me about suddenly decided to pay me a visit? Or was this a flesh and blood type of visitation?

I didn't have time to think about it though when the chimes on the front door rang. Irma was already here for our tea party.

"I saw the chief pay you a visit this morning," she said when I opened the door for her. "Is everything all right?" She followed me into the kitchen while I put away the groceries and prepared the tea.

Her house was down the sloping hill from Claire's. I wasn't sure how she was able to keep track of everything that went on here. How many hours did she spend watching from a window on the second floor? Was she spying on me, or looking out for me? Either way, it was an uncomfortable thought. I didn't want or need someone watching me. How many others in the neighborhood did she keep watch over?

Claire's warning flashed in my mind. Did I need to worry about Irma? Was I being too trusting? How many people did I need to be distrustful of? I couldn't isolate myself from everyone and still search out a killer.

Turning my mind back to the small woman, I decided she hadn't heard that Claire's death was now considered a homicide. What would she think of that development? Could she give some suggestions who might want to harm Claire? I needed to figure out who Claire's friends were, as well as her enemies. Trying to temporarily put all those thoughts aside, I explained about the chief's visit, and what the autopsy had revealed.

"Oh, my goodness, that's just awful," she exclaimed. Her face turned pale. "Who would do something like that?"

"That's what I plan on finding out," I muttered. My anger boiled up again, and she patted my hand.

"You just let the police handle this. I've already lost one neighbor. I don't want to lose another one." She leaned close, lowering her voice to a whisper. "That police chief isn't worth a pile of cow manure, but I've heard tell that the detective he has working for him is pretty sharp. If someone did this to Claire, I'll bet he'll figure it out. He isn't going to let anything happen to you. I think he's sweet on you." My face heated up at the implication that she knew of his daily visits as well.

For a woman in her seventies and living alone, she had her finger on the pulse of most everything that happened around her. If she had been watching the house for me to return, would she have seen someone break in while I was out? I needed to check the locks to see if I could tell if they had been jimmied.

Before I could decide how to ask that question, she asked one of her own. "Have you decided if you'll be staying here after the funeral?"

I shook my head. "I haven't made any definite plans, but I'm thinking about it." Until I knew who I could trust, including Irma, I wasn't going to give out very many details of my plans.

Her wrinkled face lit up. "I think that would be wonderful." She patted my hand again. "I do so miss my visits with Claire. Will you go through with her plans to open a bed and breakfast?"

I shrugged. "I haven't thought that far ahead. I'll have to see how things work out."

"What will you do with the house if you go back to South Carolina? It would be a shame to let it sit empty. I'm afraid some of those hippie-type people who have moved into town would take advantage of an empty house. Young people nowadays don't want to work. They want everything handed to them." I imagine grandparents have been saying similar things about the younger generation since the beginning of time.

Before I could answer, a knock at the back door brought a sharp sniff from Irma. "That will be Dusty. She was always bothering Claire." She struggled to stand up. "I'll leave now. Thank you for the lovely tea. You be careful of that one, too." She nodded her gray head towards the kitchen door where Dusty waited. "I don't know what her game is, but she's always poking her nose where it doesn't belong." At the front door she turned back to me. "You are still going to church with me tomorrow, right?"

"Of course, I'll pick you up at nine sharp." A satisfied smile curved her lips as she shuffled out. I didn't get the chance to ask if she'd seen anyone at the house while I was out. That would have to wait for another time.

Dusty knocked again, and I hurried to the kitchen. In the few days I'd been in Bisbee, I'd had a revolving door of visitors. I wondered again how Claire had gotten any work done on the house. "Hello, Dusty." I held the door open for her to come in. "I haven't heard anything new since this morning."

"Oh, I know. Investigations don't get resolved as fast as they do on television. I came over to rescue you from our nosy neighbor. She's a sweet old lady, but she was always bothering Claire when she was trying to get things ready to open her bed and breakfast. I think she's lonely. Her kids don't come to see her very often." How had she known Irma was here? I wasn't even sure which house was hers. How many people were watching me? The thought made me uneasy.

"Why do you come to the back door instead of the front like everyone else does?" It was time to do a little fishing of my own. Old Bisbee had been a mining town; the houses had been built for the miners on the side, top, and bottom of the many hills surrounding the mines. There were other houses higher up the mountain. Did one of them belong to her?

Her rumbling chuckle spoke of too many cigarettes smoked over the years. "My place is on the next street over and further up the hill. Climbing the stairs back there saves me from walking all the way around the block and climbing even more stairs. Bisbee is famous for its stairs, you know." She nodded in the direction of Irma's house. "They don't keep some people home though. Irma probably knows more about what goes on in this town than the police." *Maybe they both did,* I silently added.

I thought small towns were supposed to be friendly, but there was little love lost between these two neighbors. They each seem jealous of the friendship Claire had with the other woman.

Noticing the groceries I still had to put away, Dusty turned back to me. "How about letting me buy you dinner tonight? I hope I'm not asking too late. Has that young detective already asked you out?" Her teasing smile lifted the corners of her mouth.

How did she know I'd seen Dan today? Did she also know about his daily visits? Did I live in a fish bowl?

She chuckled, guessing at my thoughts. "No, you aren't the main topic of gossip in town. I had lunch with Jeff in the San Jose district. We saw the two of you leaving the café."

It took a minute for it to register who she was talking about. "You're dating the chief?" I don't know why that surprised me, but it did. Was this how the chief knew Claire?

She looked down at her hands, seemingly embarrassed. "Dating is for teenagers. I guess you could say we're keeping company or we're companions." She lifted her shoulders in a shrug. "Are you free for dinner tonight?" she asked again, changing the subject. The fact that she was dating the chief was oddly disturbing, and I didn't know why. As long as they were both single, they could date whoever they wanted. Was this how she knew the results of the autopsy so quickly this morning? How many other things did the chief tell her?

"As you know, I had lunch in town just a couple of hours ago," I answered evasively. "I'm not really hungry yet." Would that be a good enough excuse so she would back off? She didn't need to know that I only had iced tea with Dan.

"I don't usually eat dinner until closer to seven in the evenings. I want to make sure my guests are settled before I go anywhere."

Every now and then inspiration strikes me, and this was

one of those times. "I'd like to see your place sometime. Maybe you could give me a tour?" I raised my eyebrows questioningly. "Maybe you could fill me in on how much work is involved in running a B&B. That might help me decide what I'm going to do." It wasn't exactly the truth, but it sounded good.

"So you're planning on sticking around, and going ahead with Claire's plans?" Was there a hint of disappointment in her voice? Again I wondered if she had been afraid of the competition Claire was offering. Would she kill for something like that? What did that have to do with what Claire said about see or hearing something she shouldn't?

I shrugged. "I don't know what my plans are right now. It all depends on how long it takes to find the person who..." My voice trailed off. It was still hard to say the word murder out loud.

She gave my hand a pat. "I understand. I'd be happy to show you around my place. Care to go now? My guests are all out exploring the town or on wine tasting tours in the area. I have some free time." She jumped out of the chair, excited about the idea of showing off her place.

Leaving the house by the back door, I locked it behind me. "It isn't necessary to lock your doors here," Dusty chuckled. "There isn't a lot of crime in a town this size."

"I'm from the big city. Locking doors just comes natural to me." Even with the doors locked this morning someone had managed to get inside to move that table in the entry. I didn't believe for a minute that a ghost had done that.

Dusty was right; coming to the back door was much shorter for her than walking around to ring the chimes at the front door. Of course, there were about fifty steps to climb either way. With stairs everywhere in town, it was a wonder there were any older people living in Bisbee. How did they climb that many steps? Maybe that's what keeps them young and active, I decided.

"Well, this is my little slice of heaven." Dusty waved me in the door leading to a laundry room and to the kitchen beyond. All the modern equipment needed to fix meals for a big group of people filled the large airy room. Big windows offered a stunning view of the Mule Mountains. Afternoon sun brightened up the space. In the winter, the sun would keep the room toasty warm.

"On most mornings my guests come in to keep me company while I fix breakfast. I enjoy sharing a cup of coffee with them. I have a lot repeat guests, and I like to think of them as friends." Dusty did have a warm nature, and she seemed to really care about her guests. I could see how Claire had considered her a friend. Maybe we would eventually become friends as well. Only time would tell.

Once again, Claire's warning drifted through my mind. I needed to be very careful where I placed my trust until I could find out the truth. I wasn't going to allow someone to commit murder twice if I could help it.

"I have all five rooms rented this weekend, or I would show them to you." Dusty's voice broke in on my thoughts. "Running a bed and breakfast is a lot of work, but I love it. I wouldn't want to do anything else, and believe me I've tried my hand at a lot of different jobs."

"Have you always lived in Bisbee?" Getting to know the people who had been in Claire's life would help me figure out who considered her a threat.

"No, but I've lived here for more than twenty years. When I first moved here, I tried my hand at some of the artsy things around town," she chuckled, giving her salt-and-pepper head a shake. "I sort of pictured myself as one of those hippie-types that Irma is always grousing about. The only trouble with that idea is there isn't an artistic bone in this here body." She patted her broad hips.

"This old house was in pretty bad shape when I bought it for a song. I've fixed it up real nice if I do say so myself. Now it supports me in a manner I've come to enjoy." She chuckled again.

While we talked, she led me into the dining room. A table big enough to seat twelve without crowding anyone sat in the middle of the large room. "I think this used to be considered the parlor, but I decided it was put to better use as the dining room," she explained. "I moved the living room out there." She waved her arm towards an arched doorway. "I call it the common room where folks can enjoy a cup of coffee or tea in the afternoon. I always put out fresh cookies. I keep some DVD's for the guests to borrow as well as a bunch of books." She nodded at the built-in bookcase. "When people get tired of all the sightseeing, they just want to crash at night. Each room has a big television."

Through a set of French doors I could see a beautiful garden. "Do you do your own work out there as well?" Flowering plants and shrubs I couldn't name grew in abundance. There were lawn chairs for her guests to use.

"Oh no," she gave her head a vigorous shake. "I have a black thumb, not a green one. When I tried my hand at gardening, I killed more plants than you could shake a stick at." She laughed nervously. "My nephew lives in a little shed we fixed up out back for him. He keeps all the plants blooming. He even grows the vegetables and herbs I use in the kitchen."

For a brief moment she gave me a hard stare. I didn't know what it meant. Just as quick, she gave me a big smile, continuing with her story. "What I don't use, he sells at the farmer's market in Vista Park every Saturday morning." At my blank look, she explained further. "That's in the Warren district. There's a ball park there as well." I still had a lot to learn about the quirky little town.

"Bisbee is made up of four districts, or neighborhoods," she went on, explaining more history of the town. "They started out as separate mining camps. Old Bisbee is the historical part of town, dating back to the eighteen hundreds when mining was in full swing. That's where we live. If you stick around long enough, you'll have to go on a ghost walk. They can be really interesting. A lot of the old houses claim to be haunted."

I didn't believe in ghosts, or that one had moved that table in my entry. But who would come into the house just to move a table? It didn't make sense. I still hadn't had a chance to go through the rest of the house to make sure nothing was missing or disturbed.

I looked back at the flowers. "If I decide to stay here, maybe your nephew can give me a few pointers. I don't have any idea what kind of plants grow in Arizona." I couldn't tell from her expression if she was pleased by that suggestion, or dismayed.

When four people wandered into the common room looking for a cookie and a cup of coffee, I decided it was time for me to head home and let Dusty take care of her guests. "Dinner tonight?" Her question stopped me from leaving.

"That sounds nice." I surprised myself with the answer. Climbing down one set of uneven steps and up another, I realized I meant it. I wasn't used to spending so much time alone.

When I walked in the back door, I saw the flashing light on the phone indicating a message. With all the visitors today, I'd forgotten to see who had called earlier. Listening to the message I was surprised to hear the lawyer's voice. I hadn't expected to hear from him again.

"Miss Connors, I just heard about the autopsy report. To say I'm shocked is an understatement. Please accept my condolences. If there is anything I can do for you, please give me a call. I'm here to help you."

How far did news travel in the west? Maybe because he was her lawyer, someone had called him. I didn't know if he expected me to return his call, but I decided it wasn't necessary. There wasn't anything I needed from him. Unless he could provide the name of her killer, that is. I dismissed the thought and the call.

Very little had been disturbed when the table in the entry had been moved, but I could see small things that had been shifted around. What was the purpose? In the short time I'd been in the house, I hadn't catalogued every item of value. Nothing obvious was missing though. If someone was trying to scare me, they were doing a very poor job of it. I wasn't scared, I was angry. I needed to find out where to direct that anger.

~~~

Night life in Bisbee was as different from what I was used to as the town itself. The little bistro where I ate lunch was now closed, but there were many other restaurants to choose from. People spilled out of several small sports bars onto the sidewalk, sitting at tables to enjoy a glass of beer or wine while watching a game on several big screen televisions. The crowds got rowdy when their team scored, but it never got out of hand. No one got drunk enough to pick a fight.

People greeted us as we walked through town. All the locals seemed to know Dusty, and she knew them. I could see now why Claire loved living here. But someone had wanted her dead, I reminded myself. That wasn't very friendly.

It was late when Dusty dropped me off at my front door. "Thank you for dinner. I had a good time."

"Maybe we can do it again before you head back home. Do you know yet when you'll be leaving?" Her question came out of nowhere. Some people seemed very eager for me to leave town. I wondered why that was.

"I haven't made any plans," I told her again. "I won't be going anywhere until Claire's murderer is found. Thanks again, Dusty." I quickly shut the car door cutting off anything other questions. People were too willing to ignore what had happened to Claire. I wanted to know why.

CHAPTER SEVEN

Walking into the small church the following morning, I felt at peace for the first time since arriving in Bisbee. Everyone was very welcoming, offering their condolences when Irma introduced me. It was common knowledge that Claire's death was now considered a murder. I could see the speculation, even fear, in many of their eyes. Their whispers buzzed through the congregation. This wasn't like a big city where murders were more common place. Still I was grateful they had the decency not to bring the subject up to me.

To my surprise, Jake sat down in the pew beside me, mere minutes after Irma and I sat down. Leaning around me, she gave him a dark scowl, but kept her thoughts to herself. Even more surprising was Dan Tobin sitting several rows in front of us. I couldn't explain why it was comforting to know that he attended church. It just was.

When Dan filed past me after the service, he winked at me, but didn't stop to talk. The fact that Jake was standing beside me might have something to do with it. Still, I hoped to see him later.

Pastor Bennett welcomed me with a warm smile. "I'm glad you were able to join us this morning. I hope you'll come again."

"Thank you, I enjoyed your message. As long as I'm here, I plan on attending. I just don't know how long that will be."

"I understand your suspicions have been confirmed." His voice dropped to a soft whisper so the others couldn't overhear. "Any time you feel the need to talk, my door is always open. Will you be taking Claire's body back to South Carolina for burial?"

"No, this was her home. She'll be buried here."

"Do you know when the police will release her body so you can plan her funeral?"

The reality of what happened hit me full in the face, stealing my breath away. Blinking rapidly, I tried and failed to keep the tears from falling.

Quietly excusing himself from those around him, Pastor Bennett led me into his office, shutting the door on the prying eyes.

"Claire isn't coming back," I whispered. "I don't know what I've been thinking. I've been so intent on finding out who killed her that I ignored the fact that she's really gone. I guess I thought that by finding out who did this to her, everything would go back to the way it was. I still expect to see her walk down the stairs at the house. That isn't going to happen though. Nothing will ever be the same again." I couldn't stop the tears from falling.

"No, Jillian, that isn't going to happen," he agreed. "But finding the person who did this will help you move on. So will planning her funeral."

"I know. I guess I need to do that soon." I wasn't ready to say good-bye to my only sister. Would I ever be? We hadn't always been close, but I did love her. "Maybe I can come by tomorrow to discuss it?" Getting my emotions under control, I stood up. "Thank you, Pastor." I held out my hand. "I'll see you tomorrow." That was all I could think of to say.

Irma was still visiting with her friends, but I was ready to leave. I didn't want anyone asking questions. Jake was catching up with old friends when I hustled Irma out to my car, and I didn't bother to tell him I was leaving. He'd figure it out on his own.

"I have a small casserole in the oven. Would you like to share it with me?" Irma asked once we were in the car.

"That's very nice of you, but Jake asked me to have lunch with him." She huffed and puffed like the wolf in *The Three Little Pigs*, but didn't comment further. Evidently she didn't want me being friends with Jake or Dusty. I could only wonder at the reason. Would she approve of my friendship with Dan? What difference did any of this make to her?

After my talk with Pastor Roy, I wanted to beg out of my lunch with Jake. I wouldn't be very good company. But Jake's big SUV pulled into the drive behind my rental. I released a weary sigh. It was too late to change my mind now.

I wanted to make sure furniture hadn't been rearranged again while I was at church, but that would have to wait. I wasn't ready to tell anyone what about that. Who would believe me anyway?

Sitting at a small table in one of the many restaurants in Old Bisbee, Jake frowned at me. "You're awfully quiet. Is everything all right? Are you feeling okay?"

"Yes, of course, I'm fine. I'm just not very good company today. I'm sorry"

"Did the pastor say something to upset you? I saw that you went into his office after church."

"It was just..." My voice trailed off. I didn't want to talk about a funeral right now.

He reached across the table to take my hand. "I'm sorry. I shouldn't have pressed you to go out with me. I know this has been hard for you." He looked at the food I'd barely touched. "Would you rather take your lunch home to eat when you're feeling more like it?"

Nodding my head, I was grateful for his understanding. His kind gesture was almost my undoing though as tears burned at the back of my eyes. I was glad he didn't try to follow me inside when we got back to the house. If things were moved around yet again, how would I explain it to him?

When he bent down towards me, I turned my head so his lips landed on my cheek instead of my lips. Straightening back to his full height, he gave a sad smile. "I have to go back to Tucson in the morning, but I'll be back on Saturday. Do you know when you'll have the funeral yet? I want to be here."

I shrugged. "I don't know how long it takes to plan one. I'll let you know."

He squeezed my hand. "I'll call you." I watched as he drove away.

As before, the table had been moved to the opposite side of the entry. Whoever was doing this must not like the way Claire had arranged things. Did they rearrange things like this while she was alive, or was it just me? I decided to leave the table where they placed it. Maybe my human poltergeist would leave me alone if I left things where they put them.

Upstairs more things had been moved around, but I still couldn't tell if anything had been taken. Was someone searching for a particular item, or just messing with me? Calling the police would only make me look ridiculous, so I didn't bother.

When someone knocked on the back door, I released a weary sigh. "Why can't people leave me alone?" I muttered. What would Dusty want now? She was the only one to come calling at the back door.

Instead of Dusty, I was surprised to find a young man in his late teens or early twenties standing there. His long, light brown hair hung over his face, blocking the vision in one eye. His clothes were old, and slightly tattered. The knees had patches on them. His fingernails were short and chipped with dirt imbedded in them. "I'm Jules," he said, like that explained who he was.

I hadn't seen any homeless people panhandling on the street corners, but that didn't mean there weren't any in Bisbee. "Hi. May I help you?" I held onto the door knob, hoping I could slam it shut if he tried to push his way inside.

"My aunt said you wanted some help with your garden."

"You're Dusty's nephew?" Surprise caused my voice to be higher than normal. I'm not sure what I expected when she said her nephew lived behind her house, but this young man wasn't it.

"Yeah." A man of few words, I thought. I wasn't sure what I was supposed to say next. "What do you want me to show you? I took care of the garden for Claire. You want to do it yourself now?" His surly attitude was intimidating.

"Your aunt didn't say you did that for Claire. I suppose you could still do it." The thought of him hanging around was a little unnerving, but I didn't want to antagonize him either.

He looked over his shoulder, shuffling his feet. "Well, Dusty didn't exactly know I was doin' the work. She likes to keep things to herself."

"Okay." What was I supposed to say to that piece of information? "I'm not ready to do any gardening yet; and I don't know how long I'll be here. Maybe you could continue to take care of things the way you did for Claire."

"But you won't tell my aunt I'm doing the work, right?"

"Not if you don't want me to."

He seemed to breathe easier at that. "Claire always made it look like she was doin' the work when I came over."

He appeared to be suggesting that I do the same, so I nodded in agreement. For the first time, he smiled, making him look younger than I first guessed him to be. We stared at each other for a few minutes. I didn't know what else there was to say. "If you leave Bisbee, what will happen to the garden, and the house?" he finally asked. He appeared to be more interested in the garden than the house. Too bad I didn't have a good answer to give him.

I shrugged. "I'll have to decide that later." He looked disappointed, but he nodded his head. Had Dusty sent him here for the express purpose of asking that question? What difference did it make to her?

"Claire liked all the blooming flowers," he continued. More comfortable talking about flowers, he quickly changed the subject. "They take a little extra work. I can show you how to pick off the dead-heads now if you want."

I wasn't sure what a dead-head was, but I followed him outside. For the next hour, he explained what each plant was, and showed me how to pick off the dead blossoms without damaging the plants. As an apartment dweller all my life, the only flowers I had dealings with came in a vase or a small pot. Growing them was foreign to me.

"If you pick the dead blossoms off, the plants will keep producing more flowers," he explained patiently. As long as he was talking about the plants, he had plenty to say. He was more of a plant person than a people person, I decided with a chuckle.

After Jules left, I tried to figure out what I was going to do next. I still didn't know if I wanted to quit my job, or simply take an extended leave of absence. Maybe I could take a year off from teaching to see how things worked out here. The idea of running a bed and breakfast was foreign to me. I could possibly apply for a job at the local school district. Staying here meant that I needed to have my things shipped out here.

It would be faster and cheaper to use my return ticket to fly home and pack my own things. I laughed at my habit of doing everything the cheapest way possible. I didn't have to worry about money any longer. I would gladly give the check back if it meant having Claire back as well, but that wasn't going to happen. I could always use the money to make her dream come true and open the bed and breakfast. Or at least let people think that's what I was doing. If she had died because of those plans, maybe I could smoke out the killer that way. That fast, my decision was made.

I had made arrangements with the car rental agency in Tucson to pick up the car the following day. Keeping it when I had Claire's car didn't make sense.

By seven that evening I was beginning to go stir-crazy. Sitting around with nothing to do wasn't in my nature. I had checked all the flowers in the garden for any more dead blossoms. There weren't any. With my decision tentatively made, I wanted to get started. I wasn't sure where to begin though. What did I need to do to move forward with the bed and breakfast?

When my cell phone rang, breaking the silence of the house, I was grateful to have anyone to talk to, even a salesperson.

"Hi, Jill, it's Dan Tobin." His warm voice tickled my ear, sending a little thrill down my spine. I'd known the man for less than a week. How could he cause this kind of reaction? "If you haven't already eaten dinner, I was wondering if you'd like to join me."

"That sounds wonderful." I hadn't eaten much at lunch with Jake and forgot to eat the leftovers I brought home. With the mention of food, my stomach growled. My enthusiastic answer had me back pedaling a little. "Um, if you don't mind home cooking, I have a couple of steaks in the refrigerator I can fix." I tried to tone down my excitement. Telling myself this wasn't a date, it was just two friends sharing a meal didn't work either. Butterflies were doing somersaults in my stomach.

"Sounds great, I'll bring a bottle of wine. Is fifteen minutes too soon?" *He sounds as eager for company as I am,* I thought. If I kept telling myself that was the only reason for either of us to be so excited, maybe I would eventually believe it.

Fifteen minutes later, the doorbell chimed. I had barely had time to put on a pair of shoes and some lipstick, but I do so like a punctual man. I had left my hair down around my shoulders for church and hadn't bothered to do anything else with it. I hoped it hadn't gotten messed up while I worked in the garden with Jules.

Opening the door, I smiled up at him. "Um, hi," Suddenly tongue-tied, I was unsure what else to say. I moved back so he could enter.

He leaned down, placing a soft kiss on my cheek. What was it with men kissing me on the cheek? I was happy to settle for that from Jake, but I might like something a little more personal from Dan. "I hope you like this." He handed me a bottle of wine. "It's from one of our local wineries. It should go well with steak." He followed me to the kitchen.

"How are you with a gas grill? There's one big enough to bar-b-que the entire steer on the back patio. Claire must have been planning on letting her guests use it." Mentioning her name so casually, caused my heart to ache. I wanted to keep her alive in my memory even if it hurt. Why had this happened? I asked myself again. I had no answers yet.

"If I say so myself, I'm pretty good with a grill," Dan pretended he didn't notice my moment of misery. It was something I was going to have to get used to.

The flagstone patio at the back and side of the house was big enough for a party of twenty or more without crowding anyone. A picnic table sat at one end of the patio along with two smaller umbrella tables. There were also several comfortable lawn chairs and a porch swing.

I had also discovered a more private dining area along side of the house earlier in the week. Claire had made wonderful plans. I wished she would be here to enjoy them.

"It's really nice out here tonight. Would you like to eat outside?" The evening temperature in southern Arizona was similar to what I was used to in South Carolina only without the humidity. Or the bugs, I added silently.

"That sounds nice," Dan agreed. "The weather is another reason I decided to stay here when I left the Army. Snow in southern Arizona is almost unheard of. I don't miss that at all."

While Dan watched over the steaks, I tossed a salad and prepared some garlic bread to put in the broiler at the last minute.

"I'm sorry I don't have anything for dessert," I apologized when we finished eating. "I'm not really big on sweets."

"Dessert isn't necessary, besides I couldn't eat another bite. The food was delicious. Thank you." He placed his hand over mine. That same tingle moved through me. Would it always be like that with him? I wondered. It was something I could get used to.

"I'm glad you called. I hope we can do it again." I wasn't usually this bold around men, but I wasn't shy either. I was feeling a little out of my element at the moment.

It turns out Dan was as easy to talk to as he was on the eyes. It was midnight before either of us realized it. "I should go. I didn't mean to monopolize your entire evening. I'm sorry."

"I'm not; I've spent too many hours alone since I've been here. I've enjoyed myself tonight more than I have since I came to Arizona." A little pang of guilt attacked me, but I pushed it aside. Claire was dead, I wasn't. I walked to the door with him. He seemed as reluctant to leave as I was for him to go. I could feel God's leading in this as I have so many times in my life. I just wish Claire didn't have to die in order for me to meet Dan.

When he leaned down to place his lips gently on mine, I leaned in to him. That was all the encouragement he needed to deepen the kiss. When he finally drew away from me, we were both breathless. My arms were wrapped around his neck. He rested his chin on top of my head for a minute before drawing back to look down into my eyes. "Thanks again for a great meal, and an unforgettable evening. I'll see you tomorrow." He placed another soft kiss on my lips before leaving.

Too late, I wished I'd thought to ask if he knew Roland Granger. He hadn't lived in Bisbee all that long, but as a cop he might know the man, especially if he had been in trouble with the law before.

CHAPTER EIGHT

I was on my second cup of coffee the next morning, still basking in the glow of the evening spent with Dan when the chimes on the front door rang. It was only eight o'clock, a little early for Irma to pop over for a tea party. I didn't think a salesman would be calling this early either.

Before opening the door, I looked through the beveled glass on the door at the woman standing there. She could be anywhere between fifty and sixty. Unless the glass had distorted her features, she was angry and impatient while she waited for me to open the door.

"I want you know you aren't going to get away with this," she snapped before I could even offer a greeting. "It was bad enough when Tom left everything to that trollop who destroyed my marriage. Now you've stolen my son's inheritance. I'm going to fight this."

So this well-dressed woman was Jake's mother. I wasn't going to let her push me around. "She didn't destroy your marriage. You had been divorced from Tom several years when Claire met him."

"We could have worked it out if she hadn't blinded him. What sixty year old man wouldn't be delighted to have a woman young enough to be his daughter fawn all over him? This house should belong to my son. You aren't even related to the family. This house should stay in the Wilkins family. You have no right to even live here.

"Turning this stately old mansion into a bed and breakfast is an insult. I won't let you get away with this." 'Stately old mansion' was an exaggeration of grand proportion, but she didn't give me a chance to argue the point. "I'm the least of your worries," she continued smugly. "Sam won't stand for it either."

"Sam? Who is Sam?" Claire had never mentioned anyone by the name of Sam in Tom's family.

Myriam chuckled. "He is the resident ghost. I don't

suppose Jake happened to mention him. But of course he wouldn't. He's too much of a gentleman to scare you. But I'm telling you, Sam is very possessive of this house and everything in it. He doesn't like strangers living here. He won't like the fact that you have all the jewelry Tom gave that woman either. That is all family heirlooms, and it belongs to my son. Sam will see to it that you don't remain in a house that doesn't belong to you.

"Don't think you can blame me, or anyone in my family, for what happened to her either. I wasn't even in town. She was just idiot enough to do it herself. Or maybe Sam did it to protect what was his." With a superior smile, she spun around on her expensive high heeled shoes, and marched down the steps to a fancy car parked behind my rental.

Too stunned to move, I watched Myriam Wilkins drive away. Finally gathering my wits about me, I shut the door, and my mouth which had been hanging open in shock. She had been a Wilkins by marriage, just like Claire, yet she acted like this house should be hers. Was she upset enough with Claire's plans that she killed her? But Claire said she had seen or heard something she shouldn't have. Had more than one person wanted her dead? Where did Myriam get the idea that I thought she had killed Claire?

The chief had jumped to Myriam's defense even though I hadn't accused her of anything. How much had he revealed to her about the case? Was she the one who sent the fax to release Claire's body to the mortuary? If the chief had told her of our conversation, had he also told her that I insisted on having an autopsy done? I doubted I would ever find out the truth on that score. Making that woman angry probably wasn't a very good idea. The questions kept mounting up without any answers.

I dismissed all thoughts of her 'resident ghost'. I didn't believe in such things. I wasn't going to let her nonsense scare me. Dan and Dusty both had talked about the ghosts here in town. I wasn't going to let such a thing, real or otherwise, scare me off. I was here for the long haul.

~~~

An hour later I was sitting in Pastor Bennett's office. "It still feels like I'm lost in a never ending nightmare, and I'll wake up at any moment to find none of this was true. Will it ever get better?" Tears shimmered in my eyes.

Pastor Bennett shook his head. "Although I have lost people I love, I've never lost a loved one the way you lost your sister. Either way, the reality slowly settles in. There will still be times when it hits you hard. It will help to remember you'll see Claire again in heaven."

I nodded, drawing a deep breath, trying to control my runaway emotions. "I want the person who did this to pay," I whispered more to myself than to him. "They shouldn't get away with murder, but I don't know if I'll ever be able to prove who did this."

"It isn't your job to find her killer. You need to leave that to the police."

I gave a derisive snort at that. "Chief Daniels isn't working very hard to find out who did this."

"His job depends on keeping peace and order in town. He isn't going to ignore a murder."

"I'm not so sure about that. He doesn't appear to be very committed to doing that." I still didn't know where Myriam fit in with what happened. Should I tell him about her visit? How well did he know her? I didn't know if she had been a member of this congregation when she lived in Bisbee. I also didn't know how long he had been pastor of this church.

"This is the first murder he has had to investigate here in Bisbee," he went on. "What did he have to say about this?" He looked down at Claire's note.

My cheeks heated up, and I avoided eye contact for a minute. "Um, well, you're the first person I've shown it to." I had brought it with me hoping he could give me some suggestions on that as well as planning a funeral. The fact that I'd been with Dan for several hours the previous night and forgot to show it to him didn't escape my notice. My mind had been occupied with more pleasant matters.

85

"Why didn't you show it to him when you first found it?" he asked in disbelief.

"When I first got here, the chief insisted that Claire had taken those pills herself, either by accident or on purpose." I shrugged. "I didn't know if I could trust him. I still don't. When I told him she believed someone was trying to kill her, he suggested she was just hallucinating, or something, because she was sick. I couldn't handle that again."

"But he requested an autopsy; he must have thought there was something suspicious."

"No," I shook my head. "I paid to have that done. He didn't think it was necessary." This surprised him, and he was silent for a long moment.

"I still think you need to show him this. The autopsy proves something else was happening to her. Whether she took the pills herself or someone else gave them to her is beside the point. He can't ignore the fact that someone had been giving her poison." He looked down at the note again. "Why wouldn't she go to the police if she suspected someone was trying to kill her? She never said anything to you when you talked?"

I shook my head. "Not until our last conversation. Before that, she only said she was sick, and the doctor didn't know what was wrong with her. She had an appointment with a specialist in Tucson the week after she died." I thought for a minute. "This week," I added. Had it only been a week since I received that horrible phone call? It felt like I had lived a lifetime since then, while at the same time it was as fresh in my mind as though it happened just this morning. "The last time I spoke to her, she said someone was trying to kill her. She didn't know who or why." I drew a shaky breath.

"If the person who was poisoning her knew about the appointment, maybe he, or she, decided to finish the job before she could see another doctor."

"What does her doctor say about all this? Have you talked to him?"

"Not yet, I've been waiting for all the results to come back from the autopsy and the toxicology. What if he's involved? If he thinks I'm on to him, what will he do?" A shiver of fear passed through me.

"Miss Connors, Jillian, you can't suspect everyone. You have to put your trust in someone."

"I have. I came to you."

"Thank you" A small smile lifted the corners of his mouth. "You can also trust the police. Dan Tobin is a member of this congregation. You might think about taking the note to him. There is also a higher power where we can all place our trust. God will see you through this, and make sure the person responsible will pay. It may not be on your time schedule though. How long are you planning on staying in Bisbee?"

That was one of the questions many people had been asking me. "As long as it takes," I stated firmly.

He sounded surprised by my statement. "You're willing to move here, even temporarily?"

I paused for a moment. I might as well tell him the decision I'd made before Dan came over the previous night. I nodded. "I can see why Claire liked the town, and the people. I should have listened to her on several levels." I gave him a sad smile "The idea of opening a bed and breakfast has been growing on me, but I haven't made any final decisions." If the motive for her death had something to do with her plans for the house, I had decided to make like I was going through with them, at least until I found her killer.

By the time I left his office an hour later, we had made the arrangements for Claire's funeral. She had left instructions with Mr. Edmonds about what she wanted, so I had very few decisions to make. How long had she been aware she was dying? Why hadn't she told someone what was happening to her? I would never know the answers to those questions.

The ladies in the church would provide a luncheon after the service on the following Saturday. That was one less thing for me to worry about. At that time I would announce that I was moving to Bisbee. Maybe then people would stop pestering me. It might also prompt the killer to do something to me. The thought was frightening, but forewarned is forearmed. I would be much more careful where I placed my trust than Claire had been.

I had agreed to give the note to Dan instead of the chief. I still didn't know what good it would do. We knew the truth of what happened to her, just not who did it. I hoped Dan wouldn't be upset that I hadn't turned it over as soon as I found it.

Unfortunately, Dan was out of the office when I got to the police department. I was stuck with the chief. "Where did you get this?" He glared across his big desk at me.

"I found it under the blotter on the desk in Tom's office." I was hoping he wouldn't ask when I found it. I should have known better.

"You just found it today?" Skepticism rang out in his voice.

"No, I found it last week," I reluctantly admitted.

"And why are you just now getting around to giving it to me? You are aware it's against the law to withhold evidence, right?" He lowered his bushy eyebrows in a frown.

"This can't exactly be called a smoking gun. If I had given it to you before the results of the autopsy were in, would you have believed Claire's own words? You were perfectly willing to dismiss her death as self-inflicted, her illness as an attempt to get attention, or a hallucination. I think most people in my place would have kept the note to themselves."

Angry heat burned in his cheeks, and he continued to glare at me. "What prompted you to bring it in now?" I ignored his question. I wasn't going to tell him I was here only at the urgings of Pastor Bennett.

"If I hadn't paid for the autopsy myself, you wouldn't even know she had been poisoned."

He looked at the note again. "What did she mean that she saw or heard something she shouldn't have?"

"I have no idea. I'm not the detective here. Maybe you could actually do a little police work and find out. Maybe you should look for someone who had a motive to want her dead."

He glared at me for a long moment before changing the direction of the conversation. "Claire was a nice lady. There is no reason anyone would want her dead. Money is always a good motive for murder. You seem to be the main beneficiary here. Exactly how much are you getting?"

"I would gladly give up everything I received to have my sister back," I snapped. Jake would get the same thing I received, but he was overlooking that fact. Again I wondered just how well he knew Myriam, and to what lengths would he go to assist her.

He snickered. "Easy to say when you know very well it can't happen. Maybe I need to look at your financial situation."

"Have at it, Chief." I paused. I could see him mentally rubbing his hands together, his expression was eager. "Just as soon as you get a search warrant, you can look at anything you want. Good luck getting a judge to sign off on that, since you have no cause for a warrant. I haven't seen Claire since Tom's funeral. I was on the other side of the country when she died." All the years of watching cop and crime shows on television were paying off.

"If you have nothing to hide, why not let me look?" he asked with mock innocence, raising one eyebrow in an attempt to appear friendly.

"How about letting me look at your financial information, Chief?"

"What do you want with my information? I didn't benefit from her death," he blustered. "I had no reason to kill her."

"I had no reason to kill her or the opportunity to do so, yet you're suggesting I killed her. You need to look for a different motive," I stressed. "I'm sure there are other reasons for murder than money. If she saw or heard something she shouldn't have, why don't you try to find out what that was?" If he wasn't going to look into this, I would do it for him. Claire had a reason for leaving me that note.

"I don't need you telling me how to investigate a crime," he growled at me. I didn't argue, but I didn't agree with him either. It looked like he needed all the help he could get.

"I'm investigating a murder, you need to butt out."

"So am I." I kept my tone mild. I stood up; looking down on him "I'm not sure what that note will tell you. I would like to have it back when you're finished with it though. It's the last thing my sister wrote to me."

"Stay out of my way, or I'll have you arrested for interfering with an investigation."

"You can try, Chief, but I don't think you'll get very far. Remember, you're the one who said there was no murder in the first place." He was still sputtering as I walked out of his office.

Back in my car, I realized I hadn't told him about Claire's funeral on Saturday. I shrugged off the thought. The local grapevine would pass the information on soon enough. That proved to be true. Irma was waiting at my front door when I pulled into the drive.

"Oh, dearie, I just got the call." She took my hands as I stepped out of the car. "Claire's funeral is this Saturday. Is there anything I can do for you?" For a woman with arthritic fingers, she had a grip like iron.

"Thanks for the offer, but I think it's all covered." I led her inside, and set about making tea. After the day I'd had so far, I could use something stronger than tea. That would have to wait until I was alone. Or maybe not.

"Planning a funeral is no fun," Irma sat down at the kitchen table. "I should know; I've buried three husbands." I turned a shocked face towards her. I had no idea she'd been married three times. Of course I didn't know her any better than I knew anyone else in this town.

"What you need is a stiff shot of brandy, or some wine if you'd rather have that." She leaned close to me, whispering as though she thought someone might be eavesdropping on our conversation. "Sometimes Claire and I would share a glass of wine instead of tea."

I put away the tea fixings, and opened the refrigerator. Dan and I had finished the wine he brought the night before, but I still had the bottle I'd bought when I got groceries earlier in the week.

CHAPTER NINE

Saturday dawned bright and sunny. "Shouldn't it be gloomy when you're burying your only sister?" I grumbled at the sun. Claire had wanted no viewing, and I honored her wishes. She would be buried next to Tom.

Jake would be here this morning for the service. I wasn't sure if he would object to the burial arrangements. At this point, I didn't care what anyone thought.

When Myriam entered the church, butterflies attacked my stomach. "What is she doing here?" I wasn't aware I had spoken the words out loud until Jake turned to see who I was looking at.

"Damn." His muttered curse surprised me. He wasn't any happier about his mother's presence than I was. "Excuse me, Jillian." Without waiting for me to say anything, he marched across the room to the woman. Eavesdropping on their conversation could prove to be very enlightening. It was clear that neither of them was happy.

When he took her arm, trying to move her out of the church, she pulled her arm out of his grasp. "I'm staying, Jake. Accept it." Her voice echoed in the high-ceilinged area. She marched off like she was the queen, and the rest of us were her subjects.

"I'm sorry, Jillian," he whispered, when he came back to my side. "I didn't know she was even in town. I don't know what she hopes to prove by being here."

Probably nothing, I thought. She just wants to exercise her authority over anyone in her sphere.

Pastor Roy intercepted her as she started down the aisle to the front of the sanctuary. Whatever he said to her caused her smooth cheeks to turn a bright pink. With a curt nod of her regal head, she flounced over to the pew in the back.

The church was filling with people, and I was grateful she wouldn't make a scene, at least for now. There would be plenty of time later.

Chief Daniels stood at the door looking all official and important. Was he here on official business or personal? All the cop shows say the police attend the funerals of murder victims in the hope of spotting the killer. I didn't think it would be that easy. What was a killer supposed to look like?

Dusty was a few steps behind the chief. Had they come together? Just how serious was their relationship? What did it matter to me anyway?

I scanned the people milling around, looking for the tall detective. If there was an official reason for the police to be here, I'd rather it was Dan, and not Chief Daniels. My pulse jumped when Roland Granger walked in a few minutes before the service was to begin. What was he doing here? I didn't believe his claim that he and Claire were friends.

I could feel his eyes following me as I moved around through the crowd. He gave me a nod, his full lips quirking up like he had a secret he wasn't going to tell. Gratefully, he went into the sanctuary without trying to speak to me.

Dan came in minutes before the service was to start. His smile warmed the cold places in my heart. Instead of coming over to me though, he followed the crowd in to sit down at the back of the sanctuary. Was he here to look for a killer, or as my...friend? I didn't know exactly how to define our relationship. Did it matter to him that Jake was standing by my side?

The service was a celebration of Claire's life and an affirmation that she was now in heaven with Jesus. If we were believers, we were assured of seeing her again. Although I shed more tears, I felt God's comfort in Pastor Roy's words.

After the short graveside service, everyone gathered in the basement of the church for the luncheon. I looked around at the many faces I didn't recognize. Was her killer here? How would I even recognize them? Again I wondered what a killer looked like. Unless the person was deranged, there wouldn't be a sign taped on his forehead.

"How soon will you be going back to South Carolina?" Dusty asked, interrupting my observation of the people surrounding me. Jules was standing several paces behind her. He looked like he'd rather be anywhere but here. Today he was dressed in clean clothes, but they were still slightly tattered. Didn't Dusty give him any money for all the work he did for her? Did she keep the money he earned when he sold the excess vegetables at Vista Park?

Overhearing her question, the people around us stopped talking, anticipating my answer. This was as good a time as any to make my announcement. "I'm not leaving. I've decided to stay in Bisbee." My voice echoed throughout the room, informing every one of my decision. "My roommate will pack up my things and have them shipped to me."

"Oh, well, that's good." Dusty stammered, her smile was a little forced, but Jules's lips curved up slightly. Something wasn't quite right between these two. "Are you planning on turning the house in to a bed and breakfast like Claire wanted?" Again, ears perked up with that question.

"I'm still toying with the idea. I haven't decided what I'm going to do beyond moving here. I'm checking out what is involved." It wasn't quite a lie, but it wasn't the complete truth either, and I asked God's forgiveness. Dropping little hints, one at a time, might draw out a killer. My stomach churned nervously at the thought. I could be the next target.

I looked around to see what the reaction to my announcement was. Several people smiled at my decision, while most were just openly curious.

Irma hurried over to my side, giving me a hug. "I'm so glad you'll be my neighbor." Her faded eyes sparkled with unshed tears. "I do miss Claire." With that she hurried off to wipe her tears that had begun to run down her wrinkled cheeks.

Myriam's reaction was a whole different matter. She wasn't happy with my decision. If looks could kill, I would be dead on the floor. She took one step towards me, but Jake stepped in front of her. Whatever he said to her, this time it worked. She turned around, marching up the steps with her head held high.

"So you're really planning on moving to Bisbee?" Chief

Daniels drew my attention away from Myriam's retreating back. His tone was confrontational.

"Yes. Do you have any objections?" I cocked an eyebrow.

"No, no, why would I?" he backpedaled quickly.

"Just wondering," I shrugged. It was interesting to see the varied reactions of the people who were supposed to be Claire's friends. I was grateful Dan hadn't informed his boss of my decision. Would he have told Dusty? How much information passed between the dating companions?

Goosebumps that had nothing to do with the air conditioner blowing on me traveled over my arms. Someone was watching me; someone who wasn't happy with my decision. I turned in a circle. In the midst of a crowd, how could I tell who was paying special attention to me? Myriam had left, so unless she had snuck back in, she wasn't the cause of the sudden chill.

Roland Granger was across the large room. He gave me a brisk nod before turning and following Myriam up the basement stairs. Was he related to her? I hadn't seen him speak to her or anyone else, so maybe not. I couldn't tell if he was upset by my announcement. What difference would it make to him?

Mr. Edmonds hadn't bothered to attend the funeral. If he hadn't been Claire's attorney for very long, he probably didn't feel it necessary to attend. Looking back to the day he came to the house, I realized he hadn't offered condolence at that time either. Considering that now, I found it a little odd. I shrugged, dismissing him from my mind. Rubbing my arms, I wondered when it would be proper for me to leave.

~~~

"That damn bitch is going to keep digging until she finds me," he groused as he watched Jillian leave the church. "Why can't she just go back where she came from, and leave things alone?" He turned away. It wouldn't be good for either of them if she saw him now.

~~~

"That was quite a bombshell you dropped back there,"

Jake chuckled as we left the church a short time later. "You certainly got everyone's attention."

That was my intention, I thought. I wanted to ask why his mother was so upset, but held my tongue on that issue. I didn't want to get in between mother and son. Remembering the look she sent my way, another shiver shook me. Her hatred had been a physical thing, and I felt certain she would have gladly done away with me right then.

"Are you really planning on moving here?" he asked as he held the passenger door open for me. He had insisted on picking me up before going to the church that morning.

"Yes," I kept my answer simple. I didn't know what he would think of the idea.

He reached across the console, taking my hand. "I'm glad," was all he said for several minutes, keeping my hand in his. When he spoke again, he asked the same question Dusty had. "Are you going to turn the house into a B&B?"

"I'm still thinking about it. It's what Claire wanted. Do you mind?" I was hoping to get an honest answer from him.

He didn't take his eyes off the twisting road, but I could see the frown drawing his dark brows together. "Why would I mind?"

"Because the house is half yours," I reminded him.

"Not really, it belongs to the trust, we're just the trustees. As I told you, my business keeps me very busy right now. There is no way I could help you. Bisbee is a nice town, but I don't want to move back here on a permanent basis."

"Do you want anything in the house that once belonged to your folks?

He gave a harsh laugh. "My mother took as much of the furnishings as she could get her hands on at the time of the divorce. If there was anything of value, I'm sure it's long gone by now. She's been married and divorced twice since her divorce from Dad. She took each one of her husbands for all she could get." It didn't sound like there was much love lost between mother and son.

"Don't do this because it's what Claire wanted," he stated

quietly. "You can't live her life for her. You need to live your own life." Was this advice for himself as well as for me?

He was quiet the remainder of the short drive back to the house. Coming around to open the passenger door, he took my hand to help me stand up. Instead of releasing it, he laced his fingers through mine as he walked me to the door. He followed me into the house, still without saying anything.

Sitting down in the living room, he stared up at the portrait of his father. "I would like to have that." Without looking at me, he spoke softly. "I'm sorry for the way she acted today." I didn't have to ask who he was talking about. "She shouldn't have been there, and I don't know why she was, except to garner some attention."

Again he fell silent. When he spoke again, he changed the subject. "I'll be leaving for Tucson tomorrow afternoon. I'd like to spend a little time with you before I leave. Do you feel up to going out for dinner tonight?"

My stomach clinched at the invitation. I didn't want to give him the impression I wanted anything romantic between us. "No, I'm still full from the luncheon. The ladies put on a very nice meal." I hoped he wouldn't push it.

"Yes, they did, but you can't be full. You barely touched your food. Are you sure you're all right? You aren't getting sick, are you?" His voice held a worried note, and he leaned forward, staring at me like he could look into my very soul. A worried frown drew his dark brows together.

"No, I'm perfectly healthy," I assured him with a laugh. "I guess I just wasn't hungry. I'm still not. I think I just need to be alone for a while." I was also hoping Dan would call or come over. Unlike the chief who used it for a social event, working the crowd, Dan had spent the entire time at the funeral and luncheon watching everyone in attendance. Had he seen anything suspicious?

Jake studied me for a moment longer. "Okay, if you're sure you're all right." He waited for me to nod my head. "If you need anything, you have my numbers." He stood up, placing a soft kiss on my cheek. "I'll see you at church tomorrow. Maybe we can go somewhere just to get away for the day." I didn't commit either way. I wanted to leave my options open. I stayed in the chair until I heard his car pull out of the drive.

Although I said I wanted to be alone, once I got my wish, I realized it wasn't what I wanted after all. In the short time I'd been in Bisbee my mind had been consumed with finding Claire's killer. That issue was far from resolved, but I didn't know where to turn next.

"A watched pot never boils" was one of my mom's favorite sayings when I became impatient for something to happen. In this instance, maybe it was time to concentrate on something else.

How long did Myriam plan on staying in town? Was she going to cause problems for me? Why did she even care if I lived here? Jake said she'd remarried several times after the divorce from his father, so why was she so intent on getting anything that had belonged to Tom?

I headed upstairs to change my clothes, but was waylaid by the chimes on the front door. Hoping it was Dan, my heart gave a little leap. Retracing my steps, I pulled the door open. My smile wilted slightly. "Hello Irma." I stepped aside to let her in.

"That was a beautiful service." Irma smiled up at me. "I'm sure Claire would have been pleased."

Pleased by her own funeral? I thought. She died far too young to be happy about something like that no matter how beautiful it seemed to someone else. I kept those thoughts to myself as we went into the living room. "Would you like some tea?" I asked instead.

She appeared to be considering my question, but finally shook her head. "It's been such a sad day. I think something a little stronger would help to revive both of us. If there is any of the delicious wine you shared with me the other day, maybe that would lift both of our spirits."

"That sounds nice. I'll bring each of us a glass." Irma's eyes sparkled in anticipation, and I chuckled as I left the room.

Was the petite woman a closet drinker? If it had been a long time since her last husband passed away, maybe she had a nip or two each day to ease the loneliness.

I carried a tray with the bottle of wine and two glasses into the living room a few minutes later. I'd added some of the homemade cookies the church ladies had insisted I bring home with me. Having wine on a nearly empty stomach wasn't a good idea for either of us.

Irma took a delicate sip, closing her eyes like she was sipping the nectar of the gods. "This is delicious. I think it was one of Claire's favorites."

I agreed it was very good. Until recently, I hadn't even known there were wineries in Arizona. Maybe I could do a little exploring while I waited for things to settle down.

"I'm so glad you've decided to stay in Bisbee," she finally said. "I hope you don't mind if I continue to visit you the way I did with Claire. Are you really going to open a bed and breakfast like Claire planned? Or were you just yanking Dusty's chain?"

I nearly choked on the swallow of wine I had just taken. She patted my back until I stopped coughing. I finally lifted my shoulders in a shrug. "I'm still thinking about it. Nothing is set in stone yet." To my mind, there were too many people unduly interested in what I was going to do with the house.

The wine began to work its magic on me, and I could feel myself begin to relax. I was running out of small talk, and I let Irma carry the conversational ball. If she had come over to pump me for information, as well as have a glass of wine, she was going to be disappointed. Wine was all she was going to get today. I had no information to impart. Or was she just lonesome? I couldn't decide.

After a second glass, Irma stood up. "I guess I'd better go home. It's been a very trying day. I think I'll take a little nap." She swayed slightly.

Taking her arm to steady her, I followed her out, wondering if I should offer to walk her home. I didn't want her to fall down the uneven steps, but I didn't want to insult her either.

The decision was taken out of my hand when she gripped my arm with talon-like fingers. "I think I need a little help here," she whispered. "Maybe I shouldn't have had that second glass." She gave a twittering laugh. Maybe she'd had a glass or two before coming over to see me.

An hour later, I decided she was more lonely than tipsy. It took that long for her to show me around her house, introduce me to her three departed husbands whose pictures and ashes were sitting on the mantle in her living room, and show me all the pictures of her children and grandchildren. She had three children, one from each husband, seven grandchildren, as well as one great grandchild. "They've all moved away now," she explained sadly. "Good jobs weren't always easy to find in our little town. They try to visit me once or twice a year. Although I talk to them regularly, I do miss them," she finished on a sigh.

"My grandchildren grew up without their granny." She wiped at her eyes with a lace hanky. "That's why I enjoyed having Claire as my neighbor." She turned her teary eyes up to me. "I'm really glad you're staying here." She patted my arm that she'd continued to cling to since I helped her home. "Maybe you'll marry that nice detective, and I can be granny to your children."

I nearly gasped at her suggestion. It was far too soon to think about something like that. In truth though, my imagination had wandered down a similar road.

Exhausted from the emotion of the funeral, and the tour of Irma's house and family, I dropped into the recliner resting my head on the back of the chair. "What I need to put the icing on the cake of my day is a visit from Myriam," I muttered to the empty room. If she came around, I wouldn't bother answering the door. There was only one person I was hoping to see tonight. Otherwise, I just wanted to be left alone.

Dan had been over every evening since I joined him for lunch. I couldn't believe that had only been a week ago. I didn't know if anything would come of our friendship, but I was willing to find out. I did like Irma's suggestion.

My eyes drifted shut as exhaustion, and the wine, claimed me. My thoughts of Dan turned into sweet dreams.

CHAPTER TEN

When the grandfather clock in the corner of the living room chimed six times, I sat up, blinking my eyes. The sun was already beginning to dip behind the mountains. Stretching lazily, I reached out to turn on a lamp in the dimming light. I stopped my hand inches from the lamp. Last night this lamp had been on the table across the room. Sometime today, the lamps had been switched.

Spending so much time with Irma earlier, I hadn't had a chance to go through the rooms to see what my unknown visitor had done while I was at the funeral. My stomach began doing flip flops. Maybe they were here while I was sleeping, and I'd been too tired to hear anything. Standing up, I looked around like I expected someone to jump out at me. The fading sun cast the room in shadows making it hard to see into the corners.

Checking all the rooms downstairs, I slowly climbed the stairs to the second floor. One drawer in my bedroom was partially open. The clothes in all the drawers had been moved around. I had been in a hurry that morning when I dressed for the funeral. Had I disturbed the clothes more than I realized? It wasn't like me to dig through my things looking for something special to wear. Had I been in such a rush that I hadn't closed the drawer all the way?

I had only opened one of the drawers to get my underclothes. Who had rearranged the clothes in the rest of them? My stomach was doing somersaults. Someone had been in here, either while I was gone today, or while I was sleeping earlier. Were they still here?

Picking up the antique candlestick I'd used my first night in the house to attack the creaking noises, I cautiously moved out of my bedroom.

I went through the other bedrooms on the second floor to see what was missing or moved. Several items from Claire's room on the third floor were now in what had been the master suite. Someone had definitely been in the house, but they had only moved things around. What was the purpose of doing that if they weren't going to take anything? And if they were going to take something, why announce the fact that they had been in here by moving things around? It was one more thing that didn't make sense. Was Myriam trying to scare me away with her 'resident ghost'?

Going through Claire's room, the few items that were now in the second floor bedroom were the only things I could tell that were missing. Like the clothes in my drawers, hers had been shifted around. The search had been so subtle that if I hadn't been looking for changes, I wouldn't have noticed. If they were going to move items from her room to the bedroom downstairs, why be so careful about the search? It was like two different people had been at work here. My stomach knotted up. What were they looking for?

The police had given me the jewelry she had on at the time of her death. It was now in my room. My heart sank. Is that what the person was looking for in my room? I rushed down the long flight of stairs. I'd put the small pouch where I kept the few pieces of jewelry I'd brought with me in the night stand with Claire's Bible. Pulling it out, I dumped the contents on the bed.

A sigh of relief escaped my lips as I sat down beside the small pile. Claire's engagement and wedding rings, along with the small cross she'd always worn, were still there with my jewelry. If they weren't looking for jewelry, what were they looking for?

"Jewelry!" I exclaimed out loud. Myriam said Tom had given Claire some jewelry that was family heirlooms, and should belong to Jake. In theory I agreed, but that didn't give her or anyone else the right to come in the house and take it. Did Jake have anything to do with the furniture being moved around in an effort to frighten me off? If he wanted the jewelry, why didn't he just ask me for it? I needed to check the safe to see if the jewelry there had been taken.

Running down to the butler's pantry for the step stool, I

headed for Tom's office. When the door chimes sounded, I gave a frustrated sigh. It was a wonder Claire got anything done if she had this much company.

It was still light out when I came home from Irma's, and I hadn't turned on the front porch light. It was now shrouded in darkness. Flipping the switch next to the door, light flooded the porch. A very handsome detective smiled at me through the wavy glass in the window. My heart did a little happy dance in my chest.

"Hello." He leaned down to place a gentle kiss on my lips as he stepped inside. "Are you changing light bulbs somewhere?" He nodded at the step stool I was still holding. "I can help you with that."

"No, I just need to check something in Tom's office."

"You need a step stool to check it?" There was a frown in his voice as he followed me down the hall to see what I was up to.

Before spinning the dial on the safe, I said a silent prayer that the cases would still be there. When I first opened the safe, I hadn't bothered to look inside them. Now I wished I had. There was no way I would know if anything was missing.

The breath I'd been holding came out on a whoosh when the three cases were still there. "Thank you, God," I whispered. Dizzy with relief, I rested my head against the edge of the safe for a second. I handed the cases to Dan, and stepped off the stool.

"Okay, you want to tell me what's going on?" he frowned at me. "Why were you so worried these wouldn't be there? How could anyone take them?"

The furniture had been moved every time I was gone, but I hadn't told anyone about it, not even him. I didn't want anyone to claim I had a ghost living with me, or that I was going nuts. I didn't have a choice but to tell him now. First I needed to see what was in the cases.

Raising my finger in a wait-a-minute gesture, I opened the first case. "Oh my," I gasped. Even in the dim light from the desk lamp, the jewels winked at me.

"Wow, are those yours?" Dan was as awestruck as I was.

"I'm not really sure. Mr. Edmonds said all of Claire's personal items were mine, but Myriam said the family heirlooms Tom gave Claire should belong to Jake."

"When did she tell you that?" Dan frowned at me. "I didn't think she said anything to you today."

"She didn't," I sighed. "She stopped by earlier in the week to tell me just what she thought of me living in this house, and receiving half of the estate. She didn't like the idea of turning the house into a bed and breakfast either." I shook my head. "The woman has definite opinions about things."

I lifted a necklace from one of the other cases holding it up to the light. "How much do think all these are worth?"

He shook his head. "I have no idea." Taking the necklace out of my hand, he examined it more closely. "I'm not a jeweler, but it's my guess is this isn't an heirloom." He handed it back to me. "The design looks too modern."

"What was she talking about then?" After going through all the cases, I put them back in the safe, spun the dial, and moved the false books back in place. I didn't know if anything was missing. If there had been heirloom jewelry in those cases, it was gone now.

"You want to tell me why you were worried the jewelry might be missing? Did something happen today while you were gone?"

He followed me into the kitchen where I began taking food the church ladies had sent home with me out of the refrigerator. By now it was after seven o'clock. The fact that I hadn't eaten much at the luncheon was beginning to make my stomach growl. I handed him a bottle of wine to open. The glass I'd had with Irma had been several hours ago. Another one while I explained about the moved furniture sounded like a good idea.

"How many times has this happened?" He interrupted before I got very far with my explanation.

"Every time I leave the house I come back to find things moved around. Today someone had gone through the drawers in my room and Claire's room. I don't think anything was taken though."

"You're just now telling me that someone has been in here several times, and now searched the house. Why didn't you call me?"

I lifted my shoulders. "What could you do? Nothing is ever taken. I don't know if someone is playing a practical joke on me or what. If I didn't know better, I'd say they were trying to *Gaslight* me." This was reminiscent of the nineteen thirties or forties movie by that name that I'd seen years ago. The woman's husband was trying to drive her crazy in order to inherit her money. But no one in Bisbee would inherit my money. I didn't even know what would happen to my share of the trust if I died before I could make out a will. It was something I needed to find out.

"Maybe someone is trying to make you think there's a ghost in the house to scare you off," he added. Either way, that wasn't going to work, I told myself. I wasn't going anywhere.

We discussed all the options while moving around each other as we prepared dinner. It was like a well-choreographed dance that we'd done a hundred times before.

"Do you know if Jake or Myriam still have a key?" A case of jitters attack my stomach. The thought of that woman being in the house wasn't a pleasant one. Of course, I'd rather she be in here when I'm not, than while I'm here. There was no telling what the woman would do to me.

"Jake never mentioned anything about having a key. He always rings the chimes when he comes over. I can't imagine Tom would allow Myriam to have a key after the divorce. From what Jake said, it wasn't a pleasant one."

"Just because Tom didn't want her to have a key, doesn't mean she didn't keep one. If the little display at the funeral is any indication, I don't think mother and son see eye-to-eye on a much either."

"Well, they can't drive me crazy, and I'm not running scared, so Myriam or whoever can just stop with the tricks." I didn't mention her story of Sam the ghost.

"Obviously, someone besides you has a key. I can fix that easily enough by changing the locks. I'll come by after church tomorrow, and do that."

Setting the last dish on the table, I looked at him. "Can we not talk about this anymore? There has to be a more pleasant subject we can discuss."

He took my hand, lifting it to his lips. "I think we can manage that."

~~~

The living room had a large screen television, and we settled down with an action movie that neither of had seen before. Like Dusty, Claire had a large selection of DVD's to choose from. It was one more indication that she was getting ready to open her bed and breakfast.

It was much later when he got ready to leave. Pulling me into his arms, he rested his forehead against mine. "If anything happens tonight, even the old house creaking, call me. I'll be here to protect you." He waggled his eyebrows; giving me a mischievous grin. His lips claimed mine once again in a heart stopping kiss. *Who would I need protection from; him or the creaking old house?*

"What about a ghost?" I asked once he lifted his head. "Do you know how to get rid of one of those?"

He laughed. "I'm willing to try anything once." He opened the door to step out. Turning serious, he pulled me against his hard chest once more. "All joking aside, if you hear anything unusual I want you to call me. I'm not taking chances."

When he released me, he moved me back inside. "Lock the door, and wedge a chair under the knob. Do that to the back door as well." With one final kiss, he disappeared into the dark night. The porch light was still on, and I wondered who had witnessed our good-byes. Did it matter to anyone else?

All the talk of ghosts and other kinds of unwanted visitors left me feeling more than a little spooked. I moved a dining room chair into the entry, wedging it under the door knob like Dan suggested, and did the same in the kitchen.

Because of the nap I had after coming home from Irma's, I

wasn't tired yet even though it was close to midnight. Curling up in the recliner with my tablet, I decided to read until I got sleepy. The murder mystery I was reading didn't help to ease my fears though. Every creak and groan from the old house made me jump nervously. Finally giving it up as a lost cause, I put the tablet aside. Whether I was sleepy or not, it was time to go to bed.

In the short time I'd been living in the house, I'd become familiar with every tread on the long staircase that creaked when stepped on. I wanted to sleep with one eye open and one ear listening for any sounds. Since both were impossible, it wasn't easy to fall asleep. If someone came in while I was asleep, I convinced myself that I would hear them coming, and could protect myself. Still, I kept my cell phone beside the bed, just in case. I decided to get a baseball bat the next time I was in town. That would be more effective than the antique candlestick I placed beside my bed.

~~~~

The merry-go-round ring tone of my cell phone woke me out of a sound sleep. It felt like mere minutes after I finally fell asleep instead of hours. "Huh?" I mumbled. "Who is this?"

"Jillian, are you all right?" Dan's worried voice brought me further awake.

"Yeah, I just woke up. What's wrong?" I pushed myself up in bed. The clock on the night stand said it was after seven. After tossing and turning for several hours, I'd finally fallen into a sound sleep only four hours ago. No wonder I felt like my head was full of cotton batting.

"Nothing's wrong. I just wanted to let you know I wouldn't be in church this morning. The chief called a few minutes ago. I need to go in to work."

My stomach began to churn. "Did something happen?" I wasn't sure what kinds of crime took place in a small border town, but it couldn't be good if he'd been called in on a Sunday morning.

He sighed heavily. "I'm not sure what's up with him. He's

been acting kind of squirrelly lately. I'll call you when I can. Say a prayer for me."

"Always." He hung up before I could say anything else.

Swinging my legs over the side of the bed, I sat there for a minute trying to figure out what to do next. My mind was still in a muddle. I decided a shower would help clear my head.

At nine o'clock sharp, I pulled into Irma's driveway. She was already outside waiting for me. "Hello, dearie. How are you this fine morning?"

"I'm right as rain." I smiled at her. By this time, I'd had several cups of coffee, and was ready to face the day. I'd even made a few plans. Since I was going to stay in Bisbee, I was going to need a car of my own. My car at home wasn't worth what it would cost to have it shipped here. It wouldn't make the long drive out either. It had been on its last legs when I bought it three years ago. I didn't know if there was a car dealership in Bisbee. I'd been driving Claire's car since returning the rental, but it belonged to the trust, not me. I wasn't sure what I would do with it; probably let it sit until I could see what Jake wanted to do with it. I thought a trust was supposed to make things less complicated. In this case, it was the opposite, at least as far as I was concerned.

Irma chattered nonstop during the short ride to church, and didn't seem to notice that I didn't respond beyond an occasional nod or uh huh. Maybe all the wine she'd had the day before put her to sleep early, and she was well-rested this morning.

Jake was outside the church when I dropped Irma off before parking the car. She gave a disgusted humph when she saw him, but kept any other thoughts to herself.

After the service, Jake smiled at Irma. "I was wondering if you ladies would join me for lunch. I hate eating alone."

After the way she acted whenever he was around, I expected her to decline the offer, but the woman never failed to surprise me. "That sounds lovely, Jake. Thank you for including me." She gave his arm a friendly pat.

"What man wouldn't want to have the company of two

such lovely ladies?" Charm oozed effortlessly from the man, and I reminded myself that I needed to be cautious until I figured out who had killed my sister.

Back at the house, Irma was out of the car the instant I shut off the engine. She hurried over to Jake's SUV where he waited to assist her into the backseat. She was anxious for her lunch date. I had to chuckle. If he could charm Irma, he could probably charm a rattlesnake. He must have inherited the trait from his father, because his mother was lacking in any kind of charm.

Jake proved to be an entertaining host. Besides including Irma in his lunch invitation, he included her in all of our conversations. After dropping her off, he drove the few feet to Claire's house to take me home. In my mind, it would always be Claire's house. That's what I would call the bed and breakfast; if I actually opened it, I qualified.

"I'll be leaving for Tucson in a few hours," he said. "But I'll be back next weekend. I'd like to see you again. He laced his fingers through mine as he walked me to the door.

"I'm sure we'll see each other whenever you're in town." I deliberately misunderstood his meaning.

He chuckled. "That's not what I meant, but then I think you know that. I'd like to go out with you. As nice as Irma is, I'd like it to be without our chaperone next time."

"I don't think that's a good idea, Jake." Claire's warning to be careful of where I put my trust was never far from my mind. Until I knew who had killed her, I didn't want to get involved with anyone she might have trusted. I had to admit that wasn't the only reason.

"Why not?" A frown furrowed his brow.

I thought about telling him I didn't think his mother would approve, but that sounded rather childish even if it was the truth. Making that woman angry would only have bad results for me.

"Do you have a boyfriend back home?"

He had just offered me an excuse, but I couldn't very well lie about it if I was going to continue seeing Dan. I shook my head. "No, but…" My voice trailed off, unsure how much to say.

"But you're seeing that detective," he finished my sentence for me. He chuckled at my startled expression. "It's a small town. Nothing remains a secret for very long." He sighed. "I'll accept defeat for now, but if things change, don't be surprised if I ask again." He bent down, placing a kiss on my cheek. "I'll see you next weekend." When I started to object, he continued, "just as a friend."

I hadn't had a serious relationship in longer than I wanted to admit; now I have two men interested in me. Go figure.

CHAPTER ELEVEN

I'd been gone for several hours, giving someone ample opportunity to get in the house. It was time to see if furniture had been rearranged again, or more things searched. The table in the entry was still where I'd left it after it had been moved twice. *That's probably where my secret decorator wanted it,* I decided, giving my head a shake. How long did I have to put up with this? I went into the living room to see what had been moved there.

Before I made it any further, someone was at the door. Had Jake decided to try convincing me to change my mind about going out with him? I considered not answering, but he knew I was here. Besides, it might to Dan. A thrill moved through me at the thought, and I turned back to the door.

But it wasn't a handsome detective on my porch. Through the window, I could see the distorted image of a woman. "Oh brother," I sighed. "What does she want?"

Instead of ringing the door chimes a second time, her fist landed on the door. "I can see you standing there, so you might as well open the door. I'm not going away." Myriam gave the door another hard hit. *I hope she gets splinters.*

"What do you want, Myriam?" I only opened the door part way, keeping my leg braced against it to prevent her from pushing her way inside.

"I want you to leave my son alone," she snapped. "First your sister gets her hooks in to my husband…"

"Your ex-husband," I interrupted.

"Shut up. He was old enough to be her father. She was just after his money, and she got it. Now you're after my son. Isn't it enough that you took his inheritance? Now you're trying to turn this beautiful house in to some cheap hotel wanna be."

"I didn't take Jake's inheritance, and I'm not after him." I tried to remain calm, and not stoop to her level. Refuting her claims wasn't working though. Everything I said only made her angrier.

"Don't lie to me," she screeched. "I saw the two of you right here on this porch not ten minutes ago."

"Are you stalking me?" The butterflies in my stomach had turned to giant birds. How unbalanced was the woman? Was she dangerous? Was she the one who kept moving furniture around trying to make me believe it was a ghost?

"I said to shut up. You need to listen to me. I won't stand for you dating my son."

"I'm not dating him," I tried telling her again, but in her present state, she wasn't listening to anything I had to say.

She gave an undignified snort. "Don't deny it. I saw the two of you!"

"Then you saw him kiss…"

"That's what I just said. I saw him kiss you, so stop lying to me."

"On the cheek," I insisted, raising my voice. "He kissed me on the cheek." I didn't know why I was arguing with her. Her mind was made up. She only heard what she wanted to hear.

"I don't care. Stay away from my son." With that parting shot, she turned, stomping down the steps to her car.

I shut the door, making sure the lock was firmly in place. If she was the one rearranging the furniture and sorting through my things, a lock wasn't going to keep her out. If she wanted in bad enough, new locks wouldn't stop her either. She could break a window and come right in. The image of her climbing through a broken window in all her finery almost humorous, almost.

My hands were shaking as I sank down in the recliner. What was I supposed to do now? Calling the police would be useless. She hadn't done anything to me. I couldn't prove she was the one getting in the house and moving furniture around while I was gone. If I told Jake what she'd pulled, would that make him mad at her or me? Did I even care?

Instead of sitting around worrying about what Myriam was going to do next, I headed for the stairs. If I was really going to make it appear like I was turning the house into a bed and breakfast, I needed to find out how to go about doing that.

When the chimes on the front door rang again, I gave a frustrated sigh. "Who now?"

Irma was wringing her hands when I opened the door, a worried frown on her face. "Are you all right, Jillian? I saw that crazy Myriam leave just a few minutes ago. I'm so sorry I didn't see her sooner, or I would have called the police. There's no telling what she'll do if she gets riled up. She can be really mean."

"I'm fine, Irma." I stepped aside to let her in. "She didn't like the fact that I was with Jake."

"And how did she know about that?" She lifted an eyebrow. "Is she spying on you?"

Spying isn't the word I would use, I thought.

"She needs to go back where she came from." The small woman paced across the living room, flopping down on the couch. "She was always more trouble than she was worth."

"Would you like some tea?" It was time for a change of subject.

With a big smile, she relaxed immediately. "That sounds lovely." Myriam was all but forgotten.

It was another hour before I finally changed out of my church clothes. Things had been moved around in Claire's room again, but I couldn't tell if anything had been taken. *What was the point of this? What were they looking for?* Calling the police wouldn't do any good. I couldn't even prove that someone had been in the house. I wasn't going to be one of those helpless women who called the police at every little thing. Until I had real proof that someone had been in the house, I wouldn't, couldn't call them.

Attempting to put that thought aside, I tried to concentrate on other matters. I needed to figure out what kind of car I wanted. I also didn't want to go all the way to Tucson to buy something. Sitting down with my laptop propped up on my legs, I began looking up locations closer to home. Sierra Vista had several car dealerships to choose from. How long would it take to find something I liked? I didn't know any more about the car buying process than I did about starting and running a bed and breakfast.

After deciding where I could go to look for a vehicle, and what I wanted, my next step was to figure out what I needed to do to open a bed and breakfast. It wasn't simply a case of putting up a sign and taking in guests. I needed to get a license from the county health department, and have the kitchen inspected. Since Bisbee was the county seat, I could accomplish that right here in town. I would also need some kind of license for myself. Tomorrow was shaping up to be a very busy day.

It was getting close to dinner, and I still hadn't heard from Dan. What had the chief found for him to do on a Sunday? Pulling my cell phone out of my purse to check for messages, I realized it was still turned off. With everything that had been going on since I got home, I'd forgotten to turn it back on. There were three missed calls and three text messages, all from Dan. Each message got a little more frantic when I didn't answer.

I dialed his number and heard the ring in stereo. He was at my front door. I disconnected, and opened the door. "What happened? Are you all right? Did someone get in the house again?" His questions came at me rapid-fire. He gripped my shoulders, looking me up and down for any sign of injuries or wounds.

"Dan, I'm fine." I put my hand on his face. "I forgot to turn my phone on after church." He relaxed, pulling me against his chest. "I was imagining all sorts of things when I couldn't reach you." He cupped my face in his big hands, looking into my eyes. Slowly lowering his head, he claimed my lips. I leaned into him, wrapping my arms around his neck. I'd waited all day for this.

When he lifted his head, we were both out of breath. I took a step back. We needed to slow things down some. "How was work? Why did the chief want you to come in on a Sunday?" I wasn't sure what kind of hours detectives normally worked.

"I didn't *have* to go in today," he scoffed. "The chief just wanted me to." He gave his blonde head a frustrated shake. "He had a bunch of busy-work for me to do; nothing that couldn't wait until tomorrow." He paused for a heartbeat, and I wondered what was coming next. "He told me he didn't think it was a good idea for me to be seeing you socially since you're part of a case we're working on."

"Oh," that was the only thing I could think to say.

"He can't dictate what I do in my time off, Jillian." He lifted my chin until I was looking him in the eyes.

"I don't want you to lose your job because of me." His smoldering look left me slightly breathless.

"He can't fire me. There isn't any conflict of interest involved. You aren't a suspect in any crime." He placed another soft kiss on my lips before changing the subject. "What did you do today?"

His face grew dark when I told him about Myriam's visit. "So she doesn't want her son around you, huh? Can't say I like it either," he groused. "Did she threaten you?"

"Nothing that dramatic. She doesn't want me dating Jake." He cleared his throat, but let me continue with my tale. "She wouldn't listen when I told her I wasn't dating him. I would have explained that Irma went to lunch with us if she had stopped talking long enough." He relaxed after that. I left out the part that she didn't want me to turn the house into a bed and breakfast. He would probably agree with her on that as well.

He shook his head. "From what I've heard, mother and son are like oil and water. They don't mix very well. She still tries to run his life, and he won't listen."

"Where did you hear that? I didn't think Jake was in Bisbee all that often."

"Gossip is a big part of small town life. I don't usually pay much attention to that kind of thing, but this time it's paid off. She has been trying to run his life for years. The harder she tries, the more he fights it."

"What am I letting myself in for by staying here?" I muttered.

"I hope you won't let her scare you off." His intense gaze bore into my eyes. "I kind of like you being here. You just need to stay away from her little boy, and all will be well."

"If a ghost or a phantom decorator doesn't scare me off, Myriam won't either." I tried to make light of the situation, but my stomach churned at the thought of Myriam being on my case. The woman was beyond vindictive. I couldn't imagine Claire letting her get close enough to poison her though.

I secretly thought Myriam was the one getting into the house every time I was away. I couldn't figure out what she hoped to accomplish though. It was time for a change of subject.

It turns out that Dan is something of a car buff, and we spent the evening researching what kind of vehicle I wanted to buy. He even knew several dealerships I could check out. Giving them his name would help me get a good deal.

As I suspected, he wasn't so keen on my idea of going through the motions of starting the bed and breakfast in order to catch a killer though. "That isn't your job, Jillian. You need to leave that to the police."

"And how's that working so far?" I snapped unnecessarily. "I don't think Chief Daniels is very interested in solving this case."

"Well, the chief isn't the only policeman in this town," he answered with equal heat. "I have never deliberately let a suspect get away with a crime, and I'm not going to start now. I'm not going to let him get at you either." We stared at each other for several minutes, anger roiling between us, before we broke out in laughter.

"Okay, now that we have that off our chests, maybe we can discuss this logically." I smiled up at him, hoping I could make him see things my way.

"Logically, you need to stay out of the investigation," he countered. "When civilians get involved in a case, it only makes matters worse."

"Don't patronize me, Detective." As quickly as my temper

diffused, it ignited again. "I have very good deductive skills." I began clicking off all the points we currently knew about the case, holding up my fingers as I went. "Someone was poisoning her," I concluded, "someone she trusted. I need to figure out who that was."

"Are you going to question everyone who knew her, and accuse them of poisoning her?"

I released a frustrated breath. "Of course not. At the time she got sick she was working hard to set up her bed and breakfast. I don't know if that's what got her killed, but I have to start somewhere."

"No you don't." His voice was tight with anger. "That's my job." We were back to staring angrily at each other. "If this had nothing to do with the bed and breakfast, then what are you going to do? Will you look for another excuse to accuse people of killing her?"

"I'm not accusing anyone of anything until I have proof."

"You aren't the one who is supposed to get the proof." His patience was almost gone, and he looked like he wanted to shake me. "Leave that to me."

"It's getting late, and we're both tired." I stood up. "I think we need to call it a night."

"You're kicking me out? In the middle of an argument?" He ran his hands through his thick hair in frustration.

I gave a weary sigh. "I'm not kicking you out; I'm saying I'm tired. This discussion isn't going anywhere. For tonight, why don't we call it a draw, and agree to disagree?"

For a minute I thought he was going to argue that point as well. Finally, he stood up, giving his head a nod. "All right, I'll call you tomorrow. Remember to keep your cell phone on, and keep the doors locked." With that reprimand, he walked out. He didn't bother kissing me good-bye.

What had just happened? I flopped down on the couch. It's true that I don't know enough about police procedure to investigate a crime, but I'm not a child either. Claire said she had trusted the wrong person. I needed to find out who that was. Again I wished she had told me what was happening before it was too late.

The night had ended in a disaster causing my heart to ache, but I couldn't stand aside while Dan, or someone else, looked into her death. I had to do this for Claire.

CHAPTER TWELVE

Replaying my argument with Dan over and over all night made for a sleepless night. The sun was just peeking over the top of the mountains when I finally gave up on sleep, and stumbled down the stairs. I didn't bother to brush my hair first. There was no one around to see what tossing and turning all night had done to it. Right now, I needed coffee.

After two cups of coffee, a hot shower, and my teeth brushed, I was beginning to feel semi-human. Thinking about Dan still caused my heart to hurt, so I tried not to think about him. Tears burned behind my eyes, but I brushed them away. I didn't need a man to tell me what I could or couldn't do.

But I really like him, I argued with myself. I didn't want this to be the end for us. He said he would call me in the morning. He just didn't say when in the morning, or which morning. *Well, I'm not going to sit around waiting for that call,* I told myself. As long as I had my cell phone with me, I didn't have to stay in the house. Besides, I needed to keep busy.

With all the car information we'd gathered before our argument, I knew what I was looking for and where I needed to go. On the drive to Sierra Vista, I kept checking my phone every few minutes to make sure I still had service. I didn't know what service was like in the mountains.

I wasn't sure I would find what I was looking for on my first shopping trip. If I did, I would have a problem getting both my new vehicle and Claire's car back to Bisbee. I'd cross that bridge when I came to it.

After the way the evening ended, I hated using Dan's name as a reference at the dealerships he'd recommended. Since he still hadn't called, I could only assume he was still angry with me.

Buying a car wasn't as easy as it sounded. Most of the salesmen were just that, men. They didn't think a woman knew the first thing about buying a car, or what she wanted.

But I knew exactly what I was looking for: a low mileage, late model truck. If I actually turned the house into a bed and breakfast, a truck would come in handy.

By the time I'd looked at three cars, not trucks, I'd had it with sales*men*. "Do you have any sales*women*?" I asked at the next dealership. The look of surprise on the man's face was comical.

"Um, yes, but I can help you find what you're looking for."

"I'm sure you can, but a woman would know a little more of what a woman would like." Translation: A woman would listen to what I wanted, not assume she knew what was best for me. He stalked away, turning me over to the young woman who had been standing with him when I pulled onto the lot.

"Hi, I'm Sherry Baker. May I help you?" She reluctantly offered her hand for me to shake. Her smile was somewhat wary. I could imagine the wild story her co-worker told her about the crazy woman on the lot.

"Yes, thank you." Relating my problem with the last three salesmen I'd dealt with, she chuckled. Giving her head a nod, she looked over her shoulder at the men watching us, and gave them a thumbs-up.

"Tell me what you're looking for, and I'll see what I can do for you." Two hours later I had the truck of my dreams; a powder blue, two-year-old Ford Explorer four-door truck with low mileage. Well, mine and the bank's.

Belatedly, I wondered what the chief would have to say about my purchase. He'd already hinted that I had something to do with Claire's death in order to inherit her money. This would probably add fuel to his fire. Shaking off that thought, I admired my new truck. I'd done nothing wrong, and just because the chief didn't have the common sense to realize that piece of truth, I wasn't going to let it worry me.

Sherry had even arranged to have Claire's car towed back to Bisbee for me. I doubted the men would have gone that extra step. Driving away, I waved at the men standing around with disgruntled expressions on their faces.

The tips Dan had given me the night before were helpful in negotiating the deal, and I wanted to tell him. But I still hadn't heard from him. I wasn't sure I'd be seeing much of him in the future.

To keep from feeling sorry for myself, I pushed that thought aside. I needed to go to the county offices in Bisbee to see what I needed to do to start my own business. What special regulations were involved in running a bed and breakfast? First, I needed to have lunch. There was a variety of restaurants in Sierra Vista to pick from.

Choosing a small Mexican restaurant, I decided it was time to test out some local dishes. Either Monday wasn't a high-traffic day, or I'd made a bad choice in restaurants. I was the only customer in the place.

When the skin on the back of my neck began to prickle, I looked around for the cause. Roland Granger had just walked in. He approached my table with a friendly smile. My stomach churned. What was he doing here? Had he been following me all morning? Before I could move, he was beside my table. "Hello, Miss Connors. Mind if I join you?" He didn't wait for me to answer as he pulled out the chair across from me.

"As a matter of fact I do mind."

He sighed dramatically. "You know, I'm not a bad guy."

"No, I don't know that. You're stalking me. In my book that makes you a bad guy."

This time he chuckled. "I'm not stalking you."

"Really?" I let the sarcasm drip from my voice. "Let's see. You tried to join me for lunch once before. You came to my sister's funeral."

"She was my friend," he interrupted.

Ignoring him, I continued. "You followed me to Sierra Vista and once again you're trying to join me for lunch. In my mind that fits the definition of stalking. Maybe I should tell Detective Tobin about this." I hoped I sounded far braver than I felt.

The door of the restaurant opened, and Roland Granger turned to see who had come in. Turning back to me, he nodded his head. "I won't bother you further." There was a silent 'today' hanging at the end of his sentence. Just that quick he was out the door. He gave in a little too fast. Something was up.

Looking at the man who had scared Mr. Granger off, a gasp escaped my parted lips. It was the man I thought had been following me the same day Roland Granger tried to insinuate himself into my life. Were they both following me for separate reasons, or were they working together, taking turns hoping I wouldn't notice? Either way it was an uncomfortable thought.

Sensing my wide-eyed stare, the man dipped his head, probably hoping I wouldn't recognize him. Had they both been following me, and I just now noticed? What did either of them hope to learn by following me?

My appetite was gone. If I hadn't already ordered, I would have left. I thought about confronting him right there, but quickly decided against it. Causing a scene in the restaurant might get me arrested for disturbing the peace. Maybe I could catch him when he came outside.

When the waitress set the steaming plate in front of me, I ate quickly, barely tasting the cheese enchilada and refried beans. If he really was following me, I wasn't sure what he was hoping to discover. He already knew where I lived. Maybe I could turn the tables, and follow him to see where he would lead me.

Outside, I surveyed the few cars in the lot. They all appeared empty. If Roland Granger was in any of them, he was hiding. Moving my truck to the parking lot next to the restaurant, I waited for the man to come outside while I kept an eye out for my other stalker. It ended up being a waste of time. A half hour later, neither man had appeared. Maybe they had both decided to stop tailing me for today.

While I was waiting to pull out of the parking lot, Mr. Edmonds' fancy car pulled in. I watched him in the rearview mirror as he got out of his car and disappeared into the restaurant. It didn't seem to be the sort of place the fastidious attorney would frequent. I chided myself for judging the man. Just because he was rather pompous didn't mean he didn't like small places with good food.

Back on the road, I thought about calling Dan to tell him about my possible tail, but would he even care anymore? My phone had remained conspicuously silent all morning even though I had made sure it was fully charged and turned on before I left the house.

Keeping one eye on my rearview mirror, checking for familiar cars going my way, I kept hoping I wouldn't get lost on my way back to Bisbee. My directional skills were better than I realized, and before long I was in front of the county offices.

It had dawned on me somewhere between Sierra Vista and Bisbee that my actions contradicted what I had told Dan I wanted. If I really wanted people to believe I was going to open a bed and breakfast, I needed them to know what I was doing. With a frustrated sigh, I got out of my new truck. It was time for me to decide what I really wanted. I just hoped that was the reason they had been following me.

By the time I was ready to leave the county office, I'd filled out more forms than I had when I bought my truck. Claire had already started most of the paperwork, but I had to start all over again. Who knew there would be so much red tape involved in starting a business?

Trying to read some of the papers as I left the building, I didn't watch where I was going. In the process, I walked in to someone standing on the sidewalk. "Oh, I am so sorry." Lifting my gaze, I stared into a pair of light blue eyes that had looked at me with burning anger the night before.

His startled expression turned into a warm smile when he realized who had nearly bowled him over. "If you wanted to see me, you didn't need to run me over to do it," he teased.

"I'm sorry about last night." We spoke at the same time. "Are you all right?" I asked. "I didn't hurt you, did I?"

"Just my heart," he teased again. "But it will be all healed if you'll agree to have lunch with me now."

"I had lunch in Sierra Vista." My timing for lunch was off once again, and I could hear the disappointment in my voice.

He chuckled, but grew serious again when he saw the stack of papers I'd been looking through when I bumped in to him. "It looks like you've been filling out paperwork for a while. Is that for the B&B?"

I nodded, waiting to see if he would get upset all over again. His lips tightened slightly, but it was the only outward sign that he was still upset with my plans. He drew a deep breath, releasing it slowly. "Filling out paperwork always makes me thirsty. How about keeping me company while I eat? You can have a glass of iced tea." He lifted an eyebrow questioningly. We'd done that once before. Maybe we could forget the argument, and start over.

"Let me put these in my truck. I'll even drive if you'd like." I wanted to show off my purchase. Unfortunately, driving wasn't necessary to reach the café where he always had lunch.

"You got your truck. That was fast." A big smile spread across his face. "This is a nice one." He walked around, inspecting it.

"Thanks to all the tips you gave me, it was easy once I got the right salesperson. I can't believe the way those salesmen treated me. How do they ever sell a car to a woman?" I unlocked the doors with the remote, holding the door for Dan to inspect the interior.

"Did you kick some butt?" He cocked his head at me, a crooked grin quirking his lips upward.

"I didn't have to," I laughed. "I just asked if they had a saleswoman handy. Maybe next time those men will think twice about treating a woman customer like she's an idiot."

He waited until we were seated in the small café to bring up the subject of the bed and breakfast. "Why are you doing this?" he asked softly so other diners couldn't hear.

I lifted my shoulders, unsure what he expected me to say. "I'm doing it for Claire. I want to find out who killed her."

"How is opening a bed and breakfast going to do that?

Why would someone kill her because of a bed and breakfast?" Fear of competition, I thought. Dusty acted encouraging enough, but there was something else I couldn't put my finger on.

"Why would someone kill her period?" I countered. "She was a caring, loving person. She would give you the shirt off her back if she thought you needed it more than she did." She could also do her darnedest to force her will on you, I added silently, especially if it was me she was trying to bend to her will. I loved her, but sometimes she could go overboard on the big sister knows best routine.

"How is opening a bed and breakfast going to help find her killer?" he repeated. "That doesn't make sense." We were back at square one.

"I don't know," I said on a sigh. "I just know that she was killed when she was working towards that goal. I figure if I pick up where she left off, maybe I can figure it out."

"Don't you mean maybe the killer will come after you? Is that what you want? " My breath hitched in my throat at the thought, but he didn't give me a chance to comment. "That's not going to happen on my watch. I'm not willing to put your life on the line. You need to leave this to the police." There wasn't the anger in his voice that had been there the night before.

"I'm not asking you to put anything on the line, and I'm not asking for your permission. This is what I'm doing. That's all there is to it."

The waitress placed Dan's lunch in front of him, interrupting our staring contest. "Can we put this aside for now?" he asked, reaching across the table to take my hand. "I don't want to spend my lunch hour arguing with you."

I nodded my head. This hadn't resolved anything. We were at the same place we'd been the night before, both still stubbornly holding to our own opinions. That didn't bode well for any future between us. For the remainder of his lunch hour we avoided any controversial topics.

Leaving the restaurant, a small gasp escaped my lips. I

126

stopped so quick Dan bumped into me. The man from the restaurant in Sierra Vista was getting out of an older model car in front of a store down the street.

"What's wrong?" Dan took my arm. "Are you sick?"

Ignoring Dan's questions, I marched along the sidewalk to the man. "Jillian?" Dan's questioning voice barely penetrated the anger flowing through me.

The man still had his back to me when I grabbed his arm. He whirled around glaring down at me.

"Why are you following me? Did Roland Granger put you up to it?"

"I don't know what you're talking about, lady." He seemed nervous, but I guess that was normal since I had just accosted him on the street.

"You were in Sierra Vista, I saw you in the restaurant."

"So, I get to have lunch even when I'm running errands for my boss."

"Now you show up on the same block where I just happen to be. That's a little too much of a coincidence. I know you've been following me," I accused him again. "Is Roland Granger your boss?"

"I don't have to tell you anything, lady," he growled at me.

I noticed he didn't deny that he was following me.

Dan was standing beside me now. He kept trying to get my attention, but I continued to ignore him. The man shot him a look that clearly said 'get this crazy woman away from me,' before looking back at me. "I don't have to answer your questions. I haven't done anything wrong." He shook my hand off his arm, heading into a store.

"You want to tell me what that was all about?" Dan whispered.

"That man has been following me for days. I saw him again in Sierra Vista just today, and now he's here."

"A lot of people work or shop there, but live here. He said he was running errands for his boss.

"I want to know who his boss is."

"Why?" Dan frowned at me.

"Because he's having me followed."

Within minutes the man was back on the sidewalk, clothes were slung over his shoulder. He lifted the hangers to show me what he had. He'd picked up some dry cleaning. With a smug smile, he opened the back door of the car, placing the clothes on the seat.

I could feel my face heat up as I looked at Dan. "Okay, I was wrong, this time," I qualified. "But I know someone has been watching me." His dubious expression got my back up again. "I suppose only cops get that prickly feeling when someone is watching them," I snapped.

"I didn't say that."

"You didn't have to say anything. Non-verbal communication speaks just as loud as verbal communication." I stalked over to my truck, pulling open the door.

"I'll see you tonight?" he called.

I sent him a glare over my shoulder. *Let him decipher that non-verbal communication,* I thought. I was tired of people treating me like I didn't know what I was talking about. If he was going to continue treating me like a three year old, maybe he wasn't the man for me.

My stomach was tied up in knots. Someone had killed my sister, and was now breaking into my house, but no one seemed to care about that fact except me. That wasn't exactly the truth. Dan cared. He'd offered to change the locks for me, but he hadn't had the time to do it yet.

Looking in the rearview mirror, I could see Dan was still standing outside the police department, a scowl on his face. If the argument we'd had the previous night hadn't put a damper on our relationship, this one certainly had. My heart ached at that realization, but there was nothing I could do about it. I couldn't stand by and do nothing while a killer got away.

As usual, things were moved around when I walked in the house. So far nothing had been taken, so what was the purpose? A noise coming from the kitchen stopped me from going further. That wasn't the sound of the old house settling. I wasn't the only one in the house. Common sense should have told me to turn tail and run, but common sense had deserted me. I ran for the kitchen. I was going to catch the culprit in the act.

The back door was standing open. I was too late. I attempted to go after them, until my feet stuck to the floor. Whoever had been in here had left a big mess for me to clean up. Flour and sugar were spread everywhere. A gallon jug of syrup had been spread around, making sticky glue out of the mess.

The pantry held nothing of value beyond food. What were they hoping to find? If they were hungry, why not just take what they wanted instead of destroying things? Anger seemed to be my constant companion lately, overruling any fear I might have otherwise felt. For the next hour I scrubbed the shelves and floor, mopping up what the intruder had left behind. If the health inspector came now, I'd never get approved for my license.

When all they did was move things around, I didn't bother moving them back, hoping whoever was doing this would get tired of rearranging my furniture. This was different. Their juvenile games had turned nasty now. I debated whether to call Dan, but after our latest argument, I decided against it. This would only give him more reason to tell me to leave this to the police. I had serious doubts the chief would want to spend much time investigating a little vandalism though.

Jake said his company handled computer security. Did that include home security systems? Maybe that's what it would take to catch the intruder in the act. Could he set up something for me?

I dismissed the idea almost as soon as it formed in my mind. If Myriam was in some way involved, I didn't want to add to the feud between mother and son. There were plenty of security companies around. I could call one of them. I dismissed that idea as well. The entire town would know about it before the system was even installed. I wasn't going to give my visitor a heads up. What I wanted was something that no one knew about but me. Something that was motion activated.

Another idea struck my funny bone, and I chuckled. Next time I left the house, I'd leave a note for my mystery decorator. If they realized this wasn't accomplishing what they wanted, maybe they would stop playing games and leave me alone.

I had just finished cleaning the pantry when someone pounded on the back door. Only Dusty used the back door. Didn't she have enough to do with her guests, that she had time to pester me? It was time to set up a few rules.

"Hi, Dusty," I spoke before checking to see who was on the other side of the door. "Oh, hi, Jules," I corrected myself. "Sorry, I thought it was your aunt." His head swiveled around as though checking to see if she was standing behind him. For a brief second I thought I saw fear in his eyes. The look was so fleeting I decided I had been mistaken.

"Um, no, it's just me. I thought you might want me to see about the garden now, since you're going to stay here. You are staying, right?" He looked over his shoulder again like he still expected someone to be standing behind him.

"Yes, I'm staying." At the force of my words, his eyes grew large in his narrow face, and he took a step back. I hadn't meant to be so forceful, but after the mess I'd just cleaned up, I was more determined than ever to stay right here. No one was going to drive me off. "Um, give me a few minutes to put some things away. I'll meet you outside." He looked even more like one of the homeless people you see in the bigger cities than he had the first time he showed up at my door. Were those his work clothes, or didn't he have anything better? Again I wondered about his relationship with his aunt.

Jules proved to be very knowledgeable about all the plants and flowers in the yard. "This here is a grape arbor," he explained patiently, pointing out the plants that shaded the side patio. The arbor covered the entire side of the house offering a shady, secluded place to sit.

As though reading my thoughts, Jules explained about the grapes. "She said her husband planted it years ago to make his own wine."

"Did he make wine?" This was the first time I'd heard

anything about that.

Jules lifted his boney shoulders. "Claire never said."

"Do you know if she was going to do something like that?" He simply shrugged again at my question. Was she hoping to make wine like Tom had planned? I was discovering there was a lot I didn't know about my sister's life in Arizona. "Do you know anything about making wine?" I asked, trying to concentrate on what he was telling me. Small clusters of grapes were already forming on the leafy plants.

"I just know plants. I leave the making of things with them to others." His eyes slid away from mine. Did he know what kind of things people made with different plants? Was it something illegal? My stomach twitched with uncertainty. Was someone growing marijuana? Is that what he meant? Is that what Claire discovered? There were a lot of secrets going on in this town.

"Maybe we can explore some of those things together," I suggested, trying to keep my tone light. "I think I'd enjoy doing things like that." I didn't know if that was a lie or not. My creativity stopped at the classroom door. He kicked at the dirt with the toe of his tattered sneakers, staring at the ground. He mumbled something I couldn't understand.

"I'd better get back to the house before Dusty comes lookin' for me," he finally said. Just that quick, he disappeared down the long rock steps leading to the next street. I stared after him with my mouth hanging open. Had I said something that spooked him? He certainly was a strange young man.

~~~

When the mail arrived that afternoon, I was happy to see an envelope from Doctor Langston in Tucson. I already had the autopsy report. Maybe this would be the toxicology report I'd been waiting for.

Still standing on the porch, I worked to open the flap on the envelope. My fingers were shaking in anticipation, making the simple task nearly impossible. When I finally managed to pull the papers out, I realized I only understood about every other word. "Why can't doctors and lawyers use plain English instead of all this mumbo-jumbo?" How was I supposed to understand any of this? There was one person in town who could explain all the scientific terms. I had put off talking to Claire's doctor long enough. With both reports in hand, now was the time.

Before heading out, I wrote a little note to my mystery visitor.

Thank you for all of your decorating tips. I like the way you've rearranged things. Next time though, please leave the pantry alone. Of course, all that sticky mess was perfect for leaving fingerprints.

I kicked myself for not thinking about fingerprints until right then. Calling Dan would only have made things worse between us though, and I didn't want that.

The mental picture I had formed of Doctor Gary Murphy was way off the mark. Instead of an aging man too tired to care for his patients, he was in his mid-forties. He had red hair and so many freckles there wasn't any way to tell one from the other, making it look like he had a great tan.

"What can I do for you, Miss Connors?" He stood at the examining room door with one hand on the door knob like he was ready to make a fast get-away. I didn't have an appointment, but if this was how he treated his patients, it was a wonder any of them ever got well.

"You can explain why you couldn't diagnose what was wrong with my sister. Or why you were so willing to sign her death certificate without finding out what was wrong with her." I hadn't meant to start out so confrontational, but the words slipped out anyway.

"Do you have a medical degree?" His reddish-brown eyebrows arched up. I shook my head. "Then don't question my medical ability."

"I doubt you have *any* medical ability. My sister was being poisoned for several months before she died."

"Yes, I heard about the autopsy report," he interrupted. "I'm sorry, but I disagree with those results." Perspiration was beginning to dot his upper lip. A bead of sweat left a trail down the side of his face.

"Would you like to talk with Doctor Langston at the University of Arizona Medical Center about that? I'm sure he has the medical expertise to understand why you said what you did."

His face got a little pasty, but he tried to bluff his way through. "I ran all the standard tests for the symptoms she was complaining of. I found no evidence of poison."

I held out the toxicology report, forcing him to step further into the room. "Maybe this will help change your mind."

His hands were shaking when he reached for the papers. The room was silent as he quickly scanned the report. When he finished, he handed the papers back to me. "I could only run tests that corresponded with her symptoms," he repeated. "Unless she told me of other symptoms, my hands were tied. Tests are very expensive and insurance companies dictate which ones can be run. I'm sorry for your loss." He stepped back to the door, indicating this interview was over.

"Is that why you told Chief Daniels you felt she was faking her illness; that she was a lonely woman looking for attention? What are you trying to cover up?"

"I'm not trying to cover up anything, and I don't have to explain myself to you, Miss Connors. Good day." He was certainly nervous about something, I just didn't know what.

Before he could disappear through the door, I gave one parting shot. "Maybe you'd like to explain yourself to a medical review board. I'll be contacting them with these findings. Good day." By the time I got to my truck, my hands were shaking so bad, I had trouble putting the key in the ignition. The arrogance of the man was unbelievable!

~~~

"That damn Murphy is becoming a liability, he's getting careless," he muttered to himself as Jillian Connors left the doctor's office. No matter what excuse the man gave, he shouldn't have left that kind of information lying around to be picked up. He's running scared now. It won't be long before he comes completely unhinged. Maybe it was time to dispose

of him before that happens. Maybe it was time to take both of them out. If she finds the papers her sister picked up, it would mean the end of all my plans. I'm not going to let that happen. It was a silent vow to himself.

~~~

"That is the cutest little truck I've ever seen." Irma was waiting at the bottom of the steps when I pulled into the drive. "Did you buy it today?"

"Yes, this morning. Would you like some tea?" Maybe tea would help calm the anger that was still boiling inside me.

"That sounds lovely." She followed me up the steps anxious for our tea party to begin.

Unlocking the door, I stepped aside for her to enter ahead of me. "Oh, my." Her gasp of surprise didn't bode well for a tea party any time soon.

CHAPTER THIRTEEN

Maybe poking fun at my tormentor hadn't been such a good idea after all, I thought. Someone was upping the game, but this didn't feel like a game to me. My note was crumpled into a ball on the floor along with the smashed table.

"Who would do this?" Irma stared at the ruined table. I took a step towards the living room to see what else had been done in my absence. After the mess in the pantry and kitchen, common sense finally took hold of me, overruling that idea.

"We need to leave. They might still be in here." My voice wouldn't work above a whisper. Taking Irma's arm, we backed out of the house. "I need to call the police."

"But why would someone do something like this?" I could feel her shaking beneath my fingers. "I should have been watching while you were gone."

Minutes felt like hours before a squad car roared into the driveway, lights flashing and sirens blaring. Dan's car was seconds behind. "What happened? Are you all right?" He reached out to take me in his arms, but thought better of it since Irma and the beat cop were standing beside us. Our earlier argument was all but forgotten by both of us.

I nodded my head. All I could do was point at the door. Finger-combing my long hair into a pony tail, I waited on the porch for the men to search the house. A combination of warm sun and nerves caused sweat to run down the collar of my blouse. Nothing else had been disturbed this time. Whoever smashed the table was long gone. Maybe they realized they'd gone too far, and didn't venture any further into the house.

"Would you care to explain what this is about?" Dan waved an evidence bag containing my note in my face. Heat rushed to my cheeks, and I couldn't look at him. "Well?" He prompted, tapping the baggie against his hand.

"I got tired of finding my things messed with," I stated defensively.

"So you decided to taunt whoever is doing this?" Disbelief

135

made his voice sharp. "What would you have done if this guy stuck around until you got home?" He didn't give me a chance to say anything. "What's this about the pantry?"

Once more my cheeks began to heat up, and I looked away from him before I could answer. "I found flour, sugar, and syrup all over the kitchen and pantry when I got home today."

"I didn't see anything like that when I was searching the house."

"Um, I cleaned it up already," I whispered. The muscles in his cheeks bunched up as he clenched his jaws tight enough to break a few teeth.

"What about fingerprints? I suppose those are all gone as well?" He lifted one eyebrow in question, and I nodded sheepishly. "Why didn't you call me instead of messing with a crime scene?"

"After our argument, I wasn't sure you'd come." That was only half of it. I was so angry I hadn't even thought about calling him. I just wanted all trace of the person out of my house.

He ran his finger through his hair, glaring at me for several long minutes. "I'm still a cop," he finally said on a frustrated sigh. "No matter what, I would still do my job." He took my hand. "Argument or not, I care about you, Jillian. I don't want anything to happen to you. That's what our arguments boil down to; I don't want anything to happen to you." He caressed the back of my hand with his thumb.

We were seated in the living room. Irma had gone home with the promise to come back when all the excitement died down. Dan had sent the patrolman back on duty.

"I know," I whispered. "I'm sorry. I let anger override my common sense. I'm just so tired of people messing with me and mine. After what happened this morning, I wasn't thinking straight."

He nodded his head in agreement, but didn't comment beyond on that. "Where did you go after you left me?"

"I came straight home. That's when I found the mess in the pantry." I filled him in on the time I'd spent cleaning up and working with Jules in the garden. "When I got the tox report in the mail," I paused, my voice dropping slightly, "I left again."

"Why? Where did you go?"

I was sure this was going to cause another argument, but there was no way around it. I had to explain about my visit to Doctor Murphy. Sure enough Dan's jaw was clenched again. If he didn't stop that, he was going to need to see a dentist really soon.

"Why did you go see him?" he asked through clenched teeth.

I decided to avoid any further argument, and explain only part of my reasoning. "I thought maybe he could explain some of the technical language in the toxicology report." That had been my original intention, but the man's arrogant attitude sent good judgment out the window along with the common sense I'd lost earlier.

"Did he explain any of the 'technical language'?" He made little quote signs with his fingers. I shook my head. "So what did you do, accuse him of malpractice, or worse, murder?" His voice was soft, making it all the more menacing. His light blue eyes were little more than chunks of ice as he glared at me.

"I didn't accuse him of murder. Not exactly," I finished defensively.

Dan released a frustrated breath. "Okay, tell me what you did accuse him of."

"Nothing! I just wanted to know why he didn't find what was making her so sick. He had all sorts of excuses. It was the insurance company's fault, or it was Claire's fault because she didn't tell him the right symptoms." I flopped back on the couch. "I'm going to need a medical dictionary to understand most of what the report says. I don't even know what kind of poison she'd been given." The fight drained out of me. Not wanting him to see the tears that were threatening to spill over, I turned away from him.

"Babe, you have to let me handle this. Something is going on here that we don't understand yet. I don't want to lose you to this maniac." His voice was now a soft caress as he reached out to take my hand again. "Besides the pantry, what other things were messed with when you came home the first time?"

I had to think about that for a minute. "Nothing, I think I caught the person in the act. I heard someone in the kitchen and the door was standing open. I couldn't give chase when I got stuck to the kitchen floor."

"Thank God for that," he muttered. "What would you have done if you'd caught him?"

I lifted my shoulders in a shrug. "I didn't think about that. I'm getting tired of whatever sick game someone is playing."

"Well, I'd say the game has taken a dark turn. You can't be doing things like this." He nodded his head at the baggie.

"Are you saying this is my fault?" I pulled my hand from his grasp. "I'm not the one who keeps breaking into someone else's house."

"That's not what I said. I don't want you to get this person so angry he decides to come after you." He reached out for my hand again. This time I didn't pull away. The soft caress of his words softened my anger.

"Who is this Roland Granger you asked that man about earlier? What does he have to do with anything?"

I sighed. I didn't want to go over that ground again, but there didn't seem to be any way around it. "He's the man who's stalking me, or one of them." I watched Dan's face, trying to tell if he would believe me.

"There are two people stalking you, and you're just now telling me?"

"Well, I didn't realize he was stalking me until today, so I couldn't very well tell you about it. Besides, you didn't believe that other man was following me, why would you believe me about Roland Granger?"

He drew a deep breath, letting it out slowly. "Okay, you have my full attention. Tell me what's going on."

It didn't take long to tell him about my encounters with the man. "I don't know if the two men are working together, or if they are both following me for different reasons."

"Why would anyone follow you, let alone two men?" He sighed heavily. "I wish I knew what was going on in this town. I thought the biggest problems we'd have here were illegals crossing the border. How wrong could I be?" He pulled me off the couch and into his arms, placing a kiss in my hair.

"Okay, I'll see what I can find out about this Roland Granger. I don't know of anyone by that name here in town, but that doesn't mean anything. If you see him or the other guy again, call me. Please, don't give chase." He looked down at me, all anger wiped from his eyes.

With one last kiss, he left with the note and pieces of the table in evidence bags. I wasn't sure what good the broken table would do him. There wasn't much of it left. Maybe there would be fingerprints he could use to find out who did this. There wouldn't be any fingerprints in the pantry after I finished cleaning up. I was mentally kicking myself for that. If I hadn't jumped the gun, we might have been able to find the culprit.

~~~

Three days later, Chief Daniels paid me a visit. Whatever had happened, I knew it wasn't good. His expression said he was ready to kill. Mostly like I was the victim he had in mind.

"I'd like to know what you've been up to for the last three days." He growled at me the minute I opened the front door.

"Good morning, Chief. Come in." I held the door open for him. "I was just having some coffee. Would you care for a cup?" Did everyone in Bisbee make social calls this early in the morning? Of course, this wasn't a social call, I reminded myself. Whatever had happened, I wasn't going to let him intimidate me.

"Um, good morning. Coffee sounds good." He caught himself then, turning a scowling face at me. "Don't try to sweet talk me, young lady. I want to know what you said to Doc Murphy when you went to see him." He spoke to my back as I continued down the hall to the kitchen.

Looking at him over my shoulder, a frown drew my eyebrows together. "What's this about? Did he complain about my visit?" I asked indignantly. "After the way he ignored what happened to Claire, he had a lot of nerve complaining about me."

"Just answer my question," the chief snapped. "Why did you go see the doc? What did you say to him?"

"I wanted to know what he had to say for himself in light of the autopsy and toxicology reports. Of course he denied any wrongdoing." I gave a sniff. "He tried to blame the insurance company for not allowing him to run more tests. He even had the nerve to question the results. He can complain all he wants about my visit, but I'm not the one who did something wrong. We'll see what the medical board thinks about his medical practices. I'm sure he'll be hearing from them very soon."

"Oh, I doubt that very much," the chief said sarcastically. "He's dead."

I sat down hard in the chair. "What? When? How?"

"What are you, some kind of reporter with all the questions?" he snapped at me. "What have you been up to since you went to see him."

"You think I killed him? Why would you even think that?"

"Well, you were pretty upset with him when you first came to town. If I recall, you thought he was incompetent when he signed your sister's death certificate without an autopsy."

"Of course I was upset with him, but that doesn't mean I'd kill him. Was he murdered?" I couldn't believe this.

"I'm the one asking the questions here," he snarled. "Now answer me. What have you been up to? Where have you been in the past three days?"

"I've been right here. I haven't gone anywhere."

"Oh, yeah?" he sneered disbelievingly. "Where'd you get that truck? You had to go somewhere to buy a snazzy thing like that."

"What does my truck have to do with Doctor Murphy's death?" He wasn't making any sense.

"You ever take that thing out in the desert?" Once again, he ignored my question.

"No, of course not, why would I?"

"I told you I'm the one asking the questions. I'll ask one last time; what have you been doing since you went to see the doc? We can do this here, or I can take you to the station."

In an effort to show how serious he was, he lowered his eyebrows in a fierce frown. He really thought I had killed the doctor. I tried to remember everything I'd done since I'd been to Doctor Murphy's office. "I was only in his office for a few minutes," I whispered. "When I came home, someone had broken in the house and smashed the table in the entry. I called the police."

He gave a derisive snort. "Yeah, I heard about how you destroyed evidence in a supposed break-in. Now, tell me where you've been since then."

Once again, he didn't believe me, but I swallowed my anger. It wouldn't do any good to argue. He had all the power here. "Nowhere, I've been right here."

"Did you see the doc after that?"

"No, of course not, and I didn't kill him."

"I'll ask you again, what have you been doing?" He ignored my assertion that I hadn't killed the doctor.

This was ridiculous. Trying to describe what I'd done during those three days wasn't easy. Before I could answer one question, he would interrupt with more. When I finished, I lifted my shoulders. "I didn't do anything else, and I didn't go anywhere. He was alive when I left his office, and I only saw the man that one time." I wasn't sure I had convinced him of that fact though. I kept waiting for him to warn me not to leave town.

"There hasn't been a murder in this town for years, until you got here," he growled at me. "Now I have two to investigate." I wasn't sure what upset him more: the fact that there were two murders on his watch, or that he had to investigate them. At least he admitted that Claire had been murdered.

"I wasn't here when Claire was killed, and I didn't kill the doctor. It seems to me that maybe you've overlooked a few things over the years." His pudgy face turned beet red, whether from anger or embarrassment, I wasn't sure. "I've answered all your questions. Now answer one of mine. What does his death have to do with my visit to his office?"

"I'm working on it," was his only answer.

When he finally left, I sagged against the wall, watching him drive away. I still had no idea how Doctor Murphy died, or when he died. Why did the chief think I had anything to do with it? How was this connected to Claire's death? Or was it?

Minutes after the chief's departure, Irma was at the front door. It was a little early for her daily visit, but she probably saw the chief's car, and wanted to know what was up. How many hours did she sit at her upstairs window watching me? The idea of her sitting there with a pair of binoculars watching everyone in town would be comical if it weren't so disturbing. This town ran on gossip.

"Good morning, Irma. How are you this morning?" I stepped back to let her come in. "Would you like tea or coffee this morning? I still have some of the sweet rolls you brought over yesterday if you're hungry." Every time she came for tea, she brought over some sweet treat. I never had a chance to eat them all before she brought more.

"Oh, thank you, dearie. That sounds wonderful." She fidgeted in the chair while she waited for me to pour coffee in a cup for her and place the rolls on a plate. She could hardly wait to find out what was going on now.

The chief hadn't said our conversation was confidential. Maybe I could cut off some of the inevitable speculation before the story got out of hand by telling Irma my side.

"Why, that's just ridiculous," she scoffed indignantly when I repeated the chief's veiled accusations. "You aren't a killer any more than I am."

"Don't tell him that. He might accuse you of something next." A queasy feeling attacked my stomach. Unless two people had committed these crimes, someone in this town had committed murder twice. I couldn't get the idea out of my head that someone was upping the game to an even more dangerous level. I didn't want to get caught in their grip.

"That man is as dumb as a cow patty if he thinks he can pin a murder on either of us. You haven't gone any further than your back yard since you bought that beautiful truck." Again I wondered how many hours she spent watching out her windows. If she was my alibi, I doubted Chief Daniels would accept her word for my whereabouts.

He couldn't have any evidence against me. Lack of evidence hasn't prevented other people from being wrongfully convicted in the past. My heart dropped to my toes at the thought of going to prison for something I didn't do.

Dusty timed her visit to coincide with Irma's departure. "Oh, Jillian, I just heard the news." The grip she had on my hand was painful. "Jeff is doing everything he can to solve all these crimes. It's his duty to check out everyone who saw the doc that day. I'm sure you don't have to worry. I know you wouldn't harm anyone no matter how upset you were with them."

"What are you talking about? How do you know that I was upset with the doctor?" I pulled my hands from her grasp. How privileged was she to confidential police information?

"Oh, ah, well," she stammered. "Um, Jeff let slip the results of the toxicology report." She shrugged like it was no big deal. "That kind of information won't be a secret once the paper gets the results. I don't blame you for being upset. You had every right to confront Doctor Murphy after what happened to Claire. I'm sure you just wanted an explanation."

"Can you explain why the chief thinks I killed the doctor?" I was tired of everyone knowing my business almost before I knew it. "I went to see him hoping he could interpret what the report meant. He got defensive before I accused him of anything."

I didn't tell her that I had already called Doctor Langston in Tucson for clarification. The juice from the oleander plant had been used to poison Claire. It was a common plant, found just about anywhere. A continued dose, even as small as it probably was, would eventually have killed her. The full bottle of pain medication was overkill.

"Oh, I'm sure he doesn't think you killed the doc," she made excuses for her boyfriend. "But he has to question the people who saw him that day."

"If he questions everyone the way he questioned me, he's going to have a lot of people in this town very upset with him," I stated. "I thought for sure he was going to haul me off to jail."

She gave a nervous chuckle. "Oh, he couldn't do that. He'd need to have a warrant first."

When Dusty left, I replayed the various conversations over in my mind. Why had the doctor been killed? Who would do that? Yes, I'd been upset when I went to see him, but I didn't want to kill him. My revenge would have been to have his medical license revoked.

Obviously, he hadn't died from natural causes, or the chief wouldn't be asking questions. So someone else wanted him dead. I needed to figure out who and why.

I gave a humorless laugh. I could hear Dan tell me that it wasn't my job to figure this out. Well, if the chief wasn't going to do his job, someone had to.

Jake had called every evening since going back to Tucson. That night was no exception. "I just heard the news. What's going on in that town? Do you know who killed him?"

"Well, if you ask Chief Daniels, that would be me," I answered angrily.

"What? Has he lost what little mind he had?"

"Look, Jake, I really don't want to talk about this anymore. How is your work? Are you keeping busy?" It was the best I could do for small talk. I was grateful when the chimes rang, allowing me to cut the conversation short.

I wasn't going to get any relief from the topic though. Dan was fit-to-be-tied by the chief's accusations. "I don't know what's wrong with that man." He paced around the living room. "If he thinks for a second that I'm going to let him railroad you on this, he needs to think again."

"Why does he think I would do that?" I watched him pace

from my seat on the recliner.

Flopping down on the couch, he gave his head a shake. "I don't know why he thinks anything anymore. He's been acting weird lately, and I don't know why."

"What kind of evidence does he have?" We had shelved our earlier arguments for now. As long as we didn't discuss my plans for finding Claire's killer we were fine.

"None, that's what has him scrambling. Doc Murphy left the office shortly after you did. No one saw him after that until his body was found in the desert last night."

"So that's why he wanted to know if I'd ever taken my truck into the desert," I said more to myself than him. My stomach was doing cartwheels. "Maybe I should let him search it," I muttered, "just to prove it's never been on a dirt road."

"You don't know where it had been before you bought it," Dan contradicted. "Even if the dealer did a thorough job of cleaning it after taking it in trade, there might still be something that would indicate the previous owner had it off-road. There would be no way you could prove it wasn't you. Don't volunteer anything."

This coming from a police detective? I thought. I could be in more trouble than I realized.

Doctor Murphy had been shot execution style sometime in the last three days. His body was dumped in the desert. Whatever was going on had taken a very bad turn. I still didn't know if this was connected to Claire's death, and if so how?

After Dan left, I was too unsettled to sleep. It was time for some serious prayers. Crawling into bed with my Bible, I opened it to Psalms. King David had worse troubles than I currently had. He had relied on God for help; I needed to follow his example.

A half hour later, a gentle calm had settled over me. Whatever happened next, I knew I would make it through because God was with me. Throughout my Bible I had underlined favorite passages. Devotions that had a special meaning for me were used as bookmarks. I read each one.

Claire had always done the same thing, and I wondered if she had some of the same passages underlined or similar devotions in her Bible. Setting my Bible on the night stand, I opened the drawer, and pulled out the small book that had belonged to her. I began leafing through, reading the slips of paper she had used as bookmarks and the underlined passages.

A handwritten note fluttered onto the bed beside me. I didn't recognize the writing as Claire's, and wondered if it had been a love note from Tom. Unwilling to snoop, I almost replaced the paper without reading it when a word jumped out at me.

"Killed." Tom wouldn't use that word in a note to Claire. Lifting the small slip of paper towards the lamp, I began reading it, gasping for breath at the few words.

"Taking things that don't belong to you and eavesdropping on other people's conversations isn't good for your health. If you know what's good for you, you'll return what you took, and keep your mouth shut about what you heard. Telling anyone could get you killed."

My heart was pounding so hard I thought it was going to jump out of my chest. This is why she had been killed. But what had she taken? What had she heard? Did she even know? I read the note again. If she took something, why didn't she just return it? Why didn't she take the note to the police?

"Because she was too scared, you dummy," I answered my own question. Speaking out loud in the empty room gave me a small amount of courage, and I didn't feel quite so alone. When had she received the note? It wasn't dated, so I had no idea when she got it.

I quickly leafed through the remaining pages, looking for another threatening note. This was the only one. Whatever she'd taken was what they were looking for when the house had been searched. Why were they moving furniture around though? That didn't make sense.

Dan had put the crumpled note I'd left on the table in a plastic baggie hoping to be able to get fingerprints. Holding the paper by the corner, I got out of bed. Hurrying down the stairs, I scrambled around in the pantry for a plastic baggie, sealing the note inside. "Now where do I put it until I can give it to Dan in the morning?" Being alone so much, I had started to talk out loud to myself.

With the note locked in the safe, I tried to go to sleep. It was long past midnight by this time, but I was too wired to fall asleep.

CHAPTER FOURTEEN

I was up to watch the sun rise over the mountains surrounding the town. The beauty escaped me though. I couldn't wait until Dan got into the office. I needed to call him and the sooner the better. I had learned my lesson. I wouldn't keep this to myself.

Only minutes after hanging up the phone, Dan was at my door. I held the plastic bag out to him as he walked through the front door. For a brief moment, he ignored the baggie, pulling me into his arms, placing a kiss in my hair. He trailed kisses down my face until he claimed my lips in a heart-stopping kiss. It was several minutes later when he lifted his head, getting down to business. He quickly scanned the few words on the scrap of paper. A frown creased his forehead. "Where did you get this?"

"I found it in Claire's Bible." I tried to explain as concisely as I could how I had come across the small slip of paper.

"Why wouldn't she turn it over to the police? We might have been able to save her life." He ran his long fingers through his hair, messing it further.

I finally realized how rumpled he looked. Either he had slept in those clothes, or he hadn't slept at all. I suspected the latter was closer to the truth. There were dark circles under his eyes, and blonde stubble covered his cheeks and chin. "Didn't you go to bed after you left here last night?"

He gave a weary sigh. "The chief called me before I even made it home. He had us working a crime scene most of the night. Seems a crime wave of sorts has gripped our small town. The man is in panic mode."

"I'm sorry. I shouldn't have called you this early. This could have waited. It wasn't life threatening. Go home and get some sleep. I'll talk to you in a few hours." I reached out to take the baggie, but he pulled it out of my reach.

"I won't be going home for a few more hours anyway." He

sniffed the coffee scented air drifting in from my kitchen. "Is that coffee I smell?" he asked unnecessarily. "I could really use a cup right about now. I don't even care if it's left over from yesterday." He trailed behind me as I headed for the kitchen.

I gave a self-conscious chuckle as I pulled a mug out of the cupboard. "This is my second pot this morning. I didn't sleep much last night either, but at least I wasn't working." Pushing him into a chair, I handed him the steaming cup.

Taking a big gulp of the hot liquid, he groaned softly. "I hope he'll let us go home and shower before too much longer. Otherwise, the office is going to get pretty ripe."

"What happened? Is it something you can talk about?" The chief didn't have a problem sharing information with his girlfriend, but I was sure he wouldn't like Dan doing the same thing with me. My only knowledge about police procedure came from all the cop shows on television. That didn't mean everything said and done on them was accurate though.

"The doc's office was broken into sometime after his body was found. Someone got away with a lot of drugs." He gave his blonde head a shake. "I knew doctors had drugs in their offices, but I thought it was just samples." He sighed. "According to Milly, his nurse, he kept a lot of drugs on hand. He claimed it was because Bisbee is so far away from a major city. He wanted to be prepared for any emergency." That sounded a little fishy to me, but I kept that thought to myself for the time being.

While we talked, I fixed breakfast for both of us. He had worked all night, and would probably be working all day as well. He couldn't keep going without eating something.

Addicts would sometimes target doctors' offices to get drugs, but I didn't think doctors normally kept narcotics in their office. If it was common knowledge that Doctor Murphy kept a large quantity on hand, he would be a target for addicts and dealers alike. "Do you know how much was taken, or what kind of drugs he had?"

He shook his head. "There was very little evidence, but

Milly said she suspects that he was running a prescription drug ring out of his office."

I gave a small gasp. "Was this why Claire was killed?" My hands shook causing hot coffee to spill over the rim of my cup. "Do you think she stumbled onto his secret, and he killed her?"

Dan shook his head. "At the moment, anything I said would be pure conjecture." He gave a tired sigh. "Whatever he had in his storeroom is gone, including non-narcotic drugs. It's been completely cleaned out. Until we can figure out what he had and how much," he lifted his shoulders in a tired shrug, letting his sentence trail off.

My stomach churned. I was afraid to ask if it was just a coincidence that he was killed and his office broken into right after my visit. This had to be connected to Claire's death. The note said she'd taken something. Had Doctor Murphy kept a record of what he had and who he sold to? That could certainly incriminate a lot of people. If whatever Claire had was still in the house, would they keep breaking in here looking for it?

This couldn't be connected to the mess in my pantry and the ruined table though. Murder and vandalism were on opposite ends of the crime spectrum. A person willing to commit murder wouldn't vandalize a home. If they were looking for whatever Claire had, they wouldn't make a mess of the pantry. This made no sense. I shook my head to clear these thoughts.

"Until we can figure out exactly what kind of drugs he had in there, we're only guessing that the motive for his murder was drugs." He finally finished his thought, bringing me back to the present. He moved his shoulders, trying to work out the kinks. "With two murders to investigate, and now this, the chief is beside himself. We're going to be stretched pretty thin for the next few days."

He finished off the coffee, setting the empty cup down on the table. I brought the coffee pot over to refill it. He was going to need all the caffeine I could pour down his throat.

He looked at the note again. "I'll show this to the chief, but I can't guarantee he'll connect it to what happened to Claire or the doc. He's stubbornly clinging to the idea that somehow Claire did this to herself. The doc's murder and now the theft of the drugs," he shrugged. "I'm not really sure what he's thinking, or if he even is. He's afraid the DEA is going to get involved. They'll be all over us, which will send the chief over the edge. He doesn't always play nice with other agencies." He gave a tired chuckle.

"If the person who sent Claire that note is the same person who killed the doctor, maybe he's long gone by now." I said with more hope than I actually felt. "It just spooked me when I found it. I've never seen a genuine death threat before."

When the grandfather clock in the living room chimed seven, Dan stood up. "I'm sorry, Babe, but I have to go. I didn't even tell the chief where I was going when I took off. He's probably going to chew my butt out when I get back." He placed a light kiss on my lips. "Thanks for breakfast." He chuckled. "I won't tell the other guys you fed me. Daniels wouldn't think of skipping a meal, but he didn't care that we hadn't eaten for longer than anyone wanted to admit." With one last lingering kiss, he was gone.

I remained in the kitchen, trying to make sense of everything that was going on. Someone had been poisoning Claire for several months. It made her sick, and eventually would have killed her. Had they gotten impatient, and given her an entire bottle of pain pills to finish the job?

If she was killed because she accidently discovered Doctor Murphy's dirty little secret, why had he waited several months before killing her? Again, that didn't make any sense. Were all of these crimes connected, or were they separate? How would I ever figure it out?

Dan would tell me it wasn't my job to figure it out. Maybe not, but I wasn't willing to sit around until the chief found it convenient to investigate. I'd been in Bisbee for nearly two months, and I was no closer to figuring out what had happened to my sister than I had been the day I arrived.

She had taken something that belonged to someone else, and they were willing to kill to get it back. Did she even know what she'd taken? I somehow doubted it. Stumbling on the good doctor's drug ring isn't something she would forget. He wouldn't have waited to see if she would turn him in either. So why had someone been poisoning her for several months, only to suddenly give her an entire bottle of pain pills?

Had two people wanted her dead? My heart knocked against my ribs. That was the only thing that made sense of what was going on here. One person hadn't committed two murders. There were two killers involved; one had been poisoning Claire slowly, the other gave her the pain pills and had also killed the doctor.

Someone had also been breaking into this house. Was it the same person who killed Claire? I had believed it was Myriam trying to scare me off so I would leave Jake alone. But I had no designs on him. Until recently it had been minor things moved around, something to mess with my mind. Breaking the table in the entry and making a mess in the pantry couldn't be called dangerous. But were they going to step things up further?

The drawers in my room and Claire's had also been searched. They were probably looking for whatever Claire had taken. If they hadn't found it, did that mean they would be back? What would they do to me if they couldn't find it? I had no answers to these questions.

Trying to think logically, I went over the events since Claire's last call. She hadn't said anything about seeing or hearing something she shouldn't have, just that she believed someone was trying to kill her. She didn't explain why she thought that.

She never wrote anything down without dating it, even her grocery lists. The note I found under the desk blotter had been dated the day after she called me. She must have received the note I found in her Bible sometime after that. Were there more threatening notes somewhere in the house? Why would she hide them in different places? Two days after we talked, someone had given her an entire bottle of pain pills. What had happened from one day to the next? Would I ever learn the truth?

I started cleaning up the breakfast dishes. Maybe distracting myself would let my subconscious mind work on the problem, and the answer would come to me. Before I knew it, the morning was gone, the house was clean, and I hadn't found any other notes. If there were any others, I didn't know where Claire would have put them. The one I found was in a place that only I would look. Where would she put something that no one else would think of looking?

My subconscious mind had come to the same conclusion my conscious mind had. Two people had wanted Claire dead. One had been giving her the poisonous oleander juice, while the other had given her the full bottle of pain pills.

It was my guess that Doctor Murphy had administered the pills. If Claire had taken something or heard something that would incriminate him, he would do anything to save himself. Had she figured it out? Or had she died not knowing why someone wanted her dead? Tears of anger and grief burned in my eyes. "I promise whoever did this to you is going to pay," I whispered a vow to her. I didn't know how I was going to do that, I just knew I would do it.

When the grandfather clock chimed twelve, I realized Irma would be over soon for tea. Shortly after that Dusty would be knocking at the back door. This was becoming so predictable I could almost set my clock by their visits. During the school year, I had to follow a set routine. In the summers, I made it a habit of not following a schedule. I needed to make a few changes, shake things up a little.

Instead of waiting for Irma to arrive, I called her. "Would you like to join me for lunch?" I asked. "We could go someplace downtown."

"Why, that sounds lovely." Her excitement came through the telephone wires. In the short time I'd been here, the only place I saw her go was church on Sunday. She even had her groceries delivered. I imagined she was very lonely. An outing might do both of us some good. It would also throw Dusty off schedule. I chuckled at that thought.

"How are your plans for the bed and breakfast coming?" Irma asked as we sat down in the little café. "I know there's a lot of paperwork involved."

Why were so many people interested in my plans for the house? Was it simply because there wasn't enough going on in their own lives that they lived vicariously through the lives of others? "I think I have all the paperwork done. I'm waiting for the health department to come inspect the kitchen." I gave a small sigh. "Claire already did most of this, but I had to start all over." It seemed like such a waste of time and resources to me.

"Nothing is easy when the government is involved." She shook her head in disgust. "Once you get everything done, it will all be worthwhile." I hoped she was right.

After lunch, we wandered through the stores close to the café. I wasn't ready to go back to the empty house. Evidently Irma wasn't either. She enjoyed looking through all the stores like this was the first time she'd been in any of them. Maybe it had been a long time, and everything was new to her.

"Oh, look there," she exclaimed, pointing at someone across the street. "There's that nice Mr. Edmonds." The lawyer had just left an office across the street. Did he always go to his clients instead of them going to him?

Today he was dressed casually in jeans and a polo shirt like any other tourist in town. If she hadn't pointed him out, I wouldn't have recognized him. Maybe today he was playing tourist, I told myself.

"Yahoo, Mr. Edmonds," she called out to him, waving her ever-present lace hanky. Either he didn't hear her, or he pretended he didn't as he hurried to his fancy car. I guess he didn't want to be bothered. "He must have a lot of clients in town," she said. "I'm sure he's very busy." I didn't understand her puzzling remark, but didn't pursue it either.

When I felt the prickles on the back of my neck, I looked around for the man I'd thought had been following me. I hadn't seen him or Roland Granger since the day I bought the truck. That didn't mean they weren't still out there watching me. They were just more careful now. The fact that this was the first time I'd gone anywhere might have something to do with it as well.

I had been in town long enough to recognize some of the locals. I might not remember their names, but the faces were familiar. No one seemed particularly interested in me, however the feeling persisted. By the time we headed back to the house, my stomach was in knots. This had to stop.

It was long past Dusty's usual time to visit when we pulled into the drive in front of Irma's house. Would she be waiting on the back porch for me to get home? That would be a little over the top if you ask me.

"I wonder if Dusty will be waiting on the back patio for you to return," Irma said with a chuckle as though reading my thoughts. "She's usually here long before this." She looked at the delicate watch on her thin wrist, indicating she knew the schedule they both kept.

Dusty wasn't the only one I was currently worried about. This was the first time I'd left the house since the entry table had been destroyed and the pantry had been messed up. My stomach churned at the thought of what could be waiting for me inside. It wasn't Dusty in my back yard though. Jules was weeding the garden when I pulled the truck around to the small parking area beside the house.

"Hi Jillian," he gave me a small smile as I stepped out of the truck. "I hope you don't mind that I came over while you were gone. I wanted to do some weeding while…" He didn't finish his sentence. His voice dropped slightly as he looked towards his aunt's house. "She had to go somewhere this afternoon." His words held a cryptic meaning that I couldn't decipher.

"That's very nice of you, thank you. Would you like some iced tea? It's a little warm this afternoon." The weather was much warmer than I was used to. Without all the humidity though, it didn't feel suffocating.

"No thanks. I need to be going soon. She won't be gone much longer...now," he finished. Something about the way he said that caused my stomach to churn. It was like he was trying to tell me something. I just didn't know what.

I looked towards Dusty's place. It sat higher up another hill, looking down on this one. How much could she see from there? With binoculars, she could probably see right into my kitchen. I'd worried that Irma was watching me. But she wasn't the only one I needed to be concerned with.

He quickly collected the few tools he'd brought with him. "There are garden tools in the garage," he said. "Do you still want me to show you what to do with the plants?"

"Any time you can get away, let me know. I'd like to learn about all these plants." My words were as ambiguous as his had been, but he probably understood my meaning. I knew he would have to wait until Dusty wasn't around to come over.

He started to walk away when I stopped him with a question. "Are there any poisonous plants here?" Since such a plant had been making Claire sick, I wanted to know if it was right here in her own garden. Had she inadvertently been poisoning herself as the chief suggested?

Suddenly nervous, Jules shook his head vehemently. "She was really careful about the kind of plants she had here." Was there a slight emphasis on the word 'she'? Did he mean someone else had poisonous plants? "She said it could be dangerous if families with kids stayed here," he quickly added. With that, he disappeared down the long stone steps.

Going in the house, I cautiously made my way through each room on the ground floor looking for any rearranged furniture. Nothing had been disturbed. It was the same on the upper floors. Nothing had been moved. What was different this time? Was it because Jules was working in the backyard? Or was it because Dusty wasn't home? Where was Myriam? I hadn't seen her for a few days either.

My suspicions encompassed a lot of people. It was time to be more proactive. If people were watching me, maybe I should watch them back. I couldn't see much of Irma's house from the first floor of this house, but the third floor windows offered a nice view. I wasn't sure what I expected to see. She had very few visitors, and never went anywhere.

Dusty was another matter. The sloping hill offered an unobstructed view of her house. It was too far away to see any activity though. "Maybe I need to invest in a pair of binoculars," I told the empty house. If she was spying on me, it was only fair that I returned the favor. I was certain God wouldn't approve of my turnabout is fair-play attitude though.

CHAPTER FIFTEEN

Jake showed up on my doorstep first thing Saturday morning. His mother hadn't been around all week for which I was grateful. Would she be pounding on my door again insisting I stay away from her precious son?

"Hi Jake, you're here bright and early today." I stepped back allowing him to come in. "Coffee should be ready in a few minutes. Would you like a cup?"

He bent down, placing a kiss on my cheek. "Coffee sounds great, but I was hoping you'd let me take you to breakfast."

I hesitated before answering him. I was still seeing Dan, just not as often as either of us liked. With all of the trouble in town, the chief was keeping him very busy. What would he think if I went to breakfast with Jake? I didn't want to put a further strain on our relationship. We still didn't see eye-to-eye on my decision for the B&B.

Jake gave me a small smile. "If it would make you feel better about joining me, you can tell the detective it's a business breakfast, not a date. We are partners of sorts. I'd like to know what's going on in town, and how your plans are coming along for the house."

Making my decision, I nodded my head. Just because I was seeing Dan didn't mean I couldn't be friends with Jake. But were Jake and I friends? Did I even want to be? Claire's note was a constant reminder that I needed to be careful where I placed my trust. My stomach gave a small roll. I wished for the hundredth time that she had been a little more specific.

Pushing those thoughts aside, I smiled up at him. "Give me a few minutes to change clothes." Since I hadn't expected visitors this early, I hadn't bothered with makeup. I also needed to put on something other than shorts and a tank top. "Why don't you get yourself a cup of coffee while you wait?" I called out as I hurried upstairs.

I was still using the bedroom on the second floor. If I really planned on opening a bed and breakfast anytime soon, I needed to move my things into the bedroom above.

With plenty of restaurants and cafes in Old Town, I didn't have to worry about going anywhere near the police department for breakfast. If Dan was working this morning, I'd rather not run into him while I was with Jake. In the month or so that I'd been seeing him, I didn't know which district he lived in either. That fact suddenly struck me as a little odd. Why hadn't he ever told me where he lived? My heart skipped a beat. What was he hiding? Did he have a wife stashed somewhere here in town? My suspicions grew on a daily basis to include everyone I met.

Occupied with those questions, I didn't realize we had arrived at the café until Jake opened the passenger door to help me out. "Where did you go back there? You were miles away." He waited until we were seated at a table in the back of the small cafe before speaking.

"Sorry, I've had a lot on my mind lately." That was an understatement. I sighed wearily.

"Have they found out who killed Doctor Murphy yet? I heard that his office was broken into. Do they know if the same person did that?"

I lifted my shoulders. "As a person of interest, I'm not privy to any of the details of the case."

"Seriously?" Jake's dark eyebrows shot to the top of his forehead. "I thought you were joking about that. Chief Daniels can't think you had anything to do with that."

"Well, he doesn't have any other suspects. If he thought it would clear up his caseload, he'd gladly pin everything on me, probably even any shoplifting cases he has pending. There's just one small problem. He doesn't have any evidence against me, or anyone else for that matter."

Jake shook his head. "The man never was the brightest bulb in the pack." Irma had used a similar analogy regarding the chief. "As long as there weren't any high profile crimes, he didn't have to worry. I'll bet he's sweating bullets now, worrying about keeping his precious job. What does your detective have to say about it?"

Suzanne Floyd

My stomach twisted. "Um, we don't talk about his work," I said evasively. I didn't want to get into that kind of discussion. "Do you think the mayor, or whoever hired the chief, would fire him over this?" I hoped he wouldn't question me further about Dan.

His only reaction to my evasive answer was to lift one eyebrow. "I have no idea what would happen to the man," he answered.

Taking my hint, he changed the subject. "How are your plans coming? You are still planning on opening a bed and breakfast, right?"

By the time we finished eating, I had filled him in on all the paperwork I'd had to complete. "I'm still waiting for the health department to come inspect the kitchen. I don't know what's taking so long. Claire had been waiting for the inspector when she...died." I still stumbled over that word.

I wasn't ready to go back to the lonely house yet, but spending the entire day with Jake wasn't a really bright idea considering the wagging tongues in town. I didn't want to give him any false hope that we could be anything but friends either. Add in the mother-from-hell factor, and I was ready to call even any friendship to a halt.

My cell phone had been conspicuously silent during the meal. Either Dan was working hard, or the gossips had told him who I was with. My heart gave a sad little bump.

We wandered through the small stores, and by mid-afternoon I was ready to put an end to our day. We'd had a nice time, but in case Dan did decide to come by, I wanted to be home.

"Can I pick you up for church tomorrow?" he asked when he brought me home. "I don't have to head back to Tucson until late afternoon." He knew about my arrangement with Irma, but he asked anyway.

"I always take Irma to church. She doesn't have any other way to get there." His shoulders drooped, but he accepted my excuse graciously.

"Okay, I'll see you there." Bending his head, he placed a

160

light kiss on my lips. This time, I didn't turn away, but there was no spark. I stepped back, breaking the contact. He seemed like a nice man, just not the one for me. I also hoped his actions weren't all for show.

No one had been in the house since the entry table had been destroyed, and the mess made in the pantry. Maybe finally bringing in the police had done the trick. I should have done that the first time things had been moved around.

I occupied myself during the remainder of the afternoon polishing the furniture, and anything else I could wipe down. A nice breeze blew every day helping to keep the house cool, but it also brought in a lot of dust. How did anyone manage to keep their house clean? I was still trying to find whatever Claire had that got her killed. I didn't know if it was a piece of paper, a book, or some other item that would incriminate someone. I'd gone through all the files in the library, but came up empty handed.

When the chimes on the front door rang, butterflies filled my stomach. I hurried to the door, hoping it was Dan, only to be disappointed. A petite woman about my age gave me a sad smile when I opened the door. "May I help you?" She looked familiar, but I couldn't place where I'd seen her before.

"Hello, I'm Milly Franklin." The name didn't ring any bells. "You probably don't remember me." My blank look was a dead giveaway.

"No, I'm sorry."

"I am…or I was Doctor Murphy's nurse." She held out her hand for me to shake.

Accepting her hand in mine, I gave a non-committal nod. I didn't recall seeing her the one time I'd been to his office. That didn't mean she hadn't been there. "What can I do for you?"

"I just wanted to tell you how sorry I am for what happened to your sister. She was a nice lady. Doctor Murphy hadn't been a very good doctor lately. I just thought he was getting lazy. I had no idea he was running a counterfeit drug ring right under my nose."

I didn't know what to say to this. Thank you didn't seem appropriate, but it was all I think to say.

"Well, I won't keep you. I just wanted to tell you I'm sorry for the way he treated her."

I watched as she went down the steps to her car, before closing the door. "That was weird," I whispered. I dismissed her visit as I waited for someone more important to come over. At least I hoped he would come over.

The sun was dipping over the top of the mountains before the chimes finally sounded again. Through the wavy glass window, I could see Dan's rangy form. Holding my breath, I swung the door open. "Hi." I stepped back to allow him to enter, but he stayed on the porch.

"May I come in?" He seemed unsure of himself for the first time.

"Of course, why wouldn't you be able to come in?" I opened the door further to allow him in.

"I wasn't sure that I'd be welcome."

He wasn't making sense. "Why wouldn't you be welcome?" We were dancing around each other like a couple of teenagers on a first date.

"I've had at least a half dozen people tell me that you spent the day with Wilkins. What gives? I thought we had something going."

"Are you jealous?" I was hopeful as well as appalled. Jealousy meant he cared, but it could also be obsessive and abusive.

"Damn right I'm jealous. That guy has a pretty big reputation with the ladies. I don't want you to be another notch on his bedpost, figuratively speaking."

"I'm not going to succumb to his charms, as tempting as they are." A teasing smile tilted my lips upward.

"That's good to know." He finally stepped inside, bending down to touch his lips to mine in a soft kiss. "I just want you to be careful. There's too much going on in this town that I don't understand, and I don't want anything to happen to you."

"You can't put me in bubble wrap, Dan. I have to make my own decisions, and I have to find out who killed my sister." We were right back where we always ended up whenever we talked about the case.

He heaved a sigh. Reaching out, he took my hand. "I know. I'm sorry for acting like such an idiot sometimes." He ignored my comment about finding Claire's killer. "One thing I learned from my folks is that people who love each other don't have to agree one hundred percent of the time. It's how they handle the disagreements that count."

My breath caught in my throat at the mention of the 'L' word. It was much too soon to consider that sort of thing. He didn't notice, or ignored, my unease as he continued. "Are we okay?"

"We're okay," I whispered, allowing him to pull me into his arms, his lips claiming mine. There was the spark that was missing when Jake kissed me. All was right with my world.

Somehow we managed to make our way to the living room without much conscious thought. I was cradled against his hard chest, my head resting on his shoulder. "You haven't been around much lately. I hope that means you've found the person who killed Doctor Murphy."

His deep breath caused my head to rise and fall on his shoulder as he released the breath slowly. "No such luck. Things have been in chaos at the PD." He ran his long fingers through his hair, putting it back in some semblance of order after I'd managed to muss it up. "Daniels has been acting…weird is the only way I can describe it, since this all began. I don't know what's wrong with him, but he's driving the entire department nuts.

"The doc was running a drug ring right under the noses of everyone in town, but he wasn't the only one involved. Someone killed him, emptying his cache of drugs. Until we figure out who was working with him…" He lifted his shoulders in a shrug, letting his sentence trail off. My head bobbed up and down on his shoulder again.

"How is this thing with the doctor connected to what

happened to Claire? Or is it?" I sat up, looking at him.

Dan gave another heavy sigh. "I don't know how to answer that. The chief is of the mind that there is some sort of poisonous plant in the garden here that was making her sick without her realizing it. When it got too much for her to handle, she took those pills on her own." I started to argue, but he put his finger on my lips to stop me. "I know what you're going to say, and I don't agree with him. I'm just telling you what he's saying. He wants this cleared up. One less crime for him to investigate is fine with him."

"How can he say she did this to herself if he doesn't even investigate? She didn't have a vegetable garden, and there aren't any harmful plants in the garden. I've already checked with Jules about that."

He shook his head. "I don't know what he's thinking, or if he even is. Can we put this subject to rest for a little while? I'd rather be doing something more pleasurable." He dipped his head, placing his lips on mine.

It wasn't until the grandfather clock in the corner chimed midnight that we realized how late it had gotten. He groaned, "I've been a little short on sleep this week. I really need to go home." The evening had slipped pleasantly away without any arguments. We slowly made our way to the front door to say good bye.

"Where do you live? Do you live alone?" I wished I could recall the words the minute they were out of my mouth, but it was too late. The questions were already out there. I hadn't meant to make it sound like an accusation.

A frown furrowed his forehead. "Yes, I live alone. I rent a small house not far from the department. Where is this coming from?"

I tried for a nonchalant shrug. "You never said where you lived. I thought it might be a secret. I wondered if maybe there was a reason you didn't want me to know."

"You mean like I might have a wife stashed somewhere?" He lifted one light eyebrow slightly. Unable to meet his questioning gaze, I looked down at my bare feet.

Placing a finger under my chin, he lifted my face to his. "Now who's jealous?" he chuckled. "No, I don't have a wife. Until you came along, I didn't even have a steady girlfriend." He paused. "You are my girlfriend, right?" It seemed we were both a little insecure at the moment.

My nod was met with a sigh of relief and a big smile. "In this town of gossips, do you really think I could have gotten away with having a wife while I was seeing you?"

I hadn't thought of that. Now I felt pretty foolish.

I finally pushed him out the door when the clock chimed one. We both needed to get some sleep, or we wouldn't wake up in time to go to church in a few short hours.

~~~

I had just finished breakfast Monday morning when the chimes on the front door rang. "I really wish people wouldn't visit so early in the morning," I muttered as I headed for the door. At least Dusty was always tied up with her guests first thing in the morning. Myriam hadn't been over since I spent part of Saturday with Jake. Maybe she was here now to correct that oversight.

Thankfully it wasn't Myriam. "Yes, may I help you?" A middle-aged woman was standing on the porch. I had no idea who she was or what she wanted this early. Her dark hair was pulled back in a severe bun at the nape of her neck. Thick lensed glasses caused her eyes to bulge out.

"I'm Daphne Stevens with the County Health Department. I'm here to inspect your facility." She didn't bother to smile.

My stomach churned. Would she mark me down for having my breakfast dishes on the table? "Oh, of course, come in." I stepped aside, trying not to show how nervous I suddenly was. Her stern countenance didn't make it easy. "Um, the kitchen is this way." As she followed behind me, I could feel her hard stare in the middle of my back.

"I'm afraid you caught me as I was finishing my breakfast. I haven't had time to clean up." All I'd had was a muffin and coffee, so there wasn't much mess. I hoped she saw it that way.

"The inspections are done on surprise visits. That way

there's no chance of fudging the results." It sounded like an accusation.

"Yes, of course, I understand." She was making me very nervous with her stern tone. "Can I get you a cup of coffee?" Maybe that would help thaw her out just a little.

"This isn't a social visit, Miss Connors." Her admonishment made my face heat up with embarrassment.

"N...no, of course not. I just thought you might like some coffee since it's so early."

She made a point of looking at her watch. "It's after eight o'clock. I've been up for several hours."

I guess that put me in my place, I thought. Nothing I said was going to melt the ice the woman was encased in. I gave a mental shrug. Let's just get this over with.

"I should have been here before this, but I've been very busy." She gave a heavy sigh. "In fact, I was supposed to be here for this inspection a week ago, but things have been crazy." She was muttering as she looked in every nook and cranny. I wasn't sure what she meant; I had just gotten my license last week. I was told at the time it would be several weeks before an inspector could make it out. Claire had been waiting for the inspector to come when she died. Maybe she thought she was here for that inspection. I was afraid to ask, so I kept my mouth shut.

I could feel the woman's disapproval, but I didn't know what I'd done wrong. With a critical eye, she inspected the refrigerator, the stove and oven, and the sinks, all the while making little marks on a form she had on a clipboard. She also made a point of inspecting the pantry, moving things around, poking in the corners. I was grateful she'd been delayed. If she'd come the very day I got my license, she would have walked in on the mess someone had left for me. That wouldn't have been a good thing. Had that been the point of the mess?

"Will you be the one doing the cooking, or will you hire a cook?" she asked, breaking in on my confused thoughts.

"Um, I'll do the cooking." I'd thought about asking Irma to do the baking, but I didn't mention that now. I didn't know if she'd mark me down for that.

"Do you have your restaurant manager's license? We're very strict about that. Have you even checked into that yet?"

I opened the drawer where I kept the folder with all the forms I'd gotten at the Health Department. At least this was something I was prepared for. "Is this what you're talking about?" I handed the small laminated card to her. When she nodded her head, I breathed a sigh of relief. I'd passed that test with flying colors. I was grateful I'd been prepared when I went to the County Health Department.

"When do you plan on opening your business?" Her voice had warmed up a tad.

"I'm not sure. I'm still trying to figure everything out." I didn't tell her this might all be for show, hoping to draw out a killer.

"This inspection is only good for six months," she said. "If you wait longer than that, I'll have to come back out before you can open your business. Of course, I'll be back out if there are any other complaints."

'*Other complaints*,' I thought. I wasn't even open for business, how could there be complaints already? She seemed to be telling me something, but I didn't know what. She didn't give me a chance to question her as she continued her inspection.

Before she was finished I thought she was going to crawl under the sink to check that out as well. I didn't know what she was looking for. Were all the inspections this thorough? "Here is your rating." She finally handed me a piece of paper she took off a portable printer she had in her briefcase. I was afraid to look at what it said. She'd been so stiff and impersonal until now. "You passed," she announced with a big smile. "I'll take that cup of coffee now if it isn't too much trouble."

Had she been trying to intimidate me? If so, it worked. I'd been very intimidated. She sat down at the table where I placed a cup of coffee. "Would you like a muffin?" I wasn't sure if she would consider that too much of a social thing.

"That would be great," she heaved a tired sigh. "I didn't get any breakfast this morning. I have a teenager who just refuses to get out of bed during the summer. He thinks he should be able to stay up all night with his friends, and sleep all day." Her voice was heavy with frustration. "Being a single parent isn't an easy job, but God never said being a parent was supposed to be easy."

I didn't know what to say to any of this, so I let her ramble. By the time she left, she had eaten two muffins and had three cups of coffee. I knew all about her teenage son and her good-for-nothing ex-husband.

"I didn't mean to take up so much of your time, Jillian." She stood up, stretching her back. "Thanks for those delicious muffins. I'm sure your guests will love them."

Watching her drive away, I leaned against the door frame. Was this all a part of her routine when she inspected businesses? She must get a lot of free meals this way. Maybe she just needed someone to listen to her complaints about her son and ex-husband.

Opening the slip of paper she'd given me, I looked at my rating for the first time. "Oh, wow," I whispered. She'd given me an A+ rating. I couldn't get any better than that. It was something to work to maintain.

Maybe I should have told her I hadn't baked the muffins. Would that have made a difference? I shook my head. She gave me the rating before she tasted the muffins so I guess it didn't matter. Irma had been plying me with her delicious baked goods since I arrived. I doubted I would be able to make anything as tasty. She would be thrilled to learn the inspector liked them.

CHAPTER SIXTEEN

Pleased with my high rating, I hung the frame holding the business license and the ratings paper in a prominent place for all to see. Claire would have been proud. My heart twisted slightly. She's the one who should be enjoying this rating, not me. She did all the work to get ready for this.

I wanted to call someone, but I didn't know who. Irma would be over after lunch with Dusty to follow shortly after that. What would Dusty think of my rating? There had been an undercurrent of something in her voice each time she asked if I was really going to do this. Was she afraid the competition would take away from her business?

I wasn't sure what Daphne had meant by 'other complaints.' Had someone called in a complaint after the break-in? Did Dusty have anything to do with that?

I didn't have time to consider that possibility when the chimes rang again. I looked around to see if Daphne had left anything behind. There was nothing that I could see. The chimes rang again, and I hurried to the front door. Someone was impatient.

Seeing Myriam through the wavy glass window in the door, my stomach rolled. "What now?" I muttered.

"I can see you, young lady, open this damn door."

"What is it now, Myriam?" I kept a firm grip on the door so she couldn't push her way inside. "I'm rather busy."

She gave a disdainful sniff. "I've warned you before to leave my son alone, but you won't listen. I'm giving you a final warning."

"What are you going to do? Jake is a grown man, he can make his own decisions and see whoever he wants." I sounded far braver than I was feeling at the moment. The woman was delusional. Was she also dangerous?

"So you admit you're dating him," she snapped.

"I'm not admitting anything. I'm just saying that he can see whoever he wants. I wonder what he would have to say about you threatening me."

She blanched a little at that. "You wouldn't dare tell him. He wouldn't believe you." She quickly changed her statement. "I'm his mother. No one talks bad about me, and gets away with it."

"If he wouldn't believe me, what difference does it make if I tell him what you've been doing?" She looked momentarily confused, and I continued. "I doubt that he would be happy to learn that you've threatened me."

"I never threatened you." She drew herself up to her full height which was still several inches shorter than me in spite of her high heels.

"That's what it sounds like to me. Did you also threaten Claire? Did you give her the poison that killed her?"

She stepped back several paces. "Are you crazy? I didn't do anything to that girl."

"But you did warn her to stay away from your son, right?" I was guessing, but apparently I was right. Her hands were shaking slightly now. As long as I was on the offensive, I decided to go all out. "Are you the one who keeps breaking into my house and rearranging my furniture?"

"This isn't your house," she snapped. "It should belong to my son." I noticed she didn't deny the accusation.

Ignoring her rant, I continued. "What exactly do you think will be accomplished by breaking in here? I'm not scared of you or anyone else in this town." That wasn't the complete truth, but she didn't need to know that.

"That's ridiculous. Why would I do something like that?" Her eyes slid to the right when she said that. She was lying.

"I know it was you, Myriam, so there's no use denying it. Did my note make you so angry you just had to break that table here in the entry?"

"I did no such thing! Everything in this house belongs to my son. Why would I destroy it?" Her denial rang true this time.

"Stay out of this house and stay away from me. The next time you break in, I'll have you arrested for trespassing." It was a threat without teeth. Chief Daniels didn't believe anyone had broken into the house, and he certainly didn't think Myriam would do something like that. "I'll also tell Jake what you've been up to." That threat struck home.

Without another word, she turned on her fancy high heels, stomping down the steps to her car. With a chuckle, I sagged against the door. I'd gotten the best of her for once. At least now I knew who was getting in while I was gone. Big deal, I thought. It was the least threatening of all the crimes going on in this town.

Was this another case of two people working separately, but with the same objective in mind? I was convinced two people had tried to kill Claire. One was killing her slowly, while the other had succeeded with a more swift result. Were the same two people breaking into the house? How much danger was I in? Until I figured out why Claire had been killed, I wasn't a threat to anyone.

Dan said he would change the locks on all the doors, but he'd been tied up with Doctor Murphy's murder, and now the break-in at his office. It was time to call in a locksmith. I didn't know why I hadn't done it sooner.

Myriam had been moving the furniture around in a feeble attempt to scare me off. Someone else had made the mess in the pantry and destroyed the table, but to what end?

Someone had also searched through the drawers in my room and Claire's. If they were looking for whatever Claire had taken, I didn't think they'd found it, otherwise they wouldn't continue coming back. I gave a frustrated sigh. It was one more mystery to figure out. Until I actually opened the bed and breakfast, I needed to do some searching of my own. As long as the thing Claire had was still in the house, they wouldn't give up.

I was convinced Doctor Murphy was the one who gave Claire the pain pills that ultimately killed her. Whoever killed him was still out there. So was the person who had given her the oleander poison. I shook my head. Maybe Dan was right. I wasn't cut out to be a detective. I needed to leave this to him.

~~~

Irma arrived for afternoon tea at her usual time. She always looked forward to coming over. It appeared to be the highlight of her day. "I made some sugar cookies this morning, dearie. I thought you might enjoy them." She followed me into the kitchen with her plate. Seeing the rating I'd received, she beamed at me. "I'm so proud of you. I knew you could do it." She wrapped me in a warm hug.

I'd never be able to make baked goods to match hers. Drawing a deep breath, I took a gamble. "Would you be interested in doing some of the baking for 'Claire's House Bed and Breakfast'? You'd have to get a food handler's license." I rushed on before she could decline. "I'll help you study for it."

She gave her twittering laugh. "Why, dearie, I've had that thing for years. How do you think I supported my children between husbands? I've kept that license up-to-date just in case I ever needed it again. I was hoping to do some baking for Claire when she got this place up and running." She gave a sad little sigh.

"Does that mean you want to do it for me?" I cocked my head to look at her, a teasing smile curving my lips.

She clapped her hands like an excited child on Christmas morning. "Yes, I would like that very much." She was almost hopping in her chair, a big grin spread across her wizened face.

"Was that your plan all along? I wondered why you kept bringing me all these treats. You are one tricky lady." We both laughed. Picking up her glass of tea, she offered it to me in a toast and we touched glasses. I had fallen right into the trap she'd set for me, and I couldn't be happier about it.

Growing serious after a moment, she lowered her voice to a whisper. "Maybe we could keep this our little secret for a while." Her faded eyes moved across the back yard towards Dusty's house sitting higher on the next hill.

"Do you bake for Dusty as well?"

She gave a derisive snort at that. "That woman wouldn't ask me for a glass of water if she was on fire. She thinks I should just curl up and die, but I'm not going to accommodate her on that. I may not see as well as I used to, or be able to drive anymore, and some things are more difficult than they were twenty years ago, but there's a lot of life left in these old bones." She patted her chest.

This small woman had more spunk than many people half her age. "Does she do all her own baking?" I asked. I wasn't sure where my question was leading, but something in the back of my mind was fighting to come to the forefront. I just couldn't grasp hold of it right then.

She shrugged. "I have no idea what that woman does. She claims to use fresh ingredients from her own garden, but I wouldn't take that as gospel either."

We were having our tea on the back patio taking advantage of the afternoon breeze. It was mid-July with the temperatures reaching into the nineties. Still it didn't feel any hotter than a summer afternoon back home where the humidity was much higher.

Looking off towards Dusty's house, the sun reflected off something in one of the windows. It was gone so quick, I wouldn't have noticed it if I hadn't been looking at that very moment. A chill ran up my spine.

"Would you like more iced tea?" I stood up, moving to the back door. That sensation of being watched prickled along my neck.

"Maybe a little of that good wine instead," she suggested slyly, "to celebrate our joint endeavor?" She followed me into the house. I gratefully closed the door to shut out the eerie feeling of being spied on.

Irma overstayed her usual hour of visitation, and we both exceeded our usual limit of one glass of wine. In fact, we finished off the bottle before we were through. By the time she was ready to go home, I decided to follow her, making sure she made it without falling on the stone steps. The woman had plenty of spunk, but she was still up in years. After more than two glasses of wine, we were both slightly tipsy. Helping her on the steps might be a case of 'the blind leading the blind' though.

"Thank you for asking me to help you, Jillian." Irma grasped my hand as we made our way to her house. "It means a lot to me. Claire was such a special friend. I was devastated when she died. I feel like I have a new lease on life now." Her eyes sparkled with unshed tears while my own tears clogged my throat. I didn't know what to say to this. I settled on squeezing her hand in reply.

I was being overly sentimental, probably because of the wine, I told myself. I wasn't used to drinking in the middle of the day, or having more than one glass at a time. Still it was nice to have someone who cared for me. Dan cared, I reminded myself. How many others in this town cared about me? I had been keeping to myself until things got straightened out. I was afraid to place my trust in very many people.

I half expected Dusty to be at my back door when I returned to the house. What would I say to her? With my wine-loosened tongue, would I say too much? I was convinced the glint I'd seen was the sun reflecting off the lens of a pair of binoculars. But what was her purpose of watching me? I had nothing to hide. She knew Irma came over most afternoons.

The prickly feeling of being watched stayed with me the remainder of the afternoon leaving me rattled and uneasy. Closing the curtains in the kitchen didn't help. The feeling persisted.

Why would Dusty be watching me? Was there someone else in her house? I couldn't believe Jules would do something like that. He had been hesitant the first time he came over, but since then he had been friendly, even helpful.

An uneasy thought crossed my mind. Had the chief recruited Dusty to keep an eye on me? Did he really believe I had something to do with the doctor's murder? Against Dan's wishes, maybe it was time for me to do a little more snooping on those snooping on me. If she could watch me, I would return the favor.

CHAPTER SEVENTEEN

The investigation into Doctor Murphy's death and the drug ring had stalled, at least enough to give Dan the night off. I feared the chief had completely forgotten about Claire's murder. "I thought we could bar-be-que these steaks. It's nice enough to eat on the patio." Dan announced as he held out a package of steaks before he placed a kiss on my lips.

"Um, I don't know. The bugs might eat us before we can eat the steaks." There weren't as many bugs in the evening here as there were at home where clouds of mosquitos sometimes took over at dusk. The bug I was worried about wasn't the multi-legged kind though. This one was staring at me through binoculars.

"We'll just light a few candles to keep any stray bugs away." Following me into the kitchen, he stopped, staring at the A+ rating Daphne had given me that morning. "You're really going through with this?" He turned to look at me, a frown drawing his eyebrows together. "Why? I thought you were just trying to make people believe you were going through with it."

I shrugged. "In order to make people believe I'm doing it, I have to go through all the steps. Besides, it sounds like a good idea. Claire did all the work to make it happen. I'm just following through."

"But is this what *you* want? The bed and breakfast was Claire's dream, not yours." He pulled me into his arms. "She's gone, Babe. You can't live her life for her. Do you want to run a bed and breakfast, or be a teacher? Which one is your dream?"

Tears suddenly prickled behind my eyes. He pointed out something I'd ignored through all this. I grew up wanting to be a teacher, but that had been sidetracked with my need to catch Claire's killer. "Yes, I want to be a teacher, but if it helps to catch a killer, I'll run a bed and breakfast for a while. Besides, I can't teach here without my certificate." Telling me

I couldn't do this had only made me more determined to do it. He was using unfair tactics against me now. Using my own dream against me, he was trying to redirect me.

"Okay, so get your certificate, and let me catch the killer." Before I could argue further his lips captured mine. "I don't want to lose you," he whispered once he lifted his head. His warm breath brushed against my face. "Whether you know it or not, I've fallen in love with you, stubbornness and all."

"Isn't it a little too soon for that?" I argued weakly, although I knew in my heart I was in love with him as well.

His light blue eyes looked down at me with a seriousness I hadn't seen before. "Not for me. I fell in love with you when I first saw you."

I pulled back, looking up at him. "Really?" I drew the word out, disbelief dripped from my voice. "If memory serves, the look you gave me that first morning didn't say love. It was more like 'this woman is crazy. How do I get rid of her?' "

"Okay," he chuckled, "maybe not the minute I saw you. It took a little while. But that stubborn nature of yours quickly grew on me." He had distracted me from the paranoia that had held me in its tight grip all afternoon, and I was able to relax in his arms.

It was still light outside, but the kitchen was dim. Looking around, he noticed the closed curtains. "It's like a dark cave in here? Why do you have the curtains closed?" When I tried to pull away, he tightened his grip on my waist, refusing to let me go. "What's going on? Did someone break in here again?"

When I first told him someone was watching me, he had discounted my feelings. Would he do it again? He hadn't found out anything about Roland Granger, and I wasn't certain he believed the man existed or that he was following me. Would he say that flash of light in Dusty's window was just that, a flash, the sun glinting off the window pane? *In for a penny, in for a pound,* I thought. I might as well tell him, and get it over with.

"I think Dusty was sp…watching me this afternoon," I changed the word I was going to use.

"What do you mean watching you? Didn't you tell me she and Irma Grover are here almost every afternoon?"

"Yes, but this was different. Irma came over, and we decided to sit on the patio with our iced tea." Drawing a deep breath, I released it slowly. "I think Dusty was watching us with binoculars." I stared up at him, daring him to discount my words. Telling him about that flash of light seemed a little thin.

"Why would she do that? If she wanted in on your little tea party, why wouldn't she just come over and join you?"

"I doubt that was her intention." He cocked his head to the side questioningly, waiting for me to explain. Unfortunately, I didn't have an explanation. I lifted my shoulders in a shrug, letting them drop. "I don't know," I answered his unasked question. "Haven't you ever gotten a feeling about something that you couldn't explain?" I drew back to frown at him. "Or is that something only cops get?"

"Don't put words in my mouth. I never said anything like that." He fell silent for a long moment, looking off into the distance. "I don't know her very well. She's lived here a lot longer than I have. I know she and the chief are pretty tight. I'm not sure how long they've been dating though."

"How long has she had the bed and breakfast?" I questioned softly. He was concentrating so hard on something, I didn't want to break in on his thoughts, but maybe he could fill in some blanks.

"I'm not sure. I don't think it's been very long. She's had a bunch of different jobs in the time I've been here. It caused problems between them for a while."

"What kind of jobs? She said she tried being one of the hippy/artistic-types who live here, but she isn't artistic. Is that what you mean?"

He was lost in thought again, and I wasn't sure he heard me. I finally poked him in the ribs, prodding him to explain. "I'm not really sure what I mean. Something..." he waved his hand around his head, "I'm trying to remember something I heard when I first moved here." He shook his head like that would dislodge the piece of information he was trying to access.

"Well, try not to think about it, and maybe it will come to you. What about those steaks?" It was my turn to change the subject, giving his subconscious the chance to dredge up the missing information. I didn't want Dusty spying on us, but we weren't doing anything shameful. I wasn't going to let her ruin my time with Dan. Maybe next time I think she's spying on me, I'll lift my glass to her in a mock salute. She might get the message and leave me alone. "Do you still want to have a bar-be-que?"

"What about all those 'bugs'?" He lifted one eyebrow, a teasing grin lifting the corners of his mouth.

"We'll just light some candles," I laughed, like it was my suggestion all along. "We can eat in the grape arbor. I think that's what it's for, privacy as well as shade." The evening turned out perfect, and the arbor had been an ideal place to eat dinner. If I really opened the bed and breakfast, I would make sure my guests were aware it was there for them to use.

"Do you want to be a teacher?" he asked much later, bringing our conversation full circle.

"Yes; but I sort of promised Irma that she could bake for me when I opened the bed and breakfast. She was so excited I can't let down her now." Even I could hear the disappointment in my voice.

"Don't disappoint her then, let her do the baking. Use the inheritance you receive from Claire's estate to hire someone to run everything else. That way you will keep your dream alive as well as Claire's."

I gave myself a mental head slap. Why hadn't I thought of that? I didn't need the money I would receive from the estate if I had a job. I could use it like he suggested. If her death had anything to do with opening the bed and breakfast, maybe doing just that would draw the killer out like I hoped. I would have to be careful, but I wouldn't be actively searching either. That should appease Dan's protective tendencies.

~~~

Dusty paid me an unexpected visit early the following

morning. She must have rushed over as soon as she fed her guests, and had them on their way doing touristy things. Maybe she hadn't had any guests the night before. I didn't know the tourist cycle well enough to judge what week nights were like.

"How are things going?" Her smile was forced as her eyes moved around the room. She was looking for something. The frame with the health department rating was in plain sight. She stared at it for a long moment. "Oh, congratulations." Her reaction was a sharp contrast to what Irma's had been the day before. "The first rating is always the easiest. You don't have guests in and out of your kitchen messing things up." She tried to downplay my accomplishment.

"Why would a guest mess anything up? Wouldn't that make things bad for their visit?"

"Oh, they don't do anything deliberately. Spilling things on the floor or table can cause a mess. If it doesn't get cleaned up properly and the inspector comes, that will be a black mark against you. There are a lot of ways to get marked down. You always have to worry about the next inspection. They usually inspect twice a year, but they could come more often if there's a complaint. You'll never know when they might show up."

"You mean like when someone broke in here and spilled flour, sugar, and maple syrup all around the pantry and kitchen?" I asked innocently. "I guess that would have been really bad if the inspector came right then."

"Um, yes, that would have been bad. Who would break in here and do something like that?" Her face had paled slightly.

"Maybe it was someone who doesn't want me to open the B&B," I suggested. "I guess I need to be really careful and make sure all my doors are locked even when I'm here. I wouldn't want that person to get in again, and then call in a complaint." I gave her a hard stare. Her nervous manner was telling all sorts of tales. Was she the one who broke in? Myriam was high on my list of suspects, but I didn't think she had made the mess in the pantry.

"Well, I'd better get back home. I didn't get a chance to

see you yesterday, and I wanted to find out what the inspector had to say."

"You knew she'd been here?"

"Oh, um, yes, she was at my place, and I figured she came over here as long as she was in the area. Well, I'll see you later."

"How did your inspection go?" She had stepped out onto the patio when my question stopped her.

"Oh, the same," she nodded at the frame on the wall. "I always make sure everything is shipshape. This is my livelihood. I can't take chances." There a slight emphasis on 'my livelihood'. Did she resent the fact that I'd inherited money from Claire? She escaped down the steps before I could say anything else.

"That was interesting," I spoke out loud. I still wasn't used to the silence of the house or the town. In spite of all the tourists that go through the area, it still wasn't like a big noisy city. *If she was the one who made the mess in the pantry hoping the inspector would come that very day, how much farther would she go to stop me? Was she also the one who smashed the entry table?* I wondered.

I knew, or thought I knew, Myriam had been rearranging the furniture. Now I wasn't so sure. Why would Dusty do something like that? Something else going on here, I just didn't know what.

~~~

Going for groceries was always an adventure in Bisbee. The winding, one way streets, and streets that edged the side of big drop-offs were still a challenge for me. Once you left Old Bisbee, there was a round-about to navigate before you could reach the San Jose district and the one grocery store in town. It was that or an hour drive to Sierra Vista. I usually stayed in town.

The narrow winding streets still made me nervous, and I drove much slower than some of the others in town. An impatient driver behind me honked several times, probably hoping to make me go faster. As long as I was going the speed limit, I wasn't going to let him push me. I only had a few miles before I turned onto my street.

Suddenly the big SUV rear-ended me, sending me dangerously close to the edge of one of the many drop-offs. "No, not my new truck." The words erupted out of my mouth without any conscious thought. Clenching my jaws shut, I began praying. "Please God, keep me safe." Before I even finished my prayer, the big vehicle struck again. I stomped on the brakes with both feet, and my tires squealed. My truck was going to be ruined.

Speeding up wasn't an option. A sharp curve was directly ahead. If I missed the curve, I would sail over the edge, landing on a building below. There was no telling how many innocent people would be injured or killed if that happened. As we came into the curve, the driver came along side me, tapping my bumper, drawing me ever closer to the edge.

There was no place for me to go except over the edge. The grinding sound of metal-on-metal filled the cab. As my front tires began to slide over the edge of the road, a scream tore from my throat. Just that fast, the SUV sped off, leaving me hanging there.

I was afraid to move, but I couldn't stay where I was. I didn't know how solid the ground under my tires was. The engine was still running which meant my cell phone was connected to Bluetooth. Being careful not to make a sudden move, I managed to call Dan. Within minutes I could hear the sirens coming to my rescue. They couldn't get here fast enough for me. People were gathering around, but no one came near. Everyone was afraid of dislodging the truck, sending me over the edge.

It took much longer for the tow truck to arrive to pull me back from the edge. Once that happened, Dan pulled open the door, pulling me into his arms. His hands roamed over my body searching for injuries. He was shaking as bad as I was. "Are you hurt? You need to go to the hospital; the ambulance is on the way. I don't see any blood."

I cupped his face in my hands to stop him. "I don't need to

go to the hospital," I said breathlessly. I was having a little trouble breathing from where the seat belt tightened across my chest and stomach, and the side air bag had hit me in the head. If that was all that was wrong with me, I was very lucky. He started to argue, but I stopped him with a kiss. "I'm okay, Love, really I am," I whispered.

"Thank God." It was a soft prayer. He released a shaky sigh, but continued holding me like he was afraid I would disappear if he let go. "Tell me what happened."

Staring at the damage to my beautiful truck, tears blurred my vision for a minute. White paint marred the light blue surface. The driver's side door was dented and the bed was crumpled. "Jillian," Dan gave me a little shake. "Tell me what happened." When I still didn't answer, he began searching for injuries again. "Did you hit your head? Do you remember what happened?"

I remembered all too clearly what happened. I wished I could forget the feeling of tipping over the edge of the cliff. A shiver moved through me at the memory. "I'll be sore in the morning, but that's all. My poor truck took most of the punishment," I lamented. Telling how the big SUV had continued hitting my truck until I started over the edge was like reliving a nightmare. At the time it felt like it was happening in slow motion, at the same time it happened in the blink of an eye.

"Could you see who was driving?"

My shoulders slumped, and I gave my head a small shake. "I was too busy trying to stay on the road." I sighed. "I didn't do a very good job of it."

"You didn't go over, so you did a great job. Were you able to get the license number?" I gave my head another small shake. "Can you describe the vehicle?"

"No," I said dejectedly. "It happened too fast. All I can say is it was a big white SUV. The windows were tinted so dark I wouldn't have been able to see the driver if I'd had time to look." Tears prickled behind my eyes as the tow truck disappeared with my truck.

It didn't take long for them to locate the SUV. It was at the bottom of a ravine outside of town. Pulling it out took longer than it had to pull me off the ledge. "Was the driver still inside?" I asked fearfully. I was mad at the person who did this, but I didn't want them to die. Or maybe I did if this had anything to do with Claire's murder.

Dan gave a heavy sigh. "No, but we know who it belongs to." My heart gave a jump. Maybe we could figure something out at last. "Don't get too excited, babe," he cautioned. "The SUV belonged to Doc Murphy."

I slumped back in the chair. "Well, we know he wasn't driving it, so who was?"

"We have to wait and see what the forensic team finds. Hopefully there will be fingerprints other than the doc's." I huffed out a frustrated breath. It seemed like all I'd done was wait for one report after another since I arrived in Arizona.

CHAPTER EIGHTEEN

"Why can't she leave things alone," the lone figure muttered. Watching the activities as the big truck was pulled back from the edge was aggravating. "I wanted her to go over, not hang there." With a shrug, the figure disappeared into the crowd that had gathered to watch what was going on.

~~~

Irma insisted on mothering me for the next few days. I didn't try too hard to dissuade her either. As expected, I was stiff and sore from my experience. I had a bruise on my cheek from the air bag and one on my shoulder from the seat belt.

It would take a lot longer before my truck was running again, if ever. Another report I was waiting for was from the insurance company. Were they going to fix it, or total it?

"I can't believe someone had the nerve to take that horrible doctor's car, and try to run you off the road with it," Irma groused again. She'd been doing that for the last two days. "What's taking that CSI team so long to find fingerprints?" Surprisingly, the woman was addicted to every forensic show on television.

"The town has to rely on the county for all that. I guess my little accident isn't top priority to them."

"Accident my eye," she sniffed indignantly. "Someone deliberately tried to kill you."

Each time she mentioned that, giant birds fluttered in my stomach. They were getting bigger all the time. I wished the report would come back, so we could both forget it. Somehow I doubted it would turn up anything good.

After stopping in every day since I arrived in Bisbee, Dusty was conspicuously absent from my life. She hadn't been over since the day after the inspector had been here. I wasn't sure if she was busy or avoiding me. My guess was the latter. I couldn't decide if that meant she had something to do with what happened, or not. If she was the one behind the wheel of the doctor's SUV, how did she get it? It had been missing ever since his death.

Dan's suggestion that I get my Arizona teaching certificate had taken root in my mind. This was the perfect time to study for it. I still hadn't decided whether I would apply for a job in the school system though. I could also substitute teach, or tutor students. That would give me time to run the B&B myself. I wasn't ready to give up on that altogether.

Irma seemed younger by the day with the prospect of baking and cooking for Claire's House Bed and Breakfast. Her energy level rivaled a teenager, only she was more focused on her goals. While I recuperated, we discussed different recipes for breakfast menus. I couldn't believe some of her ideas. She really was a marvel.

Jules had started spending time each afternoon instructing me on how to care for all the plants in the yard. When he first came over he hadn't wanted Dusty to know that he was helping me, but it was different now. Why the sudden change? Had she sent him to spy on me, or didn't he care any longer if she knew?

"Dusty sent over some new plants she thought you'd like," he mumbled. He was unable to look me in the eye as he handed me the small pots.

"That was nice of her. What are they?"

"Just some things she likes to grow. She experiments with different herbs." His penetrating look seemed to be trying to tell me something while avoiding telling me the name of the plants. He kept his back to Dusty's house on the next hillside.

"Are they good for cooking?" My knowledge of herbs was limited to the spices I used in the kitchen.

"No! I mean you can't use them for cooking. They don't taste good."

"Then what are they for? I thought chefs use herbs in some of the fancy dishes they make."

He shook his head. "Some herbs can't be used for cooking," he said evasively.

"What would I do with these? Can I use the flowers in a display?"

His face lost some color. "N...no, that wouldn't be a good idea. You don't want to take them in the house."

Okay, now he had my full attention. He was trying to tell me something without saying it out loud. "Why did she send them over if they aren't good for cooking or decoration?"

He lifted his shoulders without answering. "I have to go." He quickly turned away; his shoulders drooped in what I could only call defeat, his head was bowed. He wasn't happy about giving me those plants. What was wrong with them?

I took my cell phone out of my pocket taking a picture of each plant. There were literally thousands of different plants in the world, if not hundreds of thousands. Somehow I needed to figure out what these were. Why wouldn't he tell me what they were? Why had Dusty sent them over to me? His ominous warning gave me the jitters. Maybe I would just throw them away.

Snatches of different conversations kept popping up in my mind. Dusty had told me she had a black thumb and couldn't grow anything. Yet Jules clearly said she liked growing different plants, and liked experimenting with herbs. Which was it; she either couldn't grow anything or she liked experimenting with herbs? I tended to believe Jules.

Something he said the day he told me about the grape arbor came to mind. "I just know plants. I leave the making of things with them to others." He never explained what he meant by that.

I stared at the small plants on the patio table. They looked innocent enough, but so did a lot of other plants that could be deadly. My stomach twisted. Was this how Claire had died? Had Dusty given similar plants to her without warning her not to use them in food? Where were they now?

I spent the rest of the afternoon examining each plant in the garden. They all looked different from the ones Jules had brought me. Trying to look up a specific plant on the internet would be difficult since I didn't know the name of the plant. A plant nursery was my best hope in finding out what they were. That meant a trip to Sierra Vista.

CHAPTER NINETEEN

"Do you know anything about herbs?" Irma came over at her usual time after lunch. She loved to cook; maybe she would know what the plants were. "Do you use them in any of your recipes?"

She shook her head. "I do experiment with different things, but I know enough to be careful with some things. Even a common spice like nutmeg can be deadly if you go overboard with it. Some plants should never be taken internally." She almost sounded like a doctor now.

I let the subject drop until I could go to Sierra Vista with the small pots. Until I knew what the plants were, I wasn't going to put them in the ground. When Dan came over later that night, I asked him a similar question.

"No," he chuckled. "My cooking skills are limited to bar-be-que. Why? Are you planning on growing some herbs for the house?" We had finally come to an understanding about the bed and breakfast and catching Claire's killer. We just wouldn't talk about either in order to avoid an argument. That might not be the healthiest way to deal with a disagreement in a relationship, but for now it worked for us.

"No, Dusty sent Jules over with some plants. I'm trying to figure out why she would do that, and what they are."

"Didn't he tell you what they are?" He frowned. Apparently he thought it was as curious as I had.

"No, he didn't say. In fact, he avoided answering me." For several minutes Dan stared at the small plants sitting on the table. Something was bothering him. "What are you thinking?"

"I'm not sure, but..." His words trailed off as he strained to dislodge a memory.

"I don't know anything about plants, but Jules said you couldn't use these in cooking. I know some herbs can be poisonous."

We both stopped what we were doing to stare at the little

plants. "Why would Dusty give me poisonous plants?" I whispered. "Is she the one who poisoned Claire?"

He gave his forehead a slap. "That's what I've been trying to remember."

"What are you talking about?"

"You know how rumors persist long after the incident happened? When I first came here there was talk about someone using herbs as a healing agent. It backfired though, and a number of people got pretty sick. It had happened maybe ten years before I arrived, I'm just not sure exactly when. People were still talking about it though. Every now and then, I still hear people mention the incident."

"Who was doing it?"

He shrugged. "That's the funny part. No one ever said, not even the ones who got sick."

"Why wouldn't they tell who gave them the herbs if they got sick because of them? That doesn't make sense."

"From the talk, it wasn't done maliciously. I guess they didn't want to get the person in trouble." I could only shake my head at that flawed thinking. As long as the person got away with it, they might try to hurt someone else, this time on purpose. Was that person still in Bisbee? What was their connection to Claire? My stomach twisted.

"A real herbalist would know which herbs to use for healing and which ones could make you very sick," he continued. "Apparently this person was guessing which ones were the good herbs and which were the bad ones. Some herbs even have hallucinogenic properties. From the stories bantered around, there were some really wild 'trips' because of those herbs."

"I still don't understand why they wouldn't tell where they got the herbs. That person could still be doling them out." I looked off towards Dusty's house. "Do you think Dusty is the person in those rumors?" My voice was soft like I was afraid she could eavesdrop on our conversation as easily as watch us.

"I wish I could answer that," he sighed. "If the authorities knew the identity of the person involved, they never said. I do know that no one was ever charged."

"How long has Daniels been chief here?"

"I think he started as a beat cop. He's probably been chief fifteen years or more, why?"

"If he and Dusty have gone together that long, and he knew she was behind what happened he would do his level best to keep her name out of it."

He thought about that for a long moment before nodding his head. "You're right about that. One thing about the chief, he's loyal to a fault. As long as he's in your corner, you could do almost anything, and he would overlook it."

"That's a good thing in a friend, not so much in a cop. How do we go about finding out who that amateur herbalist was?" He cleared his throat, giving me a frown. "I mean, how do *you* go about finding that out?"

He chuckled at my backpedaling before growing serious again. "I'll ask around, but I'll have to do it quietly. If she was involved, I don't want the chief to get wind of my investigation until I have proof. I like my job, and I'd like to keep it. I don't care how good a friend someone is, if they've committed a crime, they need to suffer the consequences of their actions."

"What do we do if it's Dusty? Why would she hurt Claire?" I whispered more to myself than to Dan.

"Take it easy, babe. We don't know that she did anything to anyone. We can't accuse her of anything right now."

"I can accuse her of giving me poisonous herbs."

"Only if that's what they are. Besides, it isn't illegal to give someone a plant, even a poisonous one. This isn't the plant that was given to Claire though. Do you remember what that was?"

I flopped down in the lawn chair, huffing out a frustrated sigh. "The toxicology report was full of terms I couldn't pronounce, let alone understand. Doctor Langston said it was the juice from oleanders. It's a common plant, and grows just about anywhere. It's what was making her sick, and would have eventually killed her."

"Oleanders are everywhere," he agreed. Anyone could have given her something like that." Dan gave a frustrated sigh.

"But these aren't oleanders." I nodded my head towards the small pots on the table. "What should I do with these? I don't want them around if they can make someone sick. Why would Dusty give me something like that?"

"Good question. I'll find out what they are, then maybe have a little talk with her and Jules."

"I'm sure Jules didn't have anything to do with it," I objected. "I think he had a crush on Claire. He's always been very helpful to me."

"I'll talk to them once I know what kind of plants these are. Until then, I'll get them out of here."

~~~

I was getting used to Jake showing up on my doorstep first thing Saturday morning. It was a habit I needed to put the skids on. I didn't want to have another visit from Myriam, and I didn't want to give him false hopes that there would ever be anything between us beyond friendship.

Instead of coming in the house, he stayed on the porch to offer an apology. "I am so sorry for the way my mother has been acting. The woman simply can't accept that I'm an adult, and she can't pick my friends."

I stepped back to let him in. "Would you like some coffee? I just made a fresh pot." He followed me into the kitchen. Seated at the long farm-style table, I set a steaming cup in front of him. "Now, would you like to explain what you're talking about?" I hadn't said anything to him about Myriam's visits, but someone else had.

"I still have a few friends in this town," he said cryptically, "friends who let me know when she starts harassing someone she might disapprove of. And that amounts to any female she didn't introduce me to." With a weary sigh he continued. "I can't tell you how many women have called me with propositions from dinner to a toss in the hay. All were given my phone number by my dear mother."

He looked so miserable and put-upon I couldn't prevent the chuckle that escaped my lips. "I'm sorry, Jake. She is a little overbearing."

"You think?" He slumped further down in the chair. "Why didn't you tell me she had been bothering you?"

"When I threatened to tell you what she's been up to, she backed down." A little, I silently added. "I figured you'd find out soon enough and put a stop to it."

"I doubt I'll ever be able to do that, not completely anyway. The woman is incorrigible. She'll be the worst mother-in-law in the world. If I ever get married," he qualified.

"Maybe moving away from Arizona would help," I suggested. "That way she wouldn't know any of your friends."

He ran his fingers through his thick hair, dislodging the perfectly combed locks. "Arizona is my home, where my business is. Running isn't in my nature, not even to get away from my overbearing mother."

I felt sorry for him, but couldn't offer any other advice. He'd have to work out his problems with his mother on his own.

"Promise you'll tell me if she comes around again. I've warned her, but she hasn't taken me seriously so far. I might have to make a few threats of my own."

"She did tell me about the resident ghost who is supposed to live in the house," I said half-jokingly. I wanted to see what he would say.

His blank look told the true story. "She was lying about that, too. There is no Sam the ghost." My voice held a trace of resignation at being duped by his mother.

"Sam?" He started laughing, but I didn't get the joke. Tears of laughter glittered in his eyes. "I'm sorry, Jillian," he managed between guffaws. "Sam the ghost is a story I made up when I was in middle school to impress my friends. The tales of a long-dead relative who died in the house scared the willies out of them, so I just kept telling it. Anytime something went wrong in the house, we would just say Sam did it."

I felt like a complete fool. Even though I didn't believe in ghosts, her tales had given me some uncomfortable moments. Wait until she comes around again, I silently vowed. I wasn't sure what I would do to her, but I'd think of something.

We were each lost in our own thoughts for several long minutes. Finally, he turned his dark eyes back to me, changing the subject from his meddling mother. "If my spies in town are correct, Detective Tobin has stolen your heart, and I don't have a chance now."

"Spies?" Ghosts were forgotten, and my voice climbed into the screeching range. "Are you the one who is having me followed? Are you that guy's boss?" I pushed away from the table standing over him. My heart was knocking against my chest so hard I thought I'd end up with a broken rib.

"Jillian, hold on a minute." He made a calming gesture with his hands. "I'm not having you followed. What guy are you talking about?" Did I dare believe that blank look on his face?

"You said you have people spying on me. Why would you do that?"

"I was joking. You know how people in this town love to gossip. I've had any number of people tell me they've seen the two of you together."

"What difference does it make to anyone else who I see or what I do? Why would they bother telling you about it?"

"Because I haven't made a secret of the fact that I like you. They know I want to go out with you."

"So you're not having someone watch me?"

"No, I would never do that. Why would you even think that?"

"Because someone has been following me, that's why." My tone was harsh.

He reached out to take my hand, but I backed away. Claire's warning was never far from my mind. Had I wrongfully put my trust in him?

"Jillian, I'm not having anyone watch you, please believe me. Sit down and tell me what's going on. Please." He sounded sincere. I wanted to believe him, but did I dare?

Sitting back down, I tucked my hands in my lap so he couldn't touch me. It took me a minute to calm down enough to tell him about the man I'd seen several times, and the odd feeling of being watched. "Do you know Roland Granger?" I finally asked, watching his face to see if I could detect a lie.

He shook his head, his dark eyes never leaving my face. "I don't recall anyone by that name. Who is he?"

"One of the men who seems to be watching me," I said on a sigh.

"One of the men? How many people do you think are watching you?"

"Two, I think," I said with a shrug. I didn't mention Dusty's attempt to watch me from her kitchen. I didn't want to sound paranoid.

"What does Tobin have to say about this?" he asked.

"He checked out Roland Granger, but he couldn't find anything." I didn't want to admit Dan hadn't believed me at first. Hopefully, he was now taking it seriously.

"In other words, he didn't believe you. Maybe he isn't the man I thought he was. If everything you've said is true, why wouldn't he believe you?"

"If what I'm saying is true?" I lifted one eyebrow. "That's the same attitude he had. But I'm not lying or making it up. Someone has been watching me." He made no mention of someone running me off the road, and neither did I. Maybe his spies hadn't told that story yet. I was still waiting for the insurance company to replace the truck.

"I'm sorry. That's not what I meant, and I do believe you. Is it connected to Claire's, or Doctor Murphy's murder?" That was a question I couldn't answer. "With two murders in town, I'll bet Jeff Daniels is having a coronary. Has he done anything about finding Claire's killer?"

"As far as the chief is concerned, she killed herself. He doesn't believe that someone else gave her the overdose."

"But the autopsy proved someone had been giving her poison for some time. Isn't he at all concerned about that?"

"Probably not." I decided to go a different direction with

the conversation. Could I trust him to give me an honest answer? There was only one way to find out. I decided to give it a shot. "How well do you know Dusty Reynolds? She moved here while you were still living at home."

He frowned at the sudden shift in subject. "I never had much to do with her. We didn't run in the same circles. She's about ten or fifteen years older than me. Why are you asking about her? What does she have to do with Claire's murder?"

"Nothing," I hope, I added silently. I gave a phony laugh. "I'm just trying to get a better handle on the people who knew Claire. She doesn't strike me as the type of person my sister would be friends with."

He shook his head. "Sorry, I didn't know her when I was a kid. I know she was helping Claire set up the house as a bed and breakfast. I think they were pretty good friends."

That wasn't what I wanted to hear. Gossip and rumors ran rampant in town. Maybe I could use them to my advantage for a change. "I've heard rumors about someone giving out herbs that made some people sick. It must have happened while you were still in high school. Did you ever hear about that?"

For a split second his eyes shifted away from mine causing my heart to skip a beat. He knew what I was talking about. Would he tell me?

"Where's this conversation going? Why are you asking about something that happened a long time ago?"

"Someone was using a plant to poison Claire. I'm just trying to figure it out. I don't know how they got her to take it. If those old rumors are true, maybe that same person was trying to kill her."

"Why would they want to kill Claire? She didn't live here then." All I could do was shrug. I didn't have any answers. "Do you really think that same person is still here?" I shrugged again; I couldn't answer that either. "What does that have to do with Dusty?"

"Probably nothing. I'm just asking questions." I'd made the mistake of bringing Dusty into the conversation.

He chuckled. "Did anyone ever tell you that you're a

terrible liar? Your face turns a pretty pink every time you tell a lie." I thought I'd outgrown that little peculiarity, but apparently not.

I sighed. Beating around the bush wasn't working. I decided to try straight on. "Okay, I'm trying to find out about an amateur herbalist who gave out something that made people sick. If that person is still in town, maybe that's who tried to kill Claire. What can you tell me about that?"

"Why would they want to kill Claire? It happened a long time ago." His dark eyes penetrated mine, trying to read my thoughts. He still didn't answer my question.

"I don't know," I said with some heat. "That's what I'm trying to figure out. What do you remember?" I pressed.

He was quiet for several minutes. "There were a couple of kids who got sick from something. For a while it was all the talk at school. At first the police thought it was LSD, but it turned out it was something else. I don't know if I ever heard what it was. It happened a few times, and I never heard where they got the stuff either. Does that help you? Is that what you were looking for?"

"I guess." Disappointment colored my voice. I was hoping he had more information. "Do you think any of those kids would tell the authorities now where they got the stuff?"

He shook his head. "That was a long time ago. I don't know where most of those kids are now. They were older than me, and they weren't my friends, just kids I went to school with."

"Would you be willing to tell Dan this?"

"What's this really about, Jillian? You're after something with all these questions."

It was my turn to sigh. "I don't know. I'm grasping at straws. I could be way off base, but the chief isn't really interested in finding out who killed Claire." I couldn't very well accuse Dusty without any real proof. Dan probably wouldn't be too happy that I'd been questioning Jake on this matter either.

"Has something else happened?"

"You mean besides the doctor being murdered, and the realization that he was running a prescription drug ring out of his office? Then no, nothing else has happened." I still omitted mention of my accident. What would he think about that?

"Do you think Dusty was involved back then? Do you think the two murders are connected?"

"I can't answer either of those questions." I sighed. "There doesn't seem to be anything to connect her to either crime." Frustration weighed heavily on my shoulders.

We were still discussing what happened all those years ago when Dan appeared at my door. He didn't look happy to see Jake making himself at home drinking coffee and munching on one of Irma's cinnamon buns. He eyed me curiously before planting a possessive kiss on my lips.

When he finally released me my legs were weak, and my head was spinning. That sort of kiss was better off left for when we were alone. When Jake chuckled, my face burned with embarrassment. For a minute, I'd forgotten that he was there.

"Nice to see you, Tobin." Jake reached out to shake hands. "How are things going with all the cases piling up around here?" Jake relaxed in the chair, his muscular arms crossed over his chest.

"Can't comment on an ongoing case, Wilkins. It's a little early for social calls, isn't it?"

I poked him in the ribs, hoping he'd start acting like an adult. I should have known better. Jealousy was in full bloom. It was going to take more than a simple jab in the ribs to counteract its effect.

"This isn't a social call," Jake chuckled. "I came to apologize for my mother. She's made a pest of herself." Dan raised one eyebrow at me, but didn't comment. I'd failed to mention Myriam's multiple visits. I'd probably have some explaining to do later.

"Um, Jake was telling me about an incident that happened to some of the kids he went to school with. I thought you might be interested after our conversation yesterday."

Jake cleared his throat, and sent me a dark look. He hadn't exactly agreed to tell Dan about the long ago incidents. But he waited to see what Dan would do.

Dan frowned at him. "You know something about poisonous plants and herbs, Wilkins?"

"That's not what I said," I sighed, giving him another poke with my elbow.

"Will you stop that?" My jab was harder this time, and he rubbed his injured ribs. "How about filling me in on this interesting conversation? I'd like to hear all about it."

Dan listened without interrupting as Jake recounted his story. When he finished, Dan asked questions, trying to pull out more memories. "Do you remember any of the names of those kids who took...whatever it was?"

Jake lifted his shoulders in a shrug. "I haven't thought about that for a long time. I was probably a freshman or sophomore at the time. The few kids who got into that stuff were seniors. We didn't exactly run in the same crowd."

That's what he said about Dusty. I wanted to put her name out there, but I'd done that once. If she wasn't involved, I didn't want to start any new rumors. She seemed to be well-liked, and I didn't want to ruin her reputation if she wasn't involved with Claire's death.

"I'd appreciate it if you'd think about it some more, and get back to me," Dan said.

"What does this have to do with Claire's death?" Jake asked. "I thought she was given something from an oleander."

"Oleandercide," Dan clarified. "It's made from the juice from the oleander plant. I don't know if it does have anything to do with her death. I'm just looking at everything."

Jake was silent for a moment, then nodded his head. "I'll see if I can find any of the kids." In his line of work, he might have a good chance of looking them up. He stood up, turning to me. "I'll see you at church tomorrow. Have a nice day."

Dan followed me to the entry, keeping a close eye on Jake. When the door closed behind him, Dan pulled me into his arms, resting his cheek on top of my head. "Sorry I acted like such an idiot. He just looked so comfortable sitting there drinking his coffee. I wanted to punch him. Am I forgiven?"

I cradled his face between my hands, looking into his eyes. "You don't have anything to worry about. Jake is a friend, I think." I added the last as an afterthought.

"You think? What do you mean? Do you have a reason to think otherwise? Do you think he's involved in either murder or with this Roland Granger? I still haven't been able to find out anything about him." His eyebrows came together a line over his eyes.

"I just keep remembering Claire's note. She trusted the wrong person, and look what happened to her. I don't know who to trust. I wish I could get a handle on all of the people who were in her life. I don't know where Roland Granger fit either. He said he was her friend, but I don't believe that." I gave a frustrated sigh. "I don't know what or who to believe anymore."

For several minutes, Dan put on a show of not believing that Jake wasn't a threat to our relationship, letting me rain kisses over his face. Finally he pulled me against his chest with a growl, settling his lips against mine. "You're driving me nuts, woman."

It was some time later before we got down to more serious matters. "What did you find out about those plants Dusty sent over? Are they poisonous?" We went back to the kitchen where I poured him a cup of coffee.

"Oh yeah, they're very poisonous. I had them destroyed. Now I need to talk..." Before he could finish his sentence, I was out of my chair and at the back door. "Where are you going?"

"To talk to Dusty, I want to know why she gave me those plants. Was she hoping I'd poison myself?" I opened the door, only to have Dan take my hand, pulling me away from the door.

"First, I want to talk to Jules. We can't accuse Dusty of anything yet."

"Jules wouldn't do anything to Claire. I don't think he

wanted to give me those plants either. He was as nervous as a cat when he brought them over. He kept looking over his shoulder like he expected to find her watching him."

"I still need to talk to him."

"You aren't going to do anything to Dusty?" I asked hotly.

"That's not what I said. I want to get a few facts straight before I talk to her. You know she's going to deny any wrongdoing. I want something to back up my questions."

I huffed and puffed, flopping down in the chair I had just left. "What kind of evidence? She isn't going to admit to anything." I gave another frustrated sigh. "I can't find what Claire had that was mentioned in the note either."

"One thing at a time," Dan advised. "Let's figure out why Dusty sent those plants over to you. Once we get that part settled, we'll figure out if she's the one who gave Claire the poison. Then we'll look for whatever Claire had that someone wanted back bad enough to kill for. I just hope it's still here."

After having the house searched twice, it could very well be gone by now. With another sigh, I leaned forward, putting my head down on my arms on the table. "Is this ever going to end, God?" I whispered. My life had been so mundane; how could things suddenly be turned on end?

Dan cupped his fingers under my chin, lifting my head to look at him. "God never gives us more than we can handle. We'll get this figured out." He placed a soft kiss on my lips.

"I know," I answered on a sigh. Turning my mind back to Dusty, I sat up straight. "How do we get her to admit that she's the one who was poisoning Claire?"

He gave his head a shake. "We don't know that she did. Before we go accusing her of something, we need to have evidence against her. That isn't going to be easy to find at this point. That's why I want to talk to Jules first. He might be willing to explain why she sent you those plants. We have to start there."

"If I make her mad enough, I'll bet she'll say something she shouldn't."

Jules wouldn't be over until mid-afternoon. Since I saw

that flash in her window, Dusty had made herself scarce. She must know I saw her spying on me. Jules had taken her place each afternoon to work in the garden. Unlike the first time he'd come over, he was no longer afraid she would find out he was helping me. In fact, it appeared he no longer cared if she knew he was doing all the work. I wondered why the change. Was he spying on me for her? It was an uncomfortable thought, but I was getting used to people watching my every move.

CHAPTER TWENTY

We were still discussing Dusty's involvement in Claire's death when Irma appeared at my door. She was much earlier than usual. She knew Dan was there, but that didn't deter her. In fact, it gave her more reason to stop over with some of her pastries. "I made these special for you," she smiled up at him. If she wasn't old enough to be his grandmother, I'd suspect she was flirting with him. I chuckled at the thought.

"That's very nice of you, Irma. You make the best baked goods in town. I don't know why you don't open your own bakery."

She twittered at the compliment, her face turning a pretty shade of pink. "Oh, I had one of those years ago, but it got too much for me to do on my own. I finally closed the doors about ten years ago."

"There probably hasn't been a good bakery in Bisbee since then," Dan flirted back as he picked up one of the sticky buns, taking a big bite. The look on his face was like he had just died and gone to heaven. I might as well be invisible for all the attention they were paying me. "Why didn't you hire someone to help out?" he asked around a mouth full of buns.

She sniffed disdainfully. "Have you taken notice of the young people in town lately? Ever wondered why the shop owners all run their own business, instead of hiring help? I tried to hire several young people. When it got around to discussing hours," she gave a laugh, "I didn't get the chance to tell them what the hours were before they told me what hours they were willing to work. Not one of them was willing to start before ten in the morning and wanted to quit by two in the afternoon. What kind of business can run on those hours? That's when I closed the doors." She gave a sad shake of her gray head.

I reached for one of the buns only to have my hand slapped. "She brings you goodies all week." Dan winked at me. "Those are mine."

"Oh dearie, I didn't forget you." She picked up the cloth bag she'd brought, bringing out a similar pan of buns. "These are for you."

"Irma, you're spoiling me. I'm going to be as round as a bowling ball if I keep eating everything you bring over."

"I doubt that," she chuckled. "If you're at all like your sister, you'll lose weight simply by eating. It seemed the more that girl ate, the thinner she got. Especially in the last few months." Sadness clouded her features. "That's when she started getting sick. Who would want to poison her?" Tears appeared in her faded eyes.

Something clicked in my mind. "You brought Claire your baked goodies?"

"Of course, just like I have for you."

"When did you start bringing things over?"

"What are you getting at?" Dan asked. His gaze moved between the two of us.

Ignoring him, I concentrated on Irma. She seemed lost in thought for a minute. "We usually took turns providing the snacks when I came over for tea. She enjoyed making different things. When she told me her plans for the house, I started bringing over some of my specialties. I wanted her to know what I could do so she would let me bake for her when she opened her B&B." She looked a little embarrassed. "I'm ashamed to admit I was showing off."

"She'd been working on the house for over a year. Were you bringing things over the entire time?"

"No one knew about her plans until about six months ago," Irma explained. "That's when I started bringing them over on a regular basis. Does it make a difference?"

"Do you know if anyone was upset with her plans?"

Irma thought about that for a minute. She finally shook her head. "I never heard any complaints about her plans, and..." she paused for a heartbeat, "I hear about most things going on in this town. I can't get out as much as I used to, but I still keep my ear to the ground. My friends would have told me if anyone was upset. Everyone knew Claire was my special friend. I don't know why anyone would be upset though."

I thought about how to phrase my next question. I didn't want to introduce Dusty into the conversation too soon the way I had with Jake. I was hoping Irma would do that for me.

Dan caught on to where I was going with my questions, asking one of his own. "Do you know if anyone was helping her with her menus, anything like that?"

She sniffed disdainfully. "That Dusty kept butting in on everything Claire did. Every idea Claire had for her B&B eventually ended up in Dusty's house. Once that woman found out what Claire planned, she did her level best to stall those plans. Claire was getting frustrated with her, but she was too nice to tell her to stop coming over."

"Did she ever suggest special items for her menus though?" Dan pressed.

Irma narrowed her eyes, looking from me to Dan and back again. "Do you think she is the one who poisoned Claire?" she asked indignantly. "The nerve of the woman." She slapped her leg to emphasize her words.

"We don't know anything like that," Dan cautioned. "We're just trying to find out what happened." It had been two months since Claire's death, and the case was no further along than it had been the first day. Was this the breakthrough we'd been looking for? "You can't repeat any of this conversation." Dan cautioned, looking at her sternly.

Insulted, Irma sat up straight. "I may have a network of friends who keep me informed of all the gossip in town, but that doesn't mean I don't know when to keep my mouth shut. I want the person who killed her caught almost as much as you do." She patted my hand. "I'm so sorry. I should have known something wasn't right. She didn't visit much before Claire made her plans known. Dusty never did anything unless it benefitted her."

"Maybe we should have asked Irma about what happened to those kids back in high school," I suggested once she had gone home for her afternoon nap. "She has a memory like a steel trap; she doesn't forget anything."

Dan shook his head. "Those two women don't get along. Bringing that up after talking about Dusty would cement the thought in her mind that she was responsible for that as well. I don't want that to color anything that I learn right now. If it turns out that Dusty had something to do with Claire's death, as well as what happened in the past, I want it to come out without any prodding on my part."

"When are we, you" I quickly amended, "going to talk to Dusty?" I asked.

"I still need to talk to Jules, remember?" Dan cautioned. I wanted to scream at all the delays. At this rate we would never be able to prove anything. "I need to take this one step at a time. Giving you those plants may be the mistake we were waiting for." I pushed my hair away from my face in a frustrated gesture. How much longer did I have to wait?

Standing up, Dan pulled me out of the chair and into his arms. "Don't give up, babe. Sometimes, solving a case is simply a matter of luck and good timing." He lowered his head, placing his lips on mine. He tasted of cinnamon and sugar. When he lifted his head several minutes later, we were both breathing heavily. If he had let me go at that moment, my wobbly legs wouldn't have been able to hold me up.

~~~

Jules was nervous when he saw Dan sitting on the patio when he arrived to work in the garden. When I offered to help him, he shook his head; his long hair swished around his head. Dan let the silence draw out for several long minutes. When he finally spoke, Jules jumped in surprise.

"Those plants you brought Jillian the other day were rather interesting. I was wondering where you got something like that."

Jules was kneeling on the ground. He'd looked up when Dan spoke to him, now he dipped his head letting his hair fall over his face preventing us from seeing his expression. "Oh, um," he mumbled something we couldn't understand.

"I didn't catch that. What did you say?" Dan stood up, further intimidating the younger man. I wanted to stop the interrogation, but I knew Dan wouldn't be happy with me. "Jillian said your aunt sent them over," Dan continued when Jules didn't say anything. By now, the younger man's Adam's apple was nervously bopping up and down.

"Where would she get something like that?" Dan continued casually. "I hope she doesn't have anything like that in her yard. It would be too bad if someone accidentally ate one of the leaves." He left unsaid the fact that he knew the plants were poisonous.

"N…no, not in the yard," the younger man stammered. His eyes pleaded with me to make the questions stop, but I couldn't. We needed to know the truth.

"Not in the yard, but she has them somewhere?" Dan cocked his head curiously.

"Oh, um." I could see tears gathering in the corners of his eyes now. I felt so sorry for him. He fell back so he was sitting on the ground. He rested his head on his knees. "In the shed," he whispered. "I didn't want to bring them over, but she said I had to." When he looked at me, tears were streaming down his dirt streaked face. "I'm sorry. I should have thrown them away instead of bringing them here."

"Why does she have something like that in her shed?" Dan continued questioning him.

Jules shrugged. "She likes to experiment with different plants. I don't know why she was growing those."

A flash of light caught my eye, and I looked towards Dusty's house. She was watching to see what was going on here. Dan was concentrating on Jules, and hadn't noticed. I touched his arm, nodding across the way.

Jules jumped to his feet. "Is she watching?" He brushed at his face, leaving a trail of dirt across his already dirty face. "If she knows what I said, she'll kill me." His hands were shaking.

"No she won't, son." Dan's authoritative voice filled the air. "I won't let her touch you. Tell me what you know. Why did she send Jillian poisonous plants?"

"Because she's scared."

"Of what?" I spoke up for the first time. "I can't hurt her."

"You're going to open a B&B. She doesn't want that."

"Why?" Hopefully he knew the answer to that question.

"She's afraid you'll put her out of business like Claire would have."

Dan gave me that cop look to keep me from saying anything more. He needed to ask the questions. He turned his attention back to Jules. "Can you show me where those plants are?"

Jules actually shuddered at that, but nodded his head. "Can we wait until she isn't home though? I don't want her to know."

"If she's been watching us, she already knows. We need to go now before she destroys them." Dan offered his hand to pull him off the ground.

Jules gave a sigh of resignation, placing his hand in Dan's. Without another word, he led us down the stone steps towards Dusty's house and the shed behind it. "Is that where you live?" I couldn't help but voice the question. It was little more than a shack behind the garage.

"She won't let me stay in the house," he admitted.

Flames inside the small building shot through the roof, and Dusty came running around the corner of the garage. "What's going on here? Why are you burning down the shed?" She glared at her nephew.

"He didn't do anything. He's been with us." Dan had his cell phone out, calling 911. Within minutes the fire truck pulled into the street far below. We were using the garden hose, trying to control the flames, but it was too late to save the small structure. Now they needed to keep the fire from spreading.

"How did the fire get started?" Dan turned to Dusty once the firemen took over. There was a hint of steel hidden in his mild tone.

She moved from one foot to the other nervously. "I don't know." She lifted her broad shoulders in a shrug. "I was working in the kitchen when I saw the three of you walk back here. I came out to see what was going on. That's when I saw the flames." She couldn't look him in the face while she talked. "He must have left something on the stove when he went over to see Jillian. He's always doing things like that." She glared at Jules now.

"What stove?" he snapped. "That thing hasn't worked in over a year. You started the fire so they wouldn't find those plants."

Her face turned an angry red. "I don't know what you're talking about. That's your shed. You're the one who is always growing things. If there are poisonous plants in there, I have nothing to do with them."

"No one said anything about poisonous plants, Dusty," Dan said quietly. "How about we go in the house while the firemen finish up out here? I have a few questions I'd like to ask you."

"No, I need to stay here to make sure my garage doesn't burn down. My car is in there."

"You should have thought of that before you set the shed on fire," Jules snapped. He turned his back on her.

I followed as Dan took her arm, leading her into the house. She slumped down in a kitchen chair, refusing to look at either of us. Unable to hold my tongue any longer, I glared at her. "You killed Claire because you were afraid of the competition?" I stared at the woman my sister had considered her friend.

"No, I didn't do anything to her." Dusty vehemently denied having anything to do with her death. She looked around wildly, trying to find a way out of this. "I…it wasn't me," she finally stammered. "It was Jules." It was like a light bulb went on over her head, "my nephew." She never mentioned him without qualifying him as such. "He did it. He was afraid if I lost The Tinderbox, he wouldn't have a place to live."

"You bitch." Dan could barely contain Jules as he pushed his way into the room. "I would never have hurt Claire. She was my friend. She knew the truth, and was going to help me get away from you. This is all on you. I had nothing to do with it."

What had Claire known? Was Dusty the one who sent the threatening note? I tuned back in to what Jules was saying in time to catch the best part. "And I'm not your nephew." A satisfied smile tilted his lips. "I'm your son."

A choking sound came from the doorway, startling us. All eyes turned to see Chief Daniels standing in the doorway. "Your son?" he asked in disbelief. "You said he was your nephew." I almost felt sorry for him; almost. I would bet the man had given confidential information to Dusty. It might have been accidental, but the results were the same.

"Jeff honey, help me out here. You know I would never hurt anyone, not deliberately."

"Your son?" he squeaked. Turning on his heel, he walked away, his shoulders slumped. Was that all he cared about, I wondered.

"You would never hurt anyone deliberately as opposed to accidentally?" Dan asked. "So those kids in high school who took some pretty wild trips on whatever you gave them; that was another accident? What about the people you gave herbs to with the promise they would make them well? Instead, some of them nearly died. All that was an accident, have I got that right?"

"Yes!" She looked relieved that he understood. "I didn't know that would happen to them."

"But you knew the oleander juice you gave Claire would eventually kill her." My voice was almost a snarl. I kept a firm grip on the edge of the table to keep from leaping over it to do her bodily harm. Dan sent me another warning look, and I sank back in the chair.

"I didn't want her to die," she whined. "I just didn't want her to open another B&B so close to mine. She would have put me out of business. I just put a little bit in her tea or food." It was all I could do to keep from leaping over the table at her.

"Did you give her the pain pills that finally killed her?" Dan resumed questioning her.

"No!" She jumped out of the chair. "I didn't do that, you

have to believe me."

"You've made it rather hard for me to believe anything you say. Dusty Reynolds, you're under arrest for attempted murder." He turned her around, pulling her arms behind her back to place her in handcuffs.

"But I wasn't trying to kill her," she objected.

"I'll leave that to the jury to decide."

"What about my guests. I can't leave them on their own."

"I'll take care of them." Jules spoke up for the first time since Dan prevented him from attacking Dusty. He was no longer the sullen kid, but a responsible young man. He'd grown up before our very eyes.

"You'd do that for me?" Dusty smiled at him.

"No, but I'd do it for the guests. It isn't their fault you're being arrested." He turned his back on her.

Her face fell; her shoulders slumped in defeat as Dan moved her towards the door. "Call my lawyer," she spoke to Jules's back.

"Call him yourself," he said without looking at her. "You get one phone call." He disappeared into the dining room without looking at her again.

I could hear Dusty's wails as Dan led her to the patrol car waiting at the bottom of the steps to take her to the county jail outside of town.

"Do you think she's the one who sent that fax to stop the autopsy?" I asked as we watched the car drive away.

"That will have to wait until I get her in interrogation," he sighed. "I doubt her lawyer will let her say much though."

"What about the pain pills? Do you believe her denial about giving them to Claire?"

He thought about that for a moment, then nodded his head. "Yeah, I believe her. Your theory of two people working to kill Claire is probably closer to the truth." I was surprised he would admit I was right, but I didn't point that out.

"I need to go, babe. I'll be back as soon as I can. I don't know how long this is going to take." We went back to my house so he could get his car. He looked distracted. It couldn't be easy arresting someone you know. He leaned down to place a soft kiss on my lips, nibbling on my bottom lip for a moment. "I think I'd better go before I let you distract me from my job," he chuckled softly. "I'll call you when I can."

CHAPTER TWENTY-ONE

It's been interesting watching this little drama play out, but time is quickly running out. Maybe those stupid cops decide to pin everything on Dusty Reynolds. Could I be so lucky? Will she let this drop now? Too bad Murphy proved to be such an incompetent fool. Who knew he'd be so paranoid on top of it? An evil laugh erupted. Of course, he had reason to be paranoid. No way was I ever going to let him live after what he did.

With another laugh, the dark figure turned as the patrol car holding Dusty Reynolds moved down the street. It was time to disappear. First, I have to find those papers Murphy left lying around. If it's still in that house, I'll find it, even if it means I have to tear the house down brick by brick

~~~

Dan was back much sooner than I expected. Probably Dusty's attorney wouldn't let her answer any questions. Standing beside him was Roland Granger. I glared at both men. "I thought you didn't know him." I directed my statement at Dan, but I didn't take my eyes off Granger.

"I didn't until an hour ago."

"Will you give me a chance to explain?" Granger asked softly.

"Fine, explain." I crossed my arms over my chest, tapping my foot impatiently. I didn't bother to invite them inside. Dan frowned at me and Roland Granger chuckled, angering me further.

"I'm with the DEA. I've been investigating a drug ring in these parts for the past several months."

My jaw dropped open, and I quickly closed it. "You didn't think to mention that instead of lying about being my sister's friend?"

"You didn't exactly give me the opportunity, and I wasn't lying. I did know Claire."

"Knowing her doesn't make you her friend."

"She was a very nice lady, I liked her a lot. I'm sorry for what happened to her."

I nodded, accepting his condolence. "That still doesn't mean you were her friend. She said she'd trusted the wrong person. Was that you?"

Before Granger could answer my question, Dan spoke up. "Can we come in now, or are you going to keep us out here on the porch giving all the neighbors a show? I think they've seen enough for one day" He looked around to see if anyone was paying attention to them. "You know how efficient the gossip mill is around here. He's trying to keep a low profile so those running the drug ring don't catch on to why he's here."

I huffed and puffed several times. I was getting very good at it. Finally, I stepped back to allow them in.

"Answer my question. Did Claire place her trust in you in error?"

"I didn't kill her, if that's what you're asking. I was in Tucson when she died." He sighed. "Maybe she'd still be alive if I'd been here. Again, I'm sorry."

"There's plenty of guilt to go around," I stated. We were still standing in the entry. I wasn't ready to invite him all the way into my house. "What did your investigation have to do with Claire? Is that why someone killed her?" If he'd put her in danger, then he was just as guilty as the person who gave her the pain pills.

"The last time I talked to her, she told me she had received a threatening note, that she had something someone wanted. She didn't know what though. That was the day before she died."

"And you left her here to face her killer alone?" My fingers itched to strike out at the man.

"I was called back to Tucson. There was nothing I could do. I didn't know anyone was going to kill her."

"So you didn't believe her either," I said heatedly. Why hadn't anyone believed her? I included myself in that assessment.

"I didn't say that," Granger stated. "I was going to help her

212

find what the person wanted back." He gave a heavy sigh. "It was too late when I came back from Tucson."

"Were you investigating Doctor Murphy? Do you know who killed him? Is that person still in Bisbee?" I fired more questions at him without giving him a chance to answer the first one.

Dan moved to my side, placing his arm around my shoulder. "Babe, we're going to figure this out. Can we go sit down now?"

I slumped against his side, giving my head a nod. I was almost positive Doctor Murphy had given Claire the pain pills that finally killed her. But I had nothing to back that up. I had no idea who killed him either. Would the item Claire had accidentally taken incriminate that person? If so, did that mean he would continue to come after me? Before I could open the B&B, I had to find whatever it was. I couldn't put innocent people in jeopardy.

"Do you know who killed Doctor Murphy, or why?" I asked a second time. "Someone killed him which means he wasn't the head man. Will you ever be able to figure this out?"

It was Granger's turn to give a heavy sigh. "We know someone else is calling the shots behind the counterfeit drug ring, we just don't know who. If we can find what they want bad enough to kill for, we might be able to close this down. I don't want him to move somewhere else, and start all over again."

"But you knew all along Doctor Murphy was behind the drug ring?" He reluctantly nodded his head. "Why did you come to Claire? What did you think she could tell you?"

"Because she'd been so sick, he was giving her medication. I was hoping to trace where those drugs were coming from."

"If Claire didn't know what they were after, I certainly don't. I've looked in every possible place that she would put something important."

"But if she didn't know she had something important, she wouldn't necessarily put it in a safe place," Dan countered. "Did she have a place she kept papers for the house, maybe receipts for things she bought?"

I thought about that for several minutes. "Sure, I found a file like that in the cabinet in Tom's office. I looked through it after I found that note. It was just like you said, booklets for all the appliances, receipts for anything she bought for the house, things like that. There wasn't anything out of the ordinary. Certainly nothing that would incriminate anyone." I felt like I was letting Claire down all over again.

By the time he left, I was fairly certain Roland Granger was exactly who he said he was. That didn't mean I liked him. He'd dogged my steps for more than a month without telling me why. Something that he said niggled at the back of my mind, but I couldn't place my finger on what.

"Did Dusty say anything when you questioned her?" I needed to think about something else.

Dan's shoulders slumped. "She lawyered up. She's not saying anything. I'm hoping the chief can answer some of my questions. He and Dusty have been dating for a long time. I can't believe she did all this without him suspecting something." He shook his head. It must be hard for him to think his boss, the chief of police, would ignore what Dusty had done.

"So she's the one who sent the fax to release Claire's body to the mortuary." It wasn't a question.

"I'm guessing, but yeah, I think so. Unless she talks, I'm not sure I can prove it though." He leaned over placing a kiss on my lips. "I'm going to talk to the chief now. I'm not sure how much he knows, or how much he'll tell me. I don't know when I'll be done."

"I don't care what time it is, come here. I'll have something for you to eat.

"Do you think she had anything to do with the drug ring?" I asked before he left. "It still feels like two different crimes to me." Again something tapped at the door of my memory, but was gone too fast to catch it.

"Yeah, Granger is pretty sure they are two separate crimes, too."

"What happens to her B&B with her in jail? She's probably going to prison, right?" My stomach was tied in knots at the thought that she could get away with what she'd done.

"I don't know what happens to the B&B. That's out of my hands. I still have to talk to Jules. If he's willing to testify against her, I'd say yes, she's going to prison. Maybe she didn't intend to kill Claire, but that would have been the end result if she continued to give her the oleander juice."

With a final kiss, he left. He'd talk to the chief first, then talk to Jules hoping for some of the answers Dusty wouldn't give him.

A half hour later, he called. Something was wrong. He didn't sound very good. "It's going to be late when I leave here." His voice quivered. "Go ahead and eat."

"Why? What did the chief have to say?" He had been upset that Dusty had lied about Jules, but I didn't see why that would have Dan upset.

I could hear Dan gulp before he said anything. "The chief ate his gun." Cop slang meaning he killed himself.

I gasped. "Oh, no, honey, I'm so sorry. Why would he do that?"

"I'm not sure. I haven't read everything he wrote yet."

"A suicide note?" I asked quietly.

"More like a suicide letter. It covers more than twenty years."

"Why would he kill himself simply because Dusty lied about Jules?" That was over-reacting to the max, I thought.

"It goes much deeper than that." He didn't explain. "I have to go. I don't know how long this is going to take. It's a mess." His voice hitched in his throat.

My heart went out to him. It couldn't be easy investigating the suicide of someone he knew. "Come over when you're through there, I don't care what time it is." I'm not sure he even heard what I said. His thoughts were taken up with what the chief had done.

~~~

It was nearly midnight when I heard the gravel in the driveway crunch under a car's tires. Rushing to the window, I saw Dan step wearily out of his car. His shoulders were slumped, his feet dragging as he made his way to the porch steps.

He pulled me into his arms before he was even in the house, burying his face in my neck. "Are you all right?" I whispered.

"I'm not sure." He followed me into the kitchen where I had kept his dinner in the warming oven. "I've only handled one suicide before. That was awful, but it's ten times worse when you know the victim." He shook his head.

"What's going to happen now? Can you tell me what was in the letter he left?"

"Yeah, it's going to come out in the end." He scooped up a large helping of mashed potatoes on his fork, and put it in his mouth before he said any more. "He knew Dusty was the one who gave those kids the herbs that I told you about. She wanted to be an herbalist, but was trying to take short cuts. She didn't want to go to school for it. It was a lot of guess work on her part. He kept her name out of the investigation. The only thing he did was make her stop." He sighed tiredly. "He wasn't much of a cop or a leader."

"What about Claire? Did he know Dusty was poisoning her?"

"His letter said he didn't know about that until the toxicology report came back," he answered between bites of pork chops. "He confronted her, but she denied it. I'm not sure he believed her. I know he wanted to, but he didn't do anything about it."

"Does she know what happened?"

He nodded his head. "I went over to the county lockup and told her. I let her read a copy of his letter. She took it pretty hard. Although I'm not sure if she was more upset by his death or the fact he told all her secrets. The only secret he didn't know was that Jules was her son, not her nephew." He gave a tired shake of his head. "They put her on suicide watch just in case."

"Who is going to take his place?"

He shrugged. "That's up to the city council."

~~~

In the middle of the night, I sat up straight in bed, suddenly fully awake. "Counterfeit drugs," I said out loud. That was what Roland Granger said Doctor Murphy was dealing in, not prescription drugs as I had assumed. His nurse said the same thing when she came to see me. That's what had been bothering me. Had she known what her boss was doing? Had Dan or the chief told her that's what they suspected? I wasn't even sure whether Dan had known that's what the doctor had been dealing in until he talked to Roland Granger.

Lying down again, I tried to go back to sleep. The clock on my night stand said two-fifteen. It was far too early to get up. An hour later I threw back the sheet, and gave up the quest for more sleep. My mind wouldn't shut off long enough to let me fall asleep.

I padded down the stairs in my bare feet hoping I wouldn't wake Dan. He had been so tired the night before that he fell asleep in the living room. With five bedrooms in the house, he could have slept in one of them, but I didn't have the heart to wake him even to move that far.

Peeking in on him, a smile curled my lips, and love tugged at my heart. He looked so cute with his blonde hair falling over his forehead and a day's worth of stubble dotting his cheeks and chin. My fingers itched to comb through the silky strands. That would have to wait for several hours. He needed his sleep.

I tiptoed into the room to pick up my tablet. Maybe reading would help put me back to sleep. If not, it would pass the time until I could make coffee.

A startled screech erupted from my throat when someone grabbed my arm. I was sure whoever had killed Claire, was here to do the same to me.

"Take it easy, babe. It's just me." Dan pulled me down beside him on the couch.

I slapped at his shoulder. "Darn you. You scared me half to death." He chuckled mischievously. "How come you're awake so early?"

"I could ask you the same thing." He nibbled at my neck, sending goosebumps over my body. "What are you doing up in the middle of the night?" His words were punctuated with kisses between each one.

It took a minute to get my passion muddled mind to work enough to answer. Then I couldn't remember what woke me up. "Um, I just couldn't sleep, I guess." I buried my fingers in his thick, soft hair, returning his kisses.

It was several minutes, or an hour later, that he raised himself up on his elbows. Passion darkened his normally light colored eyes. "I think we need to stop before it's too late." He had to clear his throat to make his voice work properly. "Unless you don't want to stop," he asked with a hopeful note in his voice.

"Um, no, you're right, we need to stop?" I could hear the question mark at the end of my statement.

He chuckled, rolling slightly away from me to give our bodies some cool-down room. "Now, why are you up at O-dark-thirty?" he asked, using a term from his military days.

I had to search my mind for a minute. Recollection suddenly dawned on me, and I sat up crashing the top of my head against his chin. "Ow." We each rubbed our injured body part.

"I'm sorry. Are you all right?" The small night light in the entry didn't offer enough light for me to tell if I had hurt him. I sat up, pulling my robe closed around me. Realizing how close we came to losing control, I could feel my face heat up. I was now grateful for the lack of illumination.

"Something Granger said bothered me," I answered, "but I couldn't remember what. It woke me about an hour ago."

He frowned at me. "I checked him out, babe. He really is a DEA agent."

"Oh, I know," I sighed. I was still disappointed that he hadn't turned out to be the bad guy in all this. "That isn't what

I meant. He said that Doctor Murphy was running a counterfeit drug ring, not a prescription drug ring."

"Right, so?" Even in the semi-darkness I could see the frown that pulled his eyebrows together. He moved me further away so we could both sit up.

"His nurse said the same thing."

"When did you talk to her?"

"She stopped by a few days ago. She wanted to say how sorry she was for what happened to Claire. She said she didn't know he was running a 'counterfeit drug ring right under her nose'."

"Older woman, plump with graying hair pulled back in a bun; is that the one who came to see you?"

"No, she was young, petite. Who are you talking about?"

Dan heaved a sigh, pushing himself off the couch. "His nurse is an older woman. Her name is Milly something. I'd have to look at my notes for her last name."

"So who came to see me?"

"I don't know. She mentioned the counterfeit drugs? What else did she say?"

I tried to recall the conversation. Finally I shook my head. "It wasn't very memorable. She was only here for a few minutes. I know she said counterfeit drugs. After Granger mentioned the same thing, something kept nagging at me. I just didn't know what until now. She said something like he hadn't been a very good doctor lately." I shrugged. "I think that's all she said."

We'd made our way to the kitchen, and I had coffee started along with breakfast. It was still early, but the sun was beginning to peek over the top of the mountains.

"If she was part of the drug ring, why did she come to see me?" I asked as I poured our first cup of coffee. He shrugged. "I'll give this information to Granger, see what he can find. He has more resources than I have. I don't know what's going to happen in the department yet." The chief's suicide was still very fresh in his mind. I couldn't even imagine what it must be like for him.

CHAPTER TWENTY-TWO

When Dan left for the office, I decided to see if I could help Jules with his guests. I didn't know how many people were staying there, but he might need a little help. I should have known that Irma would be on top of things. She was already there serving up a full breakfast to six people.

I almost didn't recognize Jules when I stepped into the kitchen. The transformation was stunning. Out from under Dusty's thumb, he was a changed man. His hair was tied back in a neat ponytail, and he taken a shower. He had on a clean pair of jeans and polo shirt. He'd taken full responsibility for the guests at The Tinderbox. I was sure that he would have managed breakfast for everyone if Irma hadn't come to his rescue.

"What did you tell the guests?" I asked softly. The three of us were alone in the kitchen of The Tinderbox, but I didn't want to take the chance of being overheard.

He shrugged. "The truth always works best; I just didn't tell them all of it. I said she had to go away for a while, and as her son, I was taking over." He sighed heavily. "They'll learn all the dirty details if the trial gets on the national news. I hope that doesn't happen, but," He lifted his boney shoulders, letting his sentence trail off.

Irma patted his shoulder. "You're going to have plenty of help. Never forget that God is also looking out for you. He'll see you through this." He didn't look like he had much hope of that happening, but maybe with Irma's help we could convince him that God really was on his side. Dusty didn't have much faith in God, and hadn't given that faith to Jules.

Although Irma has enough energy to rival some teenagers I knew, that energy was beginning to wane as I walked her home. "How long have you been helping Jules this morning?"

"That poor boy," she sighed. "That woman has put him through a lot; the least I could do was help out. He was devastated yesterday. I couldn't just sit by and ignore him."

Her steps were slow as we walked down the stone steps. "I did most of the baking yesterday after I offered my help. I made a casserole for the guests this morning. Everyone seemed to enjoy it, but right now I'm ready for a nap."

"Did you know that Jules was Dusty's son, not her nephew?"

She sniffed disdainfully. "I had no idea. When she first moved here, she was alone. Jules showed up about six or seven years ago. She told everyone that he was her sister's boy, and he was staying with her for a while. She had everyone fooled, especially the poor chief. She had him wrapped around her finger."

When she was safely home, I walked the short distance to my front door. My energy was also beginning to fade. It had already been a long day after a very short night. Slipping the key into the lock, the door opened on its own. My heart jumped in my chest. Had I failed to lock it when Dan left this morning? I shook my head. I distinctly remembered turning the latch, hearing the click.

Stepping over the threshold, I couldn't see much, but nothing seemed out of place. Was Myriam still trying to perpetuate the story of Sam, her fake ghost? If so, she was going to be sorry. For once common sense overruled my anger. I pulled my cell phone out of my pocket, and dialed 911.

Minutes later, a patrol car pulled into the drive behind Dan's unmarked car. "What happened?" This time he didn't care that the officer was there, he pulled me against his chest. I could feel his heart beating against mine.

When Roland Granger's car pulled in behind the patrol car, I gave a heavy sigh. Would he always be lurking around?

"Are you all right, Miss Connors?" A dark frown drew his eyebrows together.

I sent him a 'duh' look, without saying anything. How did he think I was? Someone had broken into my home. He joined Dan and the patrol officer as they went through the house while I had to remain outside. This didn't sit too well with me, but I had little choice. I had to wait until they made sure the burglar was gone.

A half hour later I stared at the destruction in Tom's office/library. Books were scattered around the room, trinkets from his travels were shattered on the floor. The file cabinet had been emptied and the beautiful cabinet broken in a hundred pieces.

"That must have made someone pretty mad," I nodded my head at the false books. They now hung askew, exposing the safe. There were dents along the edge where someone had tried to open it with a crow bar. "Maybe they got what they were looking for, and they'll leave me alone now," I said with more hope than I felt.

Dan and Granger both shook their head. "I doubt that." Granger spoke quietly. "There's a lot of anger behind this much destruction. If they'd found what they were looking for, you probably wouldn't even know they'd been in here."

My bedroom and Claire's had also been trashed. The mattresses were pulled off the bed frames, drawers emptied on the floor and turned upside down. "Can you tell if anything is missing?" Dan looked down at me.

"In this mess, I'm not sure how I would know. Maybe Claire never had what they thought she did. Whoever did this looked in every conceivable place Claire could put something. There isn't anywhere else to look."

"What's in there?" Granger nodded at the safe. "Do you have the combination?"

"I do, but what they're looking for isn't in there. I've already looked. If Claire didn't know what she had, why would she put it in the safe? If it's here, it has to be in plain sight."

By the time the forensic team was finished, there was black fingerprint powder everywhere. It would take me the rest of the day and part of the next to clean it up. I was grateful the county inspector had already been around. Although the kitchen hadn't been touched, I was sure Daphne would never allow me to open the B&B if she saw this mess. She still might pull my license if she hears all the gory details of poisonous plants.

The day wasn't through with me yet. Mr. Edmonds appeared at my door while I was in the middle of the clean-up. "I heard about the break-in, Miss Connors. I came to see if there was anything I could do to help out." I wasn't sure what he thought he could do for me dressed in his expensive suit and tie.

"That's very nice of you, but right now I'm just cleaning up the mess." I stepped back to allow him in. Maybe if he saw the mess, he'd withdraw his offer to help. I'm sure he wouldn't want to get black powder all over his fancy clothes.

"Oh my, this is a mess. Was anything taken?" He looked around at the library. It would take a lot longer than one day to put all the books back in place. "What were they after?"

"I suppose anything of value." I lifted my shoulders in a shrug. "Maybe you could help me with that. Did Claire or Tom ever give you an inventory of what was in the house?" A thought occurred to me then. "I'm also going to need the name of the insurance company and the policy number. As you can see, there's some damage beyond the mess."

"Oh, yes of course. I'll get that for you." He looked at the safe high above my head. "I take it they weren't able to open that. Do you know what's in there?"

"Just Claire's jewelry, the trust papers weren't even in there. I'm glad you called me when you did. I had no idea where to look for something like that. My sister wasn't big on putting important papers in a safe place."

"That's a shame." He shook his head. "Maybe I can give you a hand sorting things out in here so you'll know what should be put in the safe." He looked at the file cabinet. "I can't imagine why sh...shomeone would destroy such a fine looking piece of furniture." He stammered, slurring his words.

I took a step back. He didn't appear drunk, but why else would he slur like that? I couldn't smell alcohol on his breath. Maybe he was having one of those mini-strokes. I looked for the classic signs, but there were none. So what just happened?

He took off his jacket, rolling up the sleeves of his shirt.

"I'm here to help." With shooing motions, he practically shoved me out of the room. "You take care of your room and Claire's. I'll have things in ship-shape in no time." He shut the door in my face.

"Wow, what was that about?" I stared at the closed door. At this point, I was surprised he didn't lock the door to keep me out. He must be used to issuing orders and the minions around him following them without question. I didn't have much choice at this point. He was going to help whether I liked it or not. He'd made a point of telling me to clean up my room. How did he know my room had been trashed? I dismissed the thought.

Still puzzling over his unusual behavior, I headed up the staircase. I should be happy for any help I could get, instead of trying to figure out why he was here. I was at the top of the stairs when the chimes on the front door filled the house. I was certain it would be Irma. Pivoting around, I started back down. This wasn't a good time for a tea party.

"Go back to your room." Mr. Edmonds hurried out of the library, his tone was gruff.

"It's Irma Grover from next door," I started to explain. "She comes over every afternoon for tea. I'll just tell her…"

"You won't tell her anything," he snapped. "Now go back to your room."

For several seconds I stared at him, too dumbfounded to say anything. I finally gathered myself, and took several steps down. "This is my house, Mr. Edmonds." The rest of my statement was swallowed up in shock when he pulled a rather big gun from behind his back. My feet felt frozen to the steps.

"You might as well come down the rest of the way, Miss Connors. We'll just invite Mrs. Grover in for that tea party."

N…no, that's okay. That isn't necessary." The chimes sounded again. She wasn't going to go away.

"You see, it is necessary. Now, get down here." His voice turned in to a growl. He motioned with the gun for me to move. If I didn't want to get shot, I didn't have much choice.

"Why are you doing this? What's this about?"

"Just be still." While keeping me in his line of sight, he opened the door. "Good afternoon, Mrs. Grover. What a pleasant surprise. Come in, dear." The gun was behind his back again.

I thought about rushing him, but the thought died quickly enough when he closed the door behind Irma.

"Why, hello, Mr. Edmonds. This is a pleasant surprise. I wanted to thank you again for the lovely gift Claire left me. I'm enjoying the same tea parties with Jillian that I did with her sister." Noticing the black fingerprint powder that I hadn't had time to remove from every surface, even in the entry, she gave a small gasp. "Oh, my, what happened here?" She stepped towards the living room. Mr. Edmonds stopped her quickly.

"I think that's enough for now. I want the two of you to sit over there." He pointed to the parson's bench that I had moved to the entry after the table was destroyed.

"Irma, are you all right?" I whispered, nodding at the cane she grasped in her hand. She hobbled some, but I'd never seen her with a cane before. "Did you hurt yourself helping out at Dusty's, I mean Jules's this morning?"

She winked at me. "I'm fine, dearie, but that shyster isn't going to be if I get a whack at him."

"Shut up. I don't want the two of you talking!" Edmonds glared at us across the entry. "I want to know where that ledger is. I know she took it from that fool Murphy."

"I don't know what you're talking about." I shrugged. "Maybe your friend found it when she trashed this place."

"Not likely," he snarled, as he grabbed my arm, pulling towards the library. "Open the safe. It has to be in there." He made the mistake of turning his back on someone considered a helpless old woman.

Irma whacked him in the back of both knees hard enough to send him to the floor. Unfortunately, he didn't loosen his grip on my arm, and I went to the floor with him. Her next hit was even harder, this time on the top of his head.

"Call Dan," she instructed forcefully, while she continued

to pound on Mr. Edmonds with her cane.

~~~

It was over that fast. Dan and several officers swept in minutes after my call, almost like he was expecting it. My head was swimming with the latest turn of events.

"How did you know what was going on?" I asked Irma.

"Why, dearie, you know very little in this town, and especially this neighborhood, escapes my notice. I'd seen him in the neighborhood several times since he was here about Claire's estate, yet he never stopped to see how you were doing. It was just a little off-putting today when he showed up nosing around. I kept waiting for him to leave, but he never did." She shrugged. "I thought I'd stop by to see what he was up to."

I gave the woman a hug. "I'm so glad you did. There's no telling what he would have done if he couldn't find what he was looking for."

"And what was that?" she questioned.

In answer, I turned to Dan. "He's looking for a ledger Claire took from Doctor Murphy. Maybe his accomplice found it when she trashed the house."

"What accomplice?" Dan and Irma spoke at the same time.. She didn't like being left out, and wanted to know everything that was going on.

"Probably the woman who claimed she was Doctor Murphy's nurse when she came here." It took a while to explain what I meant. Edmonds's stammering and slurred words hadn't meant he was drunk or having a mini-stroke. He'd almost said 'she' when talking about someone smashing the file cabinet. I hadn't caught on until it was almost too late.

"It turns out she's been in custody since shortly after she finished up here," Dan said. "Her name is Becky Miller. When she couldn't find what Edmonds wanted, she was in a hurry to get out of town. A patrol officer clocked her going through town at forty in a twenty-five mile zone. If she'd stopped, all she would have gotten was a speeding ticket. Instead she went the wrong way down a one-way street, crashing into another vehicle in her haste to escape." He gave his head a shake.

"If she hadn't panicked, she would have made it out of town before we connected her to any of this. As it is she's going to be in the hospital for a few days, and after that she'll be a guest of the county. There was a crow bar on the front seat of her car. I'm sure it will match the markings on your safe. She also had a very distinctive set of keys in her possession." When I gave him a blank look, he chuckled. "The keys to Doctor Murphy's SUV"

I gasped. "She's the one who tried to run me off the road?"

Dan nodded. "Apparently so. If she had left them in the SUV when she pushed it over the cliff, we wouldn't have been able to connect her to that. Crooks prove every day that they aren't very smart. Her fingerprints were all over that vehicle."

"Did she have some kind of a ledger with her? That's what Mr. Edmonds was looking for. I haven't found anything like that."

"She's looking for a plea bargain, and is singing like a canary. Edmonds wouldn't have been free for much longer." He pulled me against his chest, kissing the top of my head. "I'm sorry I didn't do a better job of protecting you. I never would have forgiven myself if anything had happened to you."

"Is he the one who gave Claire the fatal dose of pain pills?"

He gave a heavy sigh. "I'm not privy to that information. Once the County Attorney discovered that Miss Miller was involved with the doctor, he was perfectly willing to turn the entire case over to Granger and the DEA. Edmonds and Murphy were partners in the counterfeit drug ring, but that's about all I know at this point. If I had to guess, I would say that Murphy was the one to give her the pills. She wouldn't have questioned him when he gave her something."

I tried to tell myself it was enough to speculate that he was correct, but it wasn't. Mr. Edmonds and Becky Miller were just as guilty as the doctor. If they hadn't been doing something illegal, Claire wouldn't have died when she did. Dusty was still giving her the poison, but I might have made it here in time to save her. It was something I would never know. I should have come here when she first asked me to. Guilt piled up on guilt.

CHAPTER TWENTY-THREE

Daphne Stephens, the county inspector, allowed Jules to remain open while he got his own business license and food license.

"I hope you don't mind that I'll be cooking for Jules until he can make other arrangements," Irma wrung her hands when she told me her news. "I'll help you out as well," she rushed on before I could say anything.

I took her hands, giving them a squeeze. "There's no rush on my part. If I even open the B&B, it won't be for several months. I want to make sure Jules is well established. He needs all the help he can get right now."

It turns out that wasn't exactly true. He knew Dusty was bound to get caught, and had been preparing for this for months. He'd been afraid she would either send him away, or dispose of him in a more unsavory manner if he'd gone against her.

Mother hen that she is, Irma even convinced him to go to church with us. "But I let her get away with hurting people," he stated, his tone flat. "I'm not a very good person."

"God can forgive anything," she assured him. "All you have to do is ask for forgiveness, and have faith in His saving grace. Jesus won't let you down."

Dusty was going to remain in jail while awaiting trial. She had money stashed away, but couldn't access it. She had put the account in Jules's name. It was her one good act towards him.

He wasn't going to help her, but he didn't use any of the funds for himself either. "I'm not using her money," he stated emphatically. "I'll sink or swim on my own."

"She keeps asking to see him," Dan told me. "So far, he's refused."

"I can't say that I blame him. Denying that he was her son was wrong, but trying to push the blame off on him was even worse. He's been little more than her servant for years. I hope she spends a lot of time in prison for what she did to both Claire and Jules." Forgiveness isn't always my strong suit.

It was amazing that the notoriety of this entire episode didn't harm The Tinderbox. In fact, it was exactly the opposite. People were morbidly curious, wanting to hear all the gory details. Some even requested a room in the small shed where Jules had lived. Fortunately, it had burned to the ground when Dusty tried to dispose of the evidence.

She was also trying to get a plea bargain; unfortunately, she didn't have anything to bargain with. The chief had documented everything he knew about her activities, even those he only guessed at, in his lengthy suicide note. I felt bad that he killed himself, but I didn't feel any guilt for his death. He had brought it on himself. If he had been a good policeman, Dusty never would have gotten away with what she did.

Roland Granger did throw us a few crumbs on the case. "Becky Miller is spilling the beans on the counterfeit drug scam hoping for a reduced sentence," he said. "Edmonds and Miller were running a counterfeit drug ring. She was working with them, and was the doctor's lover. When Edmonds killed Doctor Murphy she was too afraid to go to the police.

"The good doctor," he said sarcastically, "kept a record of all his dealings with Edmonds. He wanted out, but Edmonds wasn't ready to close down the operation. The last time Claire was in his office, she saw Edmonds and Miller arguing with him. That was bad enough, but somehow the record Murphy had of his dealings got mixed up with her bill.

"After giving her the overdose of pain pills, Murphy tried searching the house, but came up empty. She had filed the papers along with her medical records without looking at what she had. Becky Miller found them when she destroyed the library. She had them when she was arrested. There's enough evidence to put Edmonds away for a long time."

"What did Dusty have to do with any of this?"

"Nothing," he answered. "You were right in your assumption that two people were involved in Claire's death. I'm sorry for what happened to her. They'll both pay for their part in her death." I would have to be satisfied with that.

Jake still stopped to see me whenever he was in town, but it wasn't as often as he had at first. He'd finally given up on any sort of romantic relationship with me. After all this settled down, he stopped by with a stranger. "Hello, Jillian." He bent down to place a kiss on my cheek. "I'd like you to meet William Frye. He's my attorney."

My heart gave a little jerk. I could only think of one reason he would bring an attorney to see me. He was going to try to break the trust, and take away my share. I didn't mind the loss of the money; I did mind the fact that he had deceived me all these months. He really did want everything from his father.

Guessing where my thoughts had gone, he took my hand. "Just listen to what we have to say, all right?"

"Sure, whatever," my voice dripped ice. I mentally began packing my things to move out of the house.

"What Mr. Edmonds told you was only partially true," Mr. Frye stated. "The trust can't be broken or altered as far as the money from the estate goes. But Mr. Wilkins can take himself off as a trustee."

I frowned at him. I didn't understand what he was saying. "Any revenue from the trust will still be split between the two of you," he continued to explain, "but Mr. Wilkins will no longer have any say on how the trust is handled. You will be sole trustee."

"What does that mean?"

"You no longer have to consult with Mr. Wilkins in regards to the house, Mrs. Wilkins' car, or any of the other investments. With Mr. Edmonds in jail and likely prison for a long time, Mr. Wilkins asked if I would take over as executor. I will oversee the investments and distribution of funds, but you will be the sole trustee."

I looked at Jake, dazed by this. I still wasn't sure what it really meant. He took my hand again. "I can't undo what Dad and Claire did by leaving half of everything to me, but I can step away and let you have sole say in things. That's the way it should have been right from the beginning. I'm not trying to take anything away from you."

He drew a deep breath before plunging ahead. "I do have one request before this goes into effect." He paused, waiting for me to nod my head. "I don't want my mother to find out about this. She would do her level best to stop me from doing what is right."

I quickly nodded my head, agreeing with this request. I wanted as little to do with Myriam as possible. I wasn't sure how Mr. Frye had become the executor so quickly after Mr. Edmonds arrest. I really didn't care either. Legal matters made my head hurt.

That night Dan had a surprise for me when he came over. "The town council offered me the job of police chief." He appeared stunned by this move. "I can't believe it."

"Congratulations!" I wrapped my arms around his neck, giving him a hug, planting a kiss on his lips. "That's wonderful. You'll make a great chief."

"I didn't accept yet," he cautioned. "I wanted to talk to you first."

"Whatever for?"

"I would be more of a hands-on chief than Daniels was. I want to know if you would be comfortable with that." Butterflies fluttered in my stomach. Was he saying what I thought he was saying? What I hoped he was saying? "Some women can't handle their husbands being in law enforcement. As chief I would be more involved with apprehending the criminals."

My mind shut off at the word "husband." It was a long while later when I gave him my verbal answer, but I think he understood my non-verbal communication perfectly well. "I don't mind at all. You were meant to be a policeman. You'll be the best chief this town has ever had."

Again, discussion stopped there. I couldn't believe I was this lucky. Once again God showed me that He knew what He was doing in my life. I might not be cut out to be an innkeeper, but I was cut out to be a wife, even a mother someday. It made me sad that Claire wasn't here with me, but she was with those she loved the most. I was safe in the knowledge that we would see each other again someday. Until then, I had the love of my life with me here on earth along with a wonderful substitute grandmother. What more could I ask for?

ACKNOWLEDGEMENTS

I thank God for the many wonderful gifts He has given me in this life, among them are my wonderful family. He has answered my prayers, allowing me to tell my stories and publish my books. I am so blessed.

My thanks and gratitude also go to Gerry Beamon, Sandy Roedl, and KaTie Jackson for their suggestions, editing and encouragement. I can't forget about all the information retired Phoenix Police Detective Ken Shriner has given me on police procedure. Thanks for your patience, Ken, and for answering my many questions about law enforcement. I apologize for taking literary license with police procedure in an effort to move the story forward.

OTHER BOOKS BY SUZANNE FLOYD

Revenge Served Cold
Rosie's Revenge
A Game of Cat and Mouse
Man on the Run
Trapped in a Whirlwind
Smoke & Mirrors
Plenty of Guilt
Lost Memories
Something Shady
Rosie's Secret
Killer Instincts
Never Con A Con Man
The Games People Play
Family Secrets
Picture That

Dear Reader:

Thank you for reading my book. I hope you enjoyed reading it as much as I enjoyed writing it. If you enjoyed Plenty of Guilt, I would appreciate it if you would tell your friends and relatives and/or write a review on Amazon. Check out my other books on Amazon.

Like me on Facebook at Suzanne Floyd Author, or check out my website at SuzanneFloyd.com.

Thank you,
Suzanne Floyd

P.S. If you find any errors, please let me know at: Suzanne.sfloyd@gmail.com. Before publishing, many people have read this book, but minds can play tricks by supplying words that are missing and correcting typos.

Thanks again for reading my book.

ABOUT THE AUTHOR

Suzanne is an internationally known author. She was born in Iowa, and moved to Arizona with her family when she was nine years old. She still lives in Phoenix with her husband Paul. They have two wonderful daughters, two great sons-in-law and five of the best grandchildren around. Of course, she just a little prejudiced.

Growing up and traveling with her parents, she entertained herself by making up stories. As an adult she tried writing, but family came first. After retiring in 2008, she decided it was her time. She still enjoys making up stories, and thanks to the internet she's able to put them online for others to enjoy.

When Suzanne isn't writing, she and her husband enjoy traveling around on their 2010 Honda Goldwing trike. She's always looking for new places to write about. There's always a new mystery and a romance lurking out there to capture her attention.

Made in the USA
Middletown, DE
09 July 2023

34773348R00139